PRAISE FOR *IN ANOTHER*

"The twisty plot builds to a satisfying resolution. Banner knows how to keep the reader guessing."

—*Publishers Weekly*

"What a beautiful . . . and completely engrossing book this was . . . It's a heavy hitter, this book, and one you shouldn't expect to come out of unaffected . . . the heavier moments are interspersed with some gorgeous interludes of beautifully written moments of normal life . . . A. J. Banner has written something very special here."

—*Mystery & Suspense Magazine*

"Blending mystery with a story about grief and trauma, there's plenty to focus on, and readers who enjoy domestic suspense will love this one."

—*The Parkersburg News and Sentinel*

"Sharply written and psychologically rich, Banner skillfully keeps readers on edge, gripped to the pages with her twisty plot, keeping you guessing—what is factual or speculation? Trust me, you will not see this twist coming."

—*JDC Must Read Books*

"*In Another Light* may well be Banner's best writing to date. She has cleverly penned a riveting thriller . . . *In Another Light* is thoroughly entertaining, as well as emotionally gripping and poignant."

—*Colloquium*

"A. J. Banner writes in her usual fast-paced style that will keep you turning pages and wanting more."

—*Bookreporter*

"A dull chapter nowhere in sight."
—*San Francisco Book Review*

PRAISE FOR *THE POISON GARDEN*

"[An] impressive psychological thriller . . . Banner keeps the reader guessing to the end."
—*Publishers Weekly*

"[A] sharply written and taut psychological thriller."
—*The Seattle Times*

PRAISE FOR *AFTER NIGHTFALL*

"[A] gripping psychological thriller . . . Well-laid clues allow the reader to sleuth along."
—*Publishers Weekly*

"[A] compelling psychological suspense with a strong Pacific Northwest setting."
—*The Seattle Times*

"An elegant and taut psychological thriller that keeps the reader on the edge of their seat until the final page."
—*Authorlink*

"*After Nightfall* is a chilling drama . . . Well-fleshed-out characters keep the reader wondering just what is going on."
—*New York Journal of Books*

PRAISE FOR *THE TWILIGHT WIFE*

"[A] harrowing plot that reveals memory to be both unreliable and impossible to fully wash away."

—*Publishers Weekly*

PRAISE FOR *THE GOOD NEIGHBOR*

"Could be the next *Gone Girl*."

—*Harper's Bazaar*

"Thrilling."

—*First for Women*

"Packed with mystery and suspense . . . the final destination is a total surprise. Well done."

—*New York Journal of Books*

"Breathtaking and suspenseful . . . unique and highly entertaining."

—Fresh Fiction

DREAMING
of
WATER

ALSO BY A. J. BANNER

The Good Neighbor
The Twilight Wife
After Nightfall
The Poison Garden
In Another Light

DREAMING
of
WATER

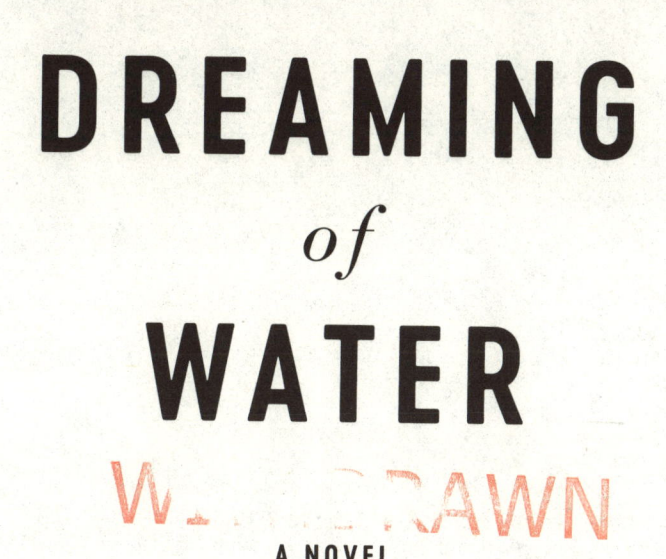

A NOVEL

A. J. BANNER

LAKE UNION
PUBLISHING

This is a work of fiction. Names, characters, organizations, places, events, and incidents are either products of the author's imagination or are used fictitiously. Any resemblance to actual persons, living or dead, or actual events is purely coincidental.

Text copyright © 2023 by Anjali Writes LLC

All rights reserved.

No part of this book may be reproduced, or stored in a retrieval system, or transmitted in any form or by any means, electronic, mechanical, photocopying, recording, or otherwise, without express written permission of the publisher.

Published by Lake Union Publishing, Seattle

www.apub.com

Amazon, the Amazon logo, and Lake Union Publishing are trademarks of Amazon.com, Inc., or its affiliates.

ISBN-13: 9781662505614 (paperback)
ISBN-13: 9781662505607 (digital)

Cover design by Eileen Carey
Cover image: © Daniel Kim Photography / Stocksy United;
© Photograph by Tom Hoover / Getty

Printed in the United States of America

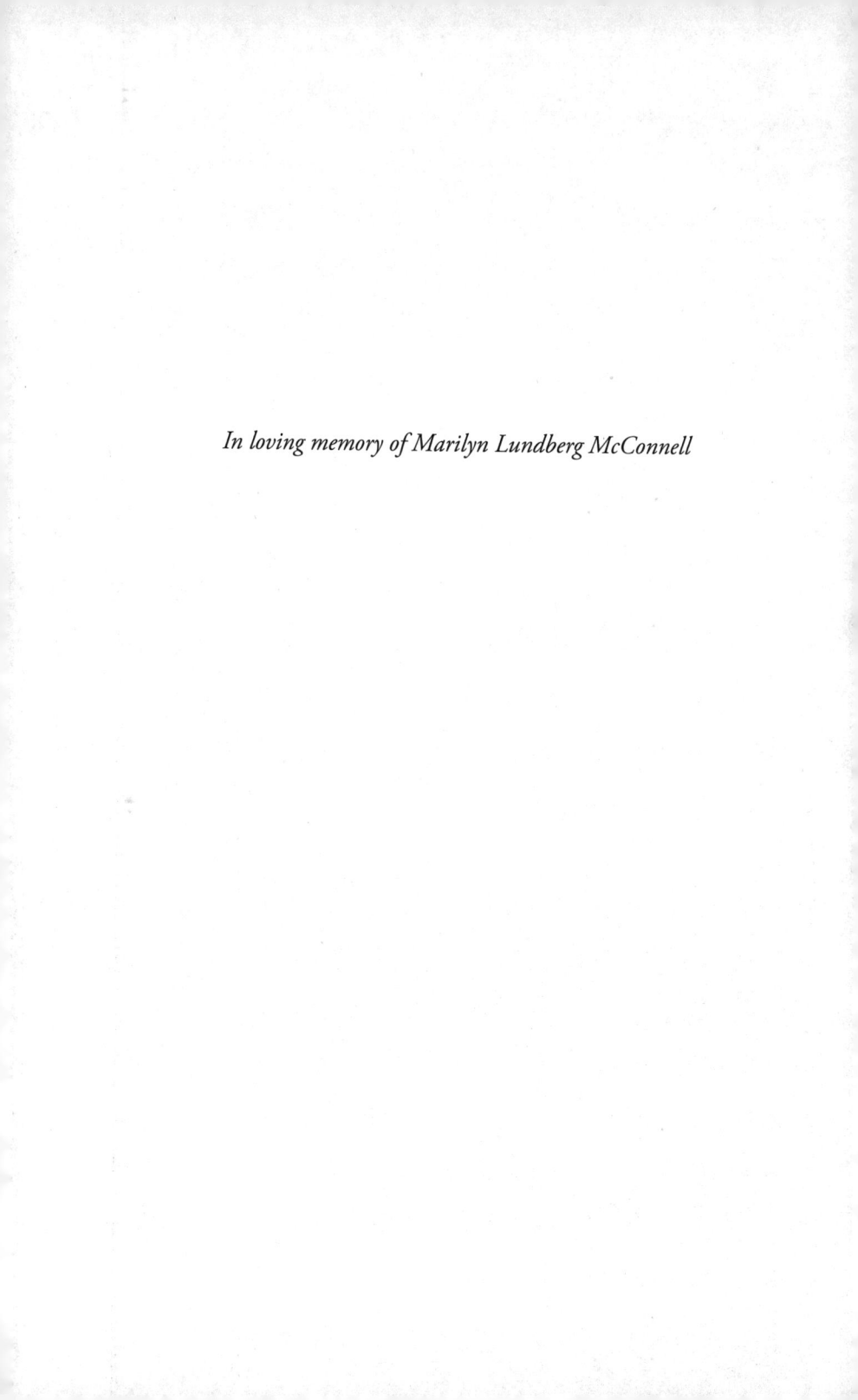

In loving memory of Marilyn Lundberg McConnell

PROLOGUE

I held her underwater...

I can't live with what I've done. My guilt twists through me like the trunk of an ancient madrone tree clinging to the cliff, desperate to survive. But I won't get a second chance. I don't deserve one. I am a killer.

Her confession has been written, the ink indelible—no erasing those damning words. She stands at the edge of a precipice, the ocean rippling away below her. Diamonds of moonlight glitter on the waves. Maybe when she falls into those icy depths, she'll become just another drowned woman whose body will never be found. All her secrets, her hopes, her regrets, will dissolve in the sea. Nobody will ever know the truth.

She should've foreseen this moment, should've understood the signs. So many things she should have said to the people she loves. But now there is no turning back. The salty wind blows cold in her face, her senses heightened, every rustle and sigh magnified. A tiny creature skitters through the underbrush—a profusion of stars brightens the sky. On this clear night, the stunning view steals her breath away. *Funny,* she thinks, *the way the world becomes more beautiful when you're about to leave it behind.*

CHAPTER ONE

One week earlier

Astrid downshifts on the winding road into Heron Bay, the brakes a little soft in her rented Corolla. She tries not to speed—she would hate to crash so close to Aunt Maude's house. How ironic it would be to make it this far after surviving awful turbulence on the flight to Seattle, only to collide with a tree. But she heard somewhere that turbulence isn't dangerous, that she should imagine the plane jiggling in a bowl of Jell-O, stuck in the air and unable to actually fall. She's not sure if this is true, and anyway, it didn't calm her in the slightest.

Her brain is in overdrive, full of anxiety. Dark memories lap at the edge of her mind, and it takes all her willpower to keep them at bay. For the first time in seventeen years, she is returning to this godforsaken town. Before that, she spent every summer in Heron Bay with her family. For two months each year, her parents closed up the Seattle house and drove three hours here to the coast. Astrid's mother, Rose, looked forward to the days spent reading and chatting with her older sister, Maude—and dancing at parties in the neighbors' house on the hill.

That is, until Astrid's three-year-old sister, Nina, drowned in a shallow reflecting pool. A freak accident, a family tragedy splashed all over the local news. Astrid and her dad escaped home to Seattle soon after Nina's death, but Astrid's mother stayed in Heron Bay for weeks, and when she finally returned to the city, she was barely a breath of her former self.

The family never again visited Heron Bay. They couldn't bear the terrible memories. They couldn't bear life without Nina. After two years of moving from state to state, struggling to outrun grief, Astrid's parents divorced.

Now, thinking back, she's surprised the marriage lasted even that long. Her father moved to the woods of Oregon, and her mother escaped to Europe, incessantly traveling, relishing the anonymity that a new place brings. She resurfaces now and then to send a postcard, and she left a new cell phone number on Astrid's voice mail a few weeks ago, but who knows how long that number will last?

Now, Astrid follows in her parents' footsteps, her life scattering into pieces behind her. No husband anymore, no real place to call home. In the rearview mirror, she looks scattered, too—dark hair frizzy and untamed, growing down past her shoulders, a few strands of gray mixed in with the black, and she is only thirty-one. Smudged mascara beneath large, wide-set eyes. Unlike her mother, who loves fashionable clothing and flashy jewelry, Astrid prefers to fade into the woodwork, wearing practical sneakers and muted colors. She works in a nondescript office in San Ramon, California, a half-hour commute from her upstairs apartment in a house in Vallejo. She spends her days peering through a microscope or magnifier, searching documents for signs of anomalies.

Her ex-husband, Trent, understood her work—he even helped her prepare for court appearances, which always made her so nervous, she thought she might faint on the stand. He played the opposing attorney, challenging her opinion that a signature was either authentic or forged. She relied on him to keep her on track, but when she ended up alone, she found herself looking in the mirror to practice for her presentations.

The breakup sent her into a tailspin, but somehow, she survived moving out of the house and setting up her own tiny space. Yet even after nearly a year, some boxes remain unpacked. The apartment feels like a way station, as if she might eventually move back in with Trent.

Wishful thinking, she knows. Her own lies and omissions ruined the marriage for good. She'd spun a fantasy life with him, pretending she shared his hopes and dreams, and she got what she deserved. What did she expect would happen? That he would forgive her?

Now she feels like a limb has been severed, an important part of her cut away. Sometimes, she still wakes expecting to find him in bed next to her, reaching out to push the hair from her eyes. Instead, she has only her memories and the occasional sound of his voice. She calls him now and then, makes up a reason. She needs his opinion about a court case or a questioned document, a forged check or counterfeit contract. He listens politely, offers a quick response, and then makes an excuse. Every time he hangs up, her heart breaks a little more. At least this getaway offers her a temporary escape.

At the edge of town, she catches the faint whiff of sulfur from the paper mill. Funny, she never noticed that smell when she was young. Along the shore side of the road, the ocean ripples across the Strait of Juan de Fuca to Whidbey and the San Juan Islands. To her left, the forest thickens as it climbs the hill behind Heron Bay.

She wouldn't have returned if not for the urgency in Aunt Maude's voice, her insistence that a typewritten letter she'd found was of the utmost importance. *The signature is handwritten. The letter will change everything we believe about the past.*

Change what? She wouldn't say.

Don't tell anyone, she said on the phone. And when Astrid pressed, asking for an emailed photo, Maude refused. *We must meet in person, and I can't come there. It would raise too many red flags. This must be our secret. The typewriter is here. The letter is in a safe place.*

Astrid agreed to visit for a week, over the long Labor Day weekend and to the following Friday. But first, she tied up loose ends, put certain projects on hold. She has no coworkers to take up the slack, to examine a contested holographic will, or forged checks, or a questioned signature on a quitclaim deed. To name only a few. *I'll be back at work soon,* she tells herself. *Aunt Maude needs me.*

She lifts her foot off the gas pedal, loosening her grip on the steering wheel. Rental cars never feel right—they tend to be ragged, abused, and slow to respond. Maybe like her, the car knows that Heron Bay was the source of all sorrows, a town haunted by its tragic past.

Every landmark should remind her of her lost little sister, but nothing looks familiar. Beneath the bright sunlight, the phantoms stay out of sight. The town seems benign. The road meanders down a wooded hillside toward the sea, the waves rippling and glinting and holding on to their secrets.

She drives past ornate Queen Anne Victorians that once defined Heron Bay as a promising seaport, but that now serve as bed-and-breakfasts and inns. The historic district could be a picture postcard, the elegant nineteenth-century buildings restored and arrested in time, from when the first settlers were sure Heron Bay would become a major terminus for the railroad. But it was not to be.

At a new traffic light on the corner, she stops on red as a young woman crosses the road in front of her, pushing a stroller toward a shop called Second Baby Toys. Astrid's breath catches, and in an instant, she sees baby Nina giggling in her jogging stroller, their mother in leggings and a sweatshirt, bouncing along the sidewalk, smiling down at her perfect little daughter. Nina was the second child and everything that Astrid was not: easygoing and sociable, photogenic and sweet-natured. Astrid was introverted, a reader, and moody.

On Oceanfront Street, she slows at a yellow light. The traffic signals weren't here before—but that was seventeen years ago. These newish buildings elude her memory: the medical clinic, a full-size grocery store, the boutiques fronted by hanging, colorful flowerpots. Tourists throng the sidewalks, licking ice cream cones and peering into shop windows.

The placid present belies the violent past. Centuries back, Native nations called this marshy forest their home until at least a third of their people died of diseases brought by invaders. Many of those who survived were forcibly moved to reservations, their homes burned. This is still their land, and they still live here. But in this quiet town, little trace remains of their struggles for freedom. *This is the way time works,* she thinks.

She has always been aware of history, of invisible ghosts—she can see what once was. Perhaps it's a curse that she can imagine the past when to everyone else, the present is perpetual. To them, it's as if the town has always been here with its lampposts and brick sidewalks, its hotels and shops along Oceanfront Street. As if nothing terrible ever happened.

On the passenger seat, her cell phone shows no service. She lost a reliable signal soon after crossing the Hood Canal Bridge and turning north. She ascends into a densely wooded escarpment. Uptown Road traverses this mostly residential district of Heron Bay. As a child, she walked this route many times to the farmers' market, the uptown shops, and the library, where Aunt Maude worked as head librarian before her retirement. For Astrid, this town was her summer home.

She turns left on Overlook Place, descends the winding road toward the sea, and pulls into her aunt's driveway at the end of the lane. Remarkably little has changed except that the trees have grown taller and the path down to the shore seems closer. The house is still pale yellow with white trim, quaint and inviting against the bright-blue sky. A hint of long-ago excitement sparks in her chest. This Victorian house always promised adventure, with its wraparound porch and stained-glass windows. The gardens offered a maze of rhododendrons and lavender, azaleas and lemongrass, rosemary bushes and privet hedges. *I can't believe I remembered all the plant names,* Astrid thinks. Aunt Maude taught them to her.

She parks behind a Honda in the driveway, gets out of the rental car, and draws a deep breath, inhaling the scents of herbs and clean air. On the north side of the property, she often took the meandering path through the woods leading up to the mansion on the bluff a quarter mile away, where the Michaels family spent summers and threw raucous parties.

Her crush on Julian Michaels feels long ago and far away. He was twenty-two years old, a university student home for the summer. Now a successful novelist, he lives on San Juan Island only a ferry ride away from his parents, who spend a few months a year here in Heron Bay, now that they've retired. They live elsewhere during the cold months, as rich people do, according to Aunt Maude.

As Astrid rolls her suitcase up the stone walkway to the front entrance, she flashes on a young Maude coming out to scoop Nina into her arms. *My little angel!*

A ceramic birdbath sits on the porch railing, a sculpted little angel perched on the rim. Aunt Maude has always loved any creature with wings. She used to hang hummingbird feeders from the eaves, and as a child, Astrid thought of her aunt as a fairy who could cast spells. Twelve years older than Astrid's mother, Maude already had tiny crow's-feet next to her eyes when Astrid was little, yet she'd always seemed youthful and bright.

Up on the covered porch, Astrid leaves her suitcase by the door and rings the bell. No answer. She rings again. Still no answer. Her phone still gets no signal. The time is 4:30 p.m. She is forty-five minutes late, but Maude must be here. The lights are on inside. Where could she have gone on a Friday afternoon? Her car sits in the driveway.

The front door is locked. But Maude mentioned a few months ago that she leaves it open for her friends. Perhaps she has started locking up.

Astrid goes back down the steps, shields her eyes, and scans the windows on the second floor, shaded by the branches of tall trees. "Aunt Maude!" No answer.

At the back of the house, the garden overflows with late-summer flowers. On the north side, the shadowy forest stretches away. No sign of anyone. "Aunt Maude!" Astrid calls out toward the woods. Her voice echoes strangely. She tries the back door to the kitchen—also locked.

Maybe Maude went for a walk on the beach. Perhaps she hid an extra house key, as she used to do years ago. On the front porch, Astrid checks underneath the flowerpots. Finally, she finds the dusty key beneath a pot of geraniums. She slides it into the lock and opens the heavy front door.

Inside, the worn entry carpet and scuffed hardwood floor bring back memories of running up and down the hall. The scent of baking lingers in the air, as if Maude has made her celebratory muffins.

The past throws itself out from the stacks of books on the living room shelves to the right. Astrid loved to explore her aunt's collection and lose herself in a good story. The old Baldwin still sits by the front bay window. Astrid spent hours playing the piano, but she stopped after that fateful summer. Grief leached away her motivation, and every time she sat at her spinet piano at home, she pictured Nina banging on the keys.

Family photos on the mantelpiece depict happier times. In one, Uncle Raj Dasgupta wraps his arms around Maude and kisses her cheek. She kept goading him to lose the beard, but he said it made him look distinguished. He was Maude's one and only husband, dead tragically of a heart attack when Astrid was only six.

Aunt Maude kept photos of Astrid and her parents and later of Nina, too . . . all of them together. Nina was blonde like Dad, and she shared his blue eyes. She might have grown up to be tall like him. Maybe an athlete or a dancer.

Astrid's throat tightens. Her father still lives in the woods of Oregon, has remarried, and is a professor of conservation biology at Portland University, but he spends most of his time in the wild.

In more recent pictures of Maude with her friends, Astrid recognizes Beatrice Michaels, the sophisticated wife of Verne Michaels, owners of the mansion on the bluff. Beatrice is regal in every shot, slim and fashionably dressed, bejeweled and elegant like Grace Kelly. She has aged well, her golden hair fading to platinum. She and Aunt Maude remained friends for all these years. Unlike Astrid's mother, Aunt Maude never blamed Beatrice for Nina's death, though the reflecting pool in which Nina drowned stood at the edge of the Michaels property. Aunt Maude said it's still there, crumbling and empty.

"Aunt Maude!" Astrid calls out again. Still no answer except for the ticking of the old grandfather clock in the passageway. She leaves her suitcase in the foyer and walks down the hall, the floorboards creaking beneath her shoes. "Aunt Maude, where are you?"

She pushes open the door to the library on the left. The walls are lined with tall shelves packed with books. A glossy, black portable typewriter sits on a shelf. When Aunt Maude said, *The typewriter is here*, she must have meant this one. Astrid remembers her mother sitting at it seventeen years ago, typing away after Nina died. Now there is only stillness, the smells of dust and old paper mixing with the scent of lavender potpourri.

A small table in a corner holds an outdated desktop computer and keyboard. The modem, router, and printer are on shelves below the computer. Beneath the single bay window, books and documents cover the desk. A jumble of papers fans out across the floor. In the corner are boxes piled up and marked LIBRARY DONATIONS. The window is open, the curtains flapping in the breeze. Sticking out from behind the desk is a blue house slipper, attached to an ankle, a leg . . .

Astrid dashes around the desk, her heart racing. Maude is lying on her back, slightly turned to her left, as if she tried to sit up or brace herself. How crumpled and thin she looks. Her face is pale, her eyes half-closed. Blood has clotted from a gash in her forehead, right above her left eye. Her wavy silver hair is tousled and translucent in the afternoon sunlight.

"Aunt Maude!" Astrid yells as she hovers above herself, distant and disbelieving. "Aunt Maude. It's me, Astrid!" *Oh no,* she thinks in a panic. *I can't be too late.*

CHAPTER TWO

The ambulance whisked Aunt Maude to Heron Bay Hospital at the south end of town. Hooked up to beeping monitors in the ICU, she looks small and frail. Three electrodes attached to her chest keep track of her vital signs, the full monitor ticking out the rhythm of her heartbeats. Her head is bandaged, her body motionless like a fallen statue. Her hair forms a silvery halo around her head.

Maude listed Astrid as next of kin, as there is nobody else now—no children, and Uncle Raj is gone. Her sister, Rose, well . . . Maude must've written her off. Astrid called her mother's latest number to leave a message. At least the cell phone still worked.

Astrid pulls up a chair next to the bed and touches her aunt's fragile wrist. An IV line snakes from her arm up to a bag of fluids; two narrow tubes deliver a liquid diet through her nose. A tube down her throat breathes for her, although she is perfectly capable of breathing on her own. The intubation is temporary. The doctors induced a coma because of her head injury. When the swelling subsides—not *if*—the tube will come out, probably within seventy-two hours. Astrid is glad her aunt is unconscious.

"Aunt Maude, you'll be okay," Astrid says, half to reassure herself. Can Maude hear anything in such a deep sleep? Does she dream while in a coma? Or does she experience nothing at all, a collapsing of hours and time? She might've tripped, fallen, and hit her head, the doctor said. But more likely, someone pushed her, and Astrid finds it difficult to believe her aunt created that mess in her library, knocking the papers off her desk. Just from a fall?

While waiting for the medics to arrive, Astrid snapped photos of the chaos—the half-open desk drawer, the books on the shelves, the filing cabinets, the black portable typewriter on a shelf.

Normally, Aunt Maude kept her library organized, even if she improvised in other areas of her life. She arranged her books according to the Dewey decimal system. She is a retired librarian, after all, but nobody mistook her for a bespectacled schoolmarm with hair tied back and a finger perpetually pressed to her lips, shushing people. She loved to chat, suggesting new books for reluctant readers. She wore flowing dresses, her hair long and wispy, and she waved her hands around when she described a story, as if casting a spell.

Come back, Aunt Maude, Astrid thinks in desperation. *I need you. You still have life left in you.* Her head throbs—her stomach hurts. She hasn't eaten since breakfast. But she can't leave Maude's side, not yet. "I'm sorry I didn't visit you before," Astrid says softly. "It was too hard to come back here."

Aunt Maude never pushed—until recently. She called, wrote letters with her fountain pen—often smudging the words—and sent gifts. She even visited Astrid in California now and then. But she never lamented the fact that her family no longer visited Heron Bay. *I should've been here for her,* Astrid thinks.

"Miss Johansen?" a soft voice says behind her. Astrid turns, and Dr. Sawari summons her to the door. Compact and quick on her feet, the doctor sports a shiny black ponytail, her eyes a startling, intense green. She seems too young to take charge of Aunt Maude's care. But then, Dr. Sawari has proven herself competent.

Astrid steps out into the hall with her. Doctors and nurses hurry by, and the air smells of bleach and perfume. Somewhere in another room, a woman is crying.

"How is she?" Astrid asks. "Will she be okay?"

Dr. Sawari offers a calibrated, sympathetic smile. "We expect the swelling to subside, but . . . we'll have to see."

"Will she come out of the coma? Will she be able to move and talk?"

"If only the stars could tell us. We'll keep a close eye on her."

"But she's not going to die."

"Not if I can help it."

"Thanks for all you're doing for her."

Dr. Sawari touches Astrid's arm. "You're welcome to stay, but you could go home and get some rest. We'll call you if anything changes."

Where is home? The last place Astrid thought of as home was the house she shared with Trent in Pacifica, where the mist rolled in thick on cool days. Not the Vallejo apartment or anywhere else. "I shouldn't leave her. I mean, what if she wakes up?"

"Nothing much is going to change in the next twenty-four hours. She's pretty far under."

"I'll . . . go back to her house, then."

"How long will you be in town?" the doctor asks.

"Only a few days. That was the plan, anyway—"

"Where is Mrs. D?" A teenage girl comes rushing down the hall, shawl flying. Reddish, curly hair peeks out from beneath a hand-knit cap. Her round face is flushed from running, a macramé purse slipping off her shoulder. A silver cross glints on a thin chain around her neck. "What happened to her?"

Astrid points to the door to Aunt Maude's room. "She's in there. I'm her niece. Are you a friend of hers?"

"Livie Dwight." The girl, maybe eighteen or nineteen years old, pulls Astrid into a tight, patchouli-scented hug. "I help her out with stuff. This is, like, so awful."

"Yes, it is. I'm glad you're here. I'm Astrid—"

"I know who you are. I've seen your pictures." Livie takes Astrid's face in her hands. "Thank God you were there. How is she?"

"She's . . . asleep." Astrid stops short of the word *coma*.

"May I see her? I signed in downstairs." Livie points to the Visitor tag pinned to her shirt.

"It's okay with me." Astrid looks at the doctor, and she nods briefly. Livie rushes into the room.

The doctor gestures to a doorway down the hall. "I forgot. The sheriff wants to ask you a few questions. I'll tell him to come back tomorrow."

"I'm happy to talk to him now."

"If you're sure." The doctor shows Astrid to a sparsely furnished waiting room, the walls a soft blue, magazines on a side table, a flat-screen television attached high on the wall, playing the news in silence. She sits in a plastic chair and stares at the palms of her upturned hands. The life line runs continuously on her left palm but breaks into two lines on her right.

"Astrid Johansen?" a man says behind her. "I'm Sheriff Burke." His deep, throaty voice sounds vaguely familiar.

"Yes, I'm Astrid." She turns to look up at the man and draws a sharp breath. "Conor."

Clad in a pale-brown shirt and green pants, a gold sheriff's star pinned to his pocket, a gun in his holster, he's an older blueprint of the teenager she remembers. She knows that slightly skewed nose, lopsided jaw. She and Conor were once friends. But he was scrawny back then. Now he's much taller and broader, with the hint of a beard and weariness in his dark-brown eyes, although he must be only thirty-two years old. As a fifteen-year-old, he was round-faced and enthusiastic. She gave him the secret, unspoken nickname *Babyface Conor*. Now he's Sheriff Conor Burke. And no hint of a baby face.

"In the flesh." He hands her a bottle of water.

"You're a saint." She takes the cold bottle and gulps from it greedily.

He sits in the chair next to her, moves it over at an angle, yanks up his pant legs. "It's good to see you after, what, a century?"

"Give or take. You filled your dad's shoes." Cillian Burke was the local sheriff when Nina died.

"He passed away two years ago."

"I'm so sorry."

"And I'm sorry about what happened to your aunt. How are you holding up?"

"Ask me when I'm conscious again. I feel like I'm sleepwalking." She tries not to think of her aunt hooked up to monitors in another room, but at least her young friend, Livie, is there. The images pass through Astrid's mind in a dreamlike haze—the medics transferring Maude to a stretcher, the ambulance doors slamming, the engine fading into the distance. A police officer—not Conor—driving her to the hospital while the sheriff went into the house, maybe to assess the scene. Must've been Conor, but she was too far away to recognize him.

"You look exhausted," he says. "Someone I can call? Your husband?"

Astrid laughs hollowly, holds up her left hand, absent a wedding ring. "The divorce was just finalized."

Conor nods, and he has the sense not to ask. He pulls a pen and notepad from his shirt pocket. A voice echoes over an intercom, shoes squeak by in the hall. In this enclosed space, she can smell the laundry detergent on his uniform and a faint minty soap.

She sips cold water from the bottle.

"Tell me what happened today," Conor says, clicking the end of the pen. He used to do that a lot, a nervous habit. At fifteen, when he worked a summer job at the local grocery store, he kept a pen in his breast pocket. He was always clicking and clicking that pen. But now he clicks his pen only once, not nervous at all.

"That's a broad question." She recounts the sequence of events: finding the door locked, the key beneath a pot, Aunt Maude lying on the floor, the mess in the library. The cold water makes her teeth chatter. Or maybe it's the air-conditioning in the hospital.

Conor jots on his notepad. "You said the house was locked—"

"She said she didn't lock her front door. Someone could've walked in without knocking, right? That same person could've locked up on their way out. Did you dust the knob for fingerprints?"

He smiles slightly. "You went in through the front door, so your fingerprints are on the knob. They likely wiped off any other prints."

"Oh, too bad."

"Did you notice anything else unusual?"

"Aside from the papers all over the floor? A desk drawer was slightly open . . . She must've known her attacker, right? I mean, she didn't have scratches on her face. Nobody broke a lamp or . . . there was no sign of a struggle."

He points to his right temple and winks at her. "Good head on your shoulders. Want to join my team? We could use you."

"My plate is full. I'm only here for a few days."

"Why come back now, after all this time?"

She explains that Aunt Maude summoned her with uncommon urgency to examine a typewritten letter with a handwritten signature. "She must've thought the letter was valuable. She sometimes finds historical stuff mixed in with library donations. Maybe an old train ticket or postcard, nothing earth-shattering. But she acted like this was different."

"So, what, she found a letter from Queen Elizabeth? Leonardo da Vinci? Benjamin Franklin?"

"I would tell you if I knew." Astrid looks up at the TV, then toward the door, wishing this room had a window. "She was going to tell me everything when I got here. I wondered if she might be a bit . . . confused." She puts the water bottle on the table. Her fingers are cold.

"Your aunt is sharp as a tack. Nothing confused about her, far as I can tell."

"You know her pretty well then."

"Yeah, we talk. I see her around."

"Small town, huh? What, ten thousand people?" Astrid pulls at a loose thread on the sleeve of her sweater.

"That's big in my book." He taps his pen on the notepad. "Give me more specifics to go on here, Astrid. What else did she say?"

"She was cryptic. Maybe someone attacked her because they were looking for the letter? Maybe they knew its value? Who would know? She must've told someone . . . or let something slip."

He shifts in his seat. "Assuming what happened to her had anything to do with the letter."

"You think that's a stretch. Do you think she just fell?"

"That's what I'm trying to find out. Why did she tell you about the letter? You in particular, I mean."

"I'm a forensic document examiner. My job is to—"

"Authenticate the letter, right?"

"I would try. It takes hours of work to analyze a document. I have to use my equipment to look at the ink in the signature, the typewritten words, the paper, that kind of thing."

He looks at her as if she is an alien with special powers. Then he jots on the notepad and clears his throat. "Uh—so, you brought all this equipment with you?"

"No—I can't transport a big microscope or light box! But I brought a few smaller things. I have to analyze the typewriting, too . . . compare the letter to typewritten samples from the typewriter on the shelf. The typebars, the type slugs, the ink ribbon. Each typewriter has its own personality, like a fingerprint. If the machine was not used to type the letter, then we'd have to find the matching typewriter."

He laughs. "Tall order. People don't exactly use typewriters anymore. It could be long gone or rusting in a landfill somewhere."

"Unless the letter was typed recently and made to look old. But my aunt wouldn't be able to tell without my help."

"You're putting a lot of weight on this supposed letter."

Astrid clasps her hands together in her lap. Her stomach growls. Her eyelids grow heavy. "Why else would someone hurt a vulnerable woman? My aunt is seventy years old! I've told you all I know. I wish I could help more, but . . ."

Conor's eyes darken, and she sees him the way he was at fifteen, skinny and barely a year older than her, his eyes sad when she told him to stop following her around. *Are you breaking up with me?* He held on to the knotted friendship bracelet he'd given her just weeks before, which she'd returned to him. *I don't feel that way about you,* she told him. *We're friends.* They were so young. She had no idea what she really felt about anyone. His face crumpled, as if his heart had broken into pieces. She stepped back away from him, uncomfortable with his raw emotion. He'd been tailing her all summer.

But now he stares off into the distance. "Nothing else you can think of, huh? Even if it seems insignificant?"

She thinks for a moment. "She left a follow-up message. I checked it right after I landed in Seattle."

"I'd like to hear it."

She extracts the phone from her purse and plays the message. "Astrid, dear," Maude begins in her musical, slightly thin voice. "I hope you've landed safely. Call me if you get lost. I meant to tell you about the key—" A distant thudding sound stops her, and then she hangs up.

Conor frowns, his expression pensive. "Play it again."

This time, Aunt Maude's voice seems to carry a slight tremor. "She's afraid," Astrid says, a shiver running through her.

"What is that thud in the background? Do you recognize the sound?" Conor asks.

Astrid shakes her head. "Could it be someone shutting a door? Dropping something?" She didn't notice it the first time, maybe due to the ambient noise in the airport.

"It could be anything," Conor says. "Or it could be nothing at all."

CHAPTER THREE

Astrid sits in the passenger seat of the sheriff's car, which smells of metal and vinyl and stale coffee. The police radio crackles, voices speaking in code. Conor sits right next to her, a stranger to her now, but she's grateful for the ride. He offered to take her to a hotel, but she told him it felt wrong not to stay in Aunt Maude's house, and anyway, she needs to look for the letter. She can't stop thinking about the thud at the end of her aunt's message. Did a book drop on the floor? Or maybe Aunt Maude was closing the piano lid. As Conor said, it could be anything. But still.

"Pretty drive, I appreciate the lift," she says, looking out at the ocean along the waterfront road.

"It's no problem," Conor replies. "This place grows on you. Was a time I couldn't wait to get out of here, but now it's good to be back. Slower pace of life."

"Aunt Maude loves it here, too. She said the dampness aggravates her arthritis, but walking helps. What if she wakes up and can't walk?"

"Best not to jump to the worst-case scenario," Conor says.

"Walking is her life. She has lived and walked here for fifty years."

"Hey, she'll be okay," Conor says.

"I hope so. She's not getting any younger."

"None of us are," he says.

She looks at his profile. Slightly bumpy nose, prominent jaw, bushy brows. "So, you left Heron Bay? Moved away somewhere?"

"I got married at eighteen, joined the army. My wife and I traveled wherever the military sent me."

My wife and I. Conor had no trouble tying the knot right out of high school. But for Astrid, relationships have been a struggle, her own marriage ending in shambles. "You must've had quite a life of travel."

"Yeah, it was the adventure of a lifetime!" His voice drips with sarcasm.

"I've touched a nerve. We don't have to talk about this."

"Afghanistan. I was deployed there for a year—without my wife, of course. Total shit show. When I got back, she wasn't too happy with me. Hell, *I* wasn't too happy with me. By the time I got myself together, she was gone. How's that for talking about this?"

"I'm truly sorry, Conor." Now she understands the weary look in his eyes.

"I'm a lot better than I was."

"I'm glad to hear it." She yawns, blinks away the sleepiness.

Conor drives through downtown now, the boutiques all closed for the evening. The crowds have dissipated from the sidewalks.

"How did you end up back here?" she asks.

"My dad needed company. My mom had left him a few months earlier. When I came back, I was only twenty-three. I'd already been to war, married, and divorced. I joined the police academy, did my training, worked my way up. Then my dad got sick with cancer."

"I'm so sorry. I remember him well." When Nina drowned, Cillian Burke was first on the scene, directing his deputies and other emergency personnel.

"I miss him," Conor says. "And my mom. She moved to the East Coast. I'm living in the family home now. I guess you could say I came full circle, settling in Heron Bay."

"Do you plan to stay?"

"I have a good life. I play baseball. I read thrillers. I love my job."

"I love mine, too," she says, although she does not love the commute from Vallejo to San Ramon through the hot, dry, crowded Bay Area. The view from her one-room suite in a large office building is not the best, but it's not bad. She can see freshly cut grass dotted by trees.

They're passing the Heron Bay Bookstore, now closed, but the lighted window display startles her—several copies of the latest hardcover thriller by Julian Michaels, *The Drowning*. The cover depicts a silhouette of a diver plunging into brightly lit ocean depths. She had read a glowing review in a national newspaper, half expecting him to have exploited the story of her sister's drowning. But the novel is about a scuba-diving tycoon who drowns in the sea under mysterious circumstances.

Astrid looks away, her eyes watery, and focuses on the road. She avoids Julian's novels, although she once peeked at his author photo inside the back cover. His chiseled features and piercing blue eyes looked unreal, airbrushed, his hair still strawberry blond. Aside from the faint lines next to his eyes, he resembled the Julian she remembered.

Conor's police radio buzzes, a voice speaking quickly. She makes out "10-92." He doesn't reply as the car turns and ascends uptown. "Are you dating anyone, now that you're unhitched?" he asks.

She shakes her head. "My colleagues try to set me up on those dating websites, but I guess I'm still getting over my marriage." *Even though it has been nearly twelve months since I moved out. Eleven months, three weeks, and four days.*

"I'm not big on those apps, either. Tinder, Matchbox—"

"Match dot com," she says, smiling at him.

"Whatever, yeah," he says, and laughs. "I went on a few dates but nothing serious . . . My friends say I've been alone too long, but you get used to it."

"I've been separated under a year. And . . . my ex is already living with my best friend. Former best friend. Leona. She moved in with him a couple of months ago." There, she voiced the truth that she could not bear to face. She imagines Leona dragging her brightly colored suitcases into the foyer of the Pacifica house, frowning at Trent's understated furniture.

"Whoa, that's got to be hard, losing your husband and your best friend at the same time," Conor says.

"He's on the rebound. They're not going to last. They're too different from each other."

Conor glances at her, then back at the road. "But they're living together. That's a big move."

"Leona is impulsive, and Trent probably went along." *He'll learn pretty quickly,* Astrid thinks. *I know Leona Kemp too well.* Leona and Astrid met in tenth grade chemistry class in San Francisco. Leona created experiments that invariably exploded, sending both her and Astrid to detention. They passed notes under the desks. Leona shoplifted makeup and tampons from the local drugstore more than once. She wore a miniskirt to the prom, danced on impulse in gym class, and wore a neon-blue pantsuit as maid of honor at Astrid's outdoor wedding to Trent. Astrid loved Leona's wildness, reveled in her bravado. They shared secrets and shopping trips and too many lunch dates to count. *I really thought we were the best of friends,* Astrid thinks, tears coming to her eyes even now. The last thing she ever expected from Leona was this deep betrayal.

Conor pulls into Aunt Maude's driveway. "Do you still want to work things out with your ex?" he asks.

"We talk every few weeks. We're still friends." The truth is, she calls Trent, but he never calls her. "Did you ever want to work things out with your wife?"

"I tried, believe me. But she was ready to leave." He nods and nods, as if trying to convince himself. "It was over. You know, you break some things, and you can't fix them, no matter how hard you try."

Maybe that was why she stayed away from Heron Bay. She broke something here that could never be fixed. "Did you two have kids together?"

He draws a deep breath. "We wanted to have a family eventually. But after I came back from Afghanistan, she said she wouldn't have a child with me, the way I was. I couldn't blame her. Now she has a kid with her new husband. They'll probably be together forever. They're a good match."

"I'm sorry things didn't work out," Astrid says, getting out of the car.

Conor gets out, too, and walks her up to the front door. "You shouldn't stay here," he says, looking toward the woods.

"I'll be okay. I promised Aunt Maude I would help with this letter. I need to look for it."

He pulls a business card from his pocket. Hands it to her. "If you need anything, my number's on there. That's my cell on the back. Day or night."

She tucks the card into the back pocket of her jeans. "I'll call you at midnight, then."

"Day or night within reason." In this different light, the waning sun shining at an angle from the west, he looks battle-weary. Then he's gone, and in the quiet evening, loneliness descends upon her.

CHAPTER FOUR

That August evening seventeen years ago, Nina slept in the bedroom next to Astrid's in Heron Bay. Aunt Maude had gone to a library fundraiser downtown. Astrid's parents danced and drank at the party up at the Michaels mansion. That was what Astrid called it—"the Michaels mansion"—as there were seven bedrooms and six bathrooms upstairs, labyrinthine hallways downstairs, and an expansive sitting room opening onto a vast stone patio where the family threw endless summer galas. She had been into the house only once to use the bathroom. Her mouth had dropped open in awe at the ornate fixtures, the sculptures and paintings, the chandeliers. And she'd thought Aunt Maude's house was spacious.

From here, in the upstairs room that became Astrid's for the summer, she could not see the Michaels mansion through the forest, but she could see her aunt's lush garden, an angled view of the glittering Pacific Ocean, and the trail heading into the woods.

In bed, she kept tossing and turning, sweating beneath the sheets. Her thin cotton nightgown clung to her back in the warm night. At fourteen, she wanted to go to parties herself. She longed to have fun with her friends instead of babysitting Nina. But every time her parents went out, they expected Astrid to stay home and watch her little sister. Nobody cared if she had any other plans.

She had checked on Nina in the room next door only a few minutes earlier. Her little sister slept deeply, her blonde hair forming a halo of loose curls around her head, her cheeks pink, her thumb in her mouth. Astrid had almost shaken her awake to warn her that her thumb would fall off, but that would've been cruel. Astrid felt like being that mean sometimes, but she never acted on her dark thoughts. Underneath the irritation, she loved her sister.

Astrid had backed out of the room, holding her breath, avoiding the squeaky floorboard. If Nina were to wake, all hell would break loose. Already, the evening had not gone well. Not five minutes after Astrid's parents had left for the party, driving all the way around on the main road instead of taking the path through the woods—her mother's red satin dress and spiked heels would not survive the muddy trail—Nina had started whimpering.

Astrid had shushed her, trying to distract her with toys and games of peekaboo, and it had worked for a while. Then out came the board books, but Nina could not be consoled. Her lips had begun to tremble, tears welling from her eyes. "Mommy gone! Mommy. I want Mommy."

That's because you're Mommy's favorite, Astrid had not said. But she had thought it. *Mommy spoils you.* Nina could not tolerate even a few hours alone. The moment Astrid had gone to the bathroom down the hall, her sister had darted out of the house in her little slip-on sneakers and taken off into the woods. Astrid ran after her, grabbed her hand. Nina dropped her whole weight onto the ground. Astrid had tried to drag her back, frustration rising inside her. Some teenagers were partying around a bonfire on the beach, including her buddy Conor Burke. She'd been down there with all of them earlier before her parents had called her back to babysit Nina.

And she had seen *him* farther down the beach. Julian Michaels, walking along the surf line, approaching the bonfire where the younger teens gathered. He wore rolled khaki pants and a loose linen shirt, his strawberry-blond hair flopping over one eye, his lanky body tanned from the sun. He looked sixteen, not twenty-two. How she longed for him.

But she'd had to leave. And babysit her sister and keep Nina from running all the way up to the party next door. She'd tried dragging her little sister home so as not to make a scene. And yet, she could not carry a three-year-old's heavy, screaming weight.

"All right, fine," Astrid had said finally. "We'll go to Mommy, okay? Stop crying."

Instantly, Nina had quieted, the tears drying on her cheeks. She'd stood, grabbed Astrid's hand, and they had run together on the trails up through the woods to the edge of the Michaels mansion, where the grown-ups clinked wineglasses and laughed and the smells of alcohol and perfume rose into the air. Astrid had tiptoed to the edge of the stone patio and caught her mother's eye. Her beautiful, curvy mother, Rose, with her black, wavy hair spilling down past her shoulders, had been sitting between Astrid's father, Bjorn, and *him*. Julian. Astrid's crush.

Lucky for her, he had been looking the other way. She couldn't bear the thought of him seeing her as the young babysitter holding her little sister's hand. Her mother had come running and snatched up Nina. "What do you think you're doing?" she'd hissed to Astrid. She frowned, her lipstick smudged.

"She wanted to come here. She was crying!" Astrid had said.

"How hard is it to babysit your sister for a couple of hours?" Her mother had hurried to the driveway, followed by Astrid's father, who'd fished in his pockets for the keys to the car, muttering to himself. Bjorn Johansen, tall and big-boned and blond like Nina, was a handsome and studious professor of conservation biology. He wore small, round glasses. Astrid's mother, more extroverted, was an interior decorator who loved parties. And Bjorn went along because he loved her.

But tonight, something was up. Astrid could tell her parents weren't happy with each other, but she didn't know why. By the tension in their shoulders and the way they didn't speak to each other but bustled around Nina, she could tell they were fighting again.

"Do you want to come back with us?" Bjorn asked Rose, not looking at her directly.

"Of course I don't," she said, tucking Nina into the car seat in the back, then kissing her forehead. "I'll be home soon, sweetie, okay? You be a good girl. I love you so much."

Nina nodded and whimpered, and Astrid's mother straightened and shut the door. "Thank God nobody else saw," she said, glancing back toward the party. The patio faced the sea, around the back of the house, out of view of the driveway. "Astrid, you have to keep an eye on her. She takes off—"

"She knows," Bjorn said, getting into the car.

"I was babysitting her. I read to her. I played with her!" Astrid stood with her hands on her hips, her lips trembling.

Her mother ignored her and instead leaned in through the driver's-side window. "Are you coming back?" she asked Astrid's dad.

"Should I? I mean, what's the point tonight?" Bjorn started.

"Don't do this. You're going all the way back?"

"I have to. I told you."

"What difference does it make?"

Astrid stood back, forgotten. "I'm walking home," she declared.

Her mother turned to look at her. "What?"

"I'm walking," Astrid said.

"Get in the car," her father said.

"I'll meet you there." She turned and left.

"Astrid!" her father shouted.

She sprinted onto the darkening trail. The woods swallowed her, and nobody came after her. When she got back to Aunt Maude's house, she found her father waiting in the foyer. He had tucked Nina back into bed in the room he and Rose shared with her.

"Will you be okay?" he asked Astrid, his blue eyes dark with concern. "I have to drive back to Seattle tonight. Your mother will be here shortly."

"You're going back to *Seattle?*" Astrid asked, her mouth dropping open. It was a three-hour drive from here.

"I have to—it's a long story. Mom will be back from the party soon."

But Mom didn't come back.

And Astrid somehow fell asleep. She must have. When she woke, her mother's laughter drifted up the stairs. Her heels tapped the wooden floor, accompanied by heavier thuds. Astrid held her breath, but nobody looked in on her. She thought she heard her mother speak nearby in the hall. "Such a likeness . . . I swear."

Then the door squeaked open to her parents' room next to hers. Silence, then a distant murmur of voices—perhaps they came from somewhere outside. Astrid drifted off again for a few minutes. When she woke, the digital clock on the nightstand read only 10:00 p.m. Her father had left at about 9:00 p.m. He must've come back. Aunt Maude was probably still at the fundraiser. She often stayed out late with her friends.

Astrid listened to the distant hooting of owls, the rush of the surf, the rustling of the trees. She drifted off a third time, and when she woke, it was 10:45 p.m. No more sounds came from inside the house. Her parents had probably gone to sleep earlier than usual.

Restless, Astrid got out of bed and looked out through the window. The balmy sea air drifted up through the screen. It was then that she saw *him* crossing at an angle through the side garden, heading toward the forest trail. Julian. Or at least, she was fairly sure it was him. Maybe he had been at the bonfire on the beach. He wore light-colored pants—not rolled up—and a black, hooded top. This was all she could make out at a distance. He walked with a familiar, long-legged lope, leaning to the left, obviously returning home through the woods.

In the moonlight, the roses and lush blooms in her aunt's garden looked unearthly, from a fairy tale. The complex smells of flowers and the sea rushed into her nose.

She glanced at the nightstand, at the old books Julian had loaned her from his parents' library, and she could hear his smooth, deep voice in her head. *What are you reading, Austen Girl?* A tingling, breathless joy filled her. That was what he had called her the first time they'd met on the beach. She'd been sitting on a driftwood log, reading. He'd sat next to her, looked at the book, *Persuasion*, and thereafter, he'd called her *Austen Girl*.

Her heart fluttered with anticipation. She leaped out of bed, yanked the window open, and almost called out to him through the screen. Then she remembered that her parents—and Nina—were likely asleep in the room next to hers. And Aunt Maude would soon be back, too.

Julian fast approached the cover of the forest.

As she whipped off her nightgown, her heart pattered. The world filled with bright possibility, her love for Julian pure and, she thought, endless. She pulled on her bra, T-shirt, jeans, and running shoes as fast as she could. She didn't bother with socks. Her fingers trembled—it was difficult to button her jeans. She tied her hair back—it was thick and wild and black—and tiptoed to the door. The house creaked a little as it settled. No sound came from anywhere else inside—no snoring, no breathing, but then, Nina didn't make a sound when she slept.

Astrid tiptoed down the stairs, a beam of moonlight falling through the hallway window. She avoided the squeaky step and held her breath at the bottom of the articulated staircase. The touch-tone phone sat on a table in the hall in another sliver of moonlight. Aunt Maude's antique furniture stood motionless. The house was quiet, save for the old grandfather clock ticking in the hall.

Astrid tiptoed back past the dining room and Aunt Maude's library. In the kitchen, the granite countertops gleamed, the white cabinets and steel appliances outlined in the pale light. She was about to open the kitchen door to the backyard, but it was already ajar. She had only to push it open and step outside, hardly daring to breathe. She made sure the door shut quietly and did not lock.

The air blew in damp from the sea, carrying the scents of roses and jasmine. A cloud crossed over the moon, night spilling like ink through the forest. Shadows moved in and out of the trees. A pungent moisture hung in the air. She set off at a sprint toward the opening into the woods, careful to stay in shadows. The branches brushed against her face, and she felt like she was flying while running in the dark. *Julian must be going home,* she thought, so she chose the trails that led back up to the Michaels house.

He can't have gone far. But he'd had quite a head start on her. She ran along the winding trail, the cloud passing away from the moon. Now she could see her way, the forest in shades of gray and silver. She listened for him, watched for his shape ahead of her, but he seemed to have disappeared into thin air. She imagined going all the way to his house, throwing a rock up at his bedroom window, but she didn't know which window was his. She had never been into his room. He was, after all, much older.

The sea glinted in the distance, and a ferry foghorn sounded from the harbor. She reached a clearing—he wasn't there. Her heart swung from elation to despair in a matter of seconds. She had so needed to find him. The stories were all lining up in her head. *I was at the beach party, yeah, and I saw you. Guess what I'm reading now?* Gone with the Wind . . .

She came out at the stone garden at the edge of the Michaels property. The garden sat nearly halfway between Aunt Maude's house and the Michaels mansion, in a forest clearing. Julian's mother, Beatrice, loved to take walks in the woods and sit in her stone garden, her sanctuary. Stone statues of all sizes surrounded Astrid—rabbits, bears, and foxes, their silhouettes a little scary in the dimness.

How had she ended up here? Generally, she avoided walking this way. The reflecting pool creeped her out, too. It was long and rectangular, the water a motionless mirror reflecting the sky. The pool was too murky for swimming, and she imagined a monster arising from the black depths, although she knew the water was shallow.

In the moonlight, something like clothing or, no, grass, maybe seagrass, floated atop the water. *How strange,* she thought. She crept in closer, her heart pounding. What if someone had thrown something into the pool? A coat? Or an animal? She would have to wade into that brackish water to rescue a dog or a deer. *The bottom must be slimy,* she thought.

But when she got close enough, she could see hair splayed out, the back of a head, a white sheet billowing in the water like a jellyfish. No, not a sheet. It was something else. Now, as she drew closer, she could see something round and shiny floating at the far end of the pool, in shadows. What was the ball doing here? This was Nina's silver ball—the one she loved so much and played with all the time.

Astrid waded in, the cold making her gasp. Icy water seeped into her shoes and froze her bare toes. She slid along the slimy bottom of the pool. The water was shallow, and yet, she could not move fast enough. She reached out to grab at the sheet, which was not a sheet but a nightgown. Nina's nightgown. She turned her sister over. *But Nina isn't here. She's in bed asleep upstairs in the alcove,* Astrid thought. *With Mom and Dad. But I should've checked. She tends to wander off . . .* Her little sister's face was pale, her eyes cloudy, her lips blue. Astrid dragged her out of the water, stumbling, and somewhere, someone with her own voice screamed for help.

CHAPTER FIVE

Astrid watches Conor's car disappear around the bend. Then she goes inside, and even though she's exhausted she can't bear to rattle around in the house alone, not just yet. She pulls on a windbreaker and walks out through the dry grass. At the edge of Maude's garden, a narrow path leads into the cedars and firs, the air cool and damp in the shade of the overhanging branches. The dirt trail soon widens and meanders deeper into the woods. She follows the path, breathing in the scents of pine and fir, listening to the muted sounds of birds overhead, a Douglas squirrel scrabbling up a tree and scolding her.

After a few minutes, the path branches off in three different directions. There was never a formal map of these trails, but she remembers the left one twisting down through the woods and eventually reaching the beach. Another branch winds around through thickets and then up switchbacks toward a spectacular lookout on the bluff. A third trail passes the stone garden—if the garden is even still there—and the reflecting pool in which Nina drowned. Even now, when Astrid thinks of the pool, her stomach clenches. She can't bring herself to take that path.

All three trails connect to each other in a complex maze. Anyone could get lost in here, but as a kid, she came to know the various curves and landmarks by heart. The forest was purely magical.

But now, she's not sure she remembers her way. As she follows the left trail, the ocean glimmers through the trees. Ages ago, she and Conor took this route many times. Instead of hiking single file, he insisted on walking next to her so that their shoulders sometimes touched. It didn't bother her at first until he gave her the woven bracelet, and then she began to notice when he came in too close.

She started keeping her distance, even stood him up once. He'd invited her to a party, but she met Julian Michaels farther down the beach instead, at the bottom of the stone steps leading up to his parents' mansion. Back then, her stomach fluttered at the thought of him.

Halfway to the beach, she backtracks and takes the turnoff that leads up to the lookout. The switchbacks climb a steep hillside—she's winded by the time she reaches the top. When did she become so out of shape? She walks in Vallejo but not up steep hills, and lately, she works too much. She loses track of time, looking up from her computer or microscope to find sunset slanting in through her office window.

As she follows the worn path to the bluff, she's suddenly dizzy. She has always been afraid of heights. But she makes herself sidle up to a signpost showing a stick figure tumbling off a cliff. The top of the sign reads FALLING CAN BE DEADLY. Below the picture are the words PLEASE STAY ON THE TRAIL. She takes one more step and peers down at shrubby trees clinging to the side of the cliff. Far below, the frothy waves dash themselves against the shore. The vast ocean stretches into the distance. A magnificent bald eagle soars overhead, letting out its peculiar, high-pitched whistling call.

Farther along the bluff, beyond a dense patch of forest, the Michaels mansion sits in a clearing, its oceanfront patio surrounded by a low stone wall. Two silhouettes stand on the patio, leaning over the wall and looking toward the sea—a slim woman and a tall man. Verne and Beatrice Michaels? The woman gesticulates expressively. The man shakes his head, and then the woman slaps his cheek. Or perhaps she merely reaches up to swat a fly or mosquito away from his face, hard to tell from a distance. The woman turns and seems to be looking straight at Astrid. *Does she see me over here, watching?*

Astrid rushes back behind the cover of trees, her heart racing. *I wasn't supposed to see that little domestic tiff.* She jogs down the trail, slowing on the steep switchbacks, and reaches the house as the sun is setting. She makes sure all the doors are locked, the porch lights lit. The forest darkens beyond the garden, and to the west, gulls cry above the waves.

She moves her suitcase into the guest room downstairs, furnished with a single bed, a watercolor painting of a driftwood-strewn beach, an antique nightstand, a Tiffany lamp, and a closet full of empty hangers. It's a neutral space holding no particular memories for her. The window offers an angled view of the garden and the ocean beyond. The evening is peaceful, only the distant sounds of surf. She changes into comfortable sweats and house slippers, hangs up a few clothes in the bedroom closet, and washes her face in the bathroom down the hall, alarmed at how tired and sad she looks.

In another life, she would've called Leona for moral support, but now Leona shares the blue tile shower with Trent, the same shower in which he made love to Astrid too many times to count. Leona wakes to the view of the misty Pacific Ocean through the bedroom window. She tells Trent her chatterbox stories about the houses she showed, the potential buyers for a villa in Sausalito or Walnut Creek. Leona kisses him goodbye in the morning and goes off to work in her little BMW, while he jets off in his practical Prius.

Didn't Leona find her friendship with Astrid more important than her obsession with Trent? *The heart does what it wants, and I couldn't help it,* Leona sobbed over the phone. She tried many times to reconnect with Astrid, sending notes of apology, leaving messages inviting her to lunch, even sending a gift for her birthday a month ago. *You're still my friend.* But Astrid understood what Conor meant about broken things. She could never bring herself to respond to Leona. Her former best friend made her choice.

In the guest room, Astrid opens her suitcase again and brings out the small, carved wooden box from Kashmir, the one Aunt Maude gave to her a few years ago. The box contains keepsakes from her marriage to Trent. She takes the box with her every time she travels, like a good-luck charm, a talisman. What would he think if he knew? She places the box on the dresser. *Maybe I should call Trent, even if Leona is there with him,* Astrid thinks. He knew Aunt Maude. She attended the wedding at Point Reyes National Seashore four years ago. Astrid's mother didn't show up, but Aunt Maude sat in the front row next to Astrid's father and his wife, all of them smiling while Astrid and Trent exchanged vows and gazed into each other's eyes with joy and adoration. Good, kindhearted, sweet Trent Hoffman, a solid, dependable accountant. Not a mean bone in his body.

Perhaps, if Astrid had fought harder to save the marriage, he might have eventually forgiven her. She can't be sure. She can still feel the softness of his touch. Can still remember every detail about him—the way he cracked his knuckles, his habit of sipping tea instead of coffee, of feeding birds and helping his neighbors bring in their groceries.

She tried to be a good wife. She listened to his complaints about work politics at a CPA firm, offered a sympathetic shoulder. She even enjoyed traveling with Trent, watching sunsets, long walks on the beach, margaritas.

At the landline in the hall, she dials his number. He picks up after two rings, the sound of his voice flooding her with relief.

"State your purpose," he says mildly. He always answers his phone this way. Never simply "hello." His tenor, slightly nasal tone has become as familiar to Astrid as a comfortable pair of slippers.

"Aunt Maude's in the hospital," she says and tells him everything. "I thought you would want to know. I mean, you were always good to her. She liked you." What she really wants to say is, *I'm sorry about everything that went wrong between us, but I don't know how to fix it, and now I'm here alone and sad in this creaky, cold house, and I needed to hear your voice*. A small part of her keeps hoping he'll show up, lift her into his arms, and declare that all is forgiven.

Trent breathes into the phone and lets out a low whistle, another habit when he's shocked or can't immediately think of what to say. "She's not going to die, sounds like. That's a plus."

Astrid looks at the grandfather clock against the wall across from her, its brass finial pointing straight up toward the ceiling. "She's on a ventilator, Trent."

"But she's coming off it soon, you said. You can take some comfort in that." His voice sounds distant, distracted. She can hear papers rustling in the background. *Is he at the office at this hour?* He did often work late.

"I worry she might take a turn for the worse or have brain damage," she says.

"You'll have to see what happens," he says, more papers rustling. "Anything I can do to help?"

Come here and tell me everything will be all right. She holds the phone a little away from her ear. "Just wanted to let you know. She was part of our life . . . together."

"Your aunt is amazing, that's for sure," he says, his voice softening. Where is he sitting, in his study at home with the window overlooking the cypress trees and the ocean beyond? Or does he have his work spread out on the dining table? She used to get on him about taking up too much room on that table.

"When she pulls out of this, I'm going to let her know that," Astrid says. A moment of silence follows. "Well, I guess that's all—"

"Wait," Trent says, his voice suddenly loud. "Don't hang up. There's something I need to tell you."

Her grip tightens on the phone. She holds her breath, imagining in a split second all the things Trent could say. *I was wrong about Leona. She's moving out. I don't care about what happened between you and me. Come back. I'm catching the next flight to Seattle. You shouldn't be alone. I made your favorite coconut curry dish with broccoli . . . I miss you. My life isn't the same without you. I'm willing to compromise . . .*

"Go ahead," she tells him.

"Leona and I . . . ," he begins, then clears his throat.

You're splitting up, I knew it, she almost says.

"We're . . . ," he continues. "We're engaged."

Of course you are, Astrid thinks, her mind going blank. *How could I have expected otherwise?* And yet, his words punch her in the gut, and she loses her breath. "You're getting married?" Her voice comes out high pitched, incredulous.

"That's what being engaged usually means," he says.

"But . . . when? Are you sure? I mean . . . you're not."

"We're not what?" he says sharply.

Compatible, interested in the same things, she doesn't say. "Um, thank you for telling me," she says. Her voice comes out raspy, her throat dry. She won't congratulate them, and why should she?

"Leona wants you to come to the wedding," he says quickly. "She's sending you an invitation. You two are friends . . . or used to be. She misses you. She wants to be friends with you . . ."

Astrid holds the phone away from her ear and starts laughing. She can't stop—the laughter makes her double over. Trent waits, not hanging up, while she gathers herself, wiping the tears from her eyes. "Are you even serious?" she says, her voice shaky and shrill. "You can tell Leona to shove her invitation up her ass."

CHAPTER SIX

Saturday morning, Astrid wakes to the chatter of birdsong. She was dreaming of ink. Striated ballpoint ink on a forged letter, dry ink on an old typewriter ribbon, the tricolor dot ink on a counterfeit contract, photocopied on watermarked cotton paper and passed off as the original. Ink on the skin of a dead boy who shot himself. The case was real, and she has dreamed of it more than once. The boy's mother believed he was killed, so she hired Astrid and another document examiner to analyze the writing on his skin. Both examiners concluded that the boy had likely written the notes on himself. His mother was devastated.

I never want to look at the body of a child again, Astrid thinks, shaking off the nightmare. *I never want to see the grief on a mother's face.* She gets up and looks out the window at the slanted sunrise glimmering on the ocean waves. *I'd forgotten the lullaby of the sea,* she thinks. What better place to be when you've just found out that your ex-husband is marrying your former best friend?

She makes coffee and calls the hospital. Aunt Maude remains in a coma, hovering in limbo between here and there, life and death. "We're hopeful," Dr. Sawari says. "She is making progress. The swelling is starting to subside."

"That gives me hope, too, thank you," Astrid says. "I'll be in to see her later on."

She goes outside and walks down the driveway until she gets a faint signal on her cell phone. Her mother has not called back. *I should've called her again last night. I always have to follow up.* But she had other things on her mind.

She goes back inside and sits in the chair next to the hall phone, nursing her coffee. She decides to call her mother. The reception might be better on the landline. Her mother answers—a surprise.

Astrid explains the situation. "I can't talk long." She looks toward the kitchen and out at the back garden, busy with fluttering birds and bright flowers.

"What are you doing in Heron Bay in the first place?" her mother says.

Nursing my wounded heart, Astrid wants to say. "Keeping an eye on things while Aunt Maude is in the hospital."

"Why would you stay there?" Rose's voice echoes distantly, as if she is speaking inside a tin can. "She shouldn't be living in that house all alone. I told her to move."

"Where would she move, Mom? She loves this place." A splinter of annoyance lodges beneath Astrid's ribs.

"Luigi invited her to come and stay—"

"Aunt Maude is not going to move to Europe!"

"Then she should find a place where she's not alone."

That's beside the point, Astrid thinks, exasperated. "I just called to let you know."

"Should I come back?" her mother asks, but she sounds halfhearted. She does not want to get on a plane, Astrid can tell. Rose and Maude have not been close for years.

"That's your choice," Astrid says.

"Well, I'm glad you're there. It's good that she has you," Rose says.

Astrid grips the phone tightly, realizing this is not the first time her mother has said such a thing. *It's good that you talk to her. I'm sure she appreciates the connection,* or *I'm sure she appreciates you staying in touch,* thus absolving herself of any responsibility to address her own special relationship with her sister. Like Astrid babysat her sister, she is now expected to babysit Maude.

I'm here because I want to help Aunt Maude, she tells herself. *Not because my mother approves or disapproves.* "I'm just letting you know, Mom. I have to go."

"Keep me posted, okay?"

Astrid hangs up, unnerved. The words *I love you* have dropped out of her conversations with her mother, frayed by unspoken grievances and distance and years. This morning, she does not have the mental strength to think about them. She can't force her mother to return, to try to mend her relationships. She doesn't seem interested in doing so, and it would have to be her own decision.

And the last thing I'll ever do is reveal my sadness, my sense of loss, or Trent's engagement to Leona. Astrid's mother would admonish her for making a mess of things.

I can't dwell on this. I have work to do to find the mysterious letter. And I need to find the password for the Wi-Fi. After a quick breakfast of toast and peanut butter, she checks Maude's filing drawers in the library, which hold all the bills and house papers. A file folder inside is marked CORRESPONDENCE. Astrid flips through letters and postcards with splashy watercolors stamped in France, Belgium, or Germany, from friends and distant cousins. Aunt Maude bundled each group of letters or postcards together according to the sender, it seems. One bundle holds notes and cards from Rose on her travels through Europe. Some of the cards are unsigned. Her handwriting swings from wide and loopy to narrow and deliberate. Her wide, carefree loops might've been penned when she'd lubed herself with alcohol or pills. Her recent, calmer handwriting, signed *Your sister, Rose,* slants far to the right with careful pushes and pulls.

No valuable or extraordinary letter reveals itself. Aside from the desk and file drawers, the library holds the old typewriter on a shelf, its case, and books on many other shelves—the most valuable tomes in the locked glass case without a key. The boxes of library donations yield no clues. Aunt Maude, who is on the board of Friends of the Library, once said that she oversees all the donations.

Astrid searches the desk again and the bookshelves. Thoughts of Trent and Leona intrude—Leona reaching up to touch Trent's face, to kiss him. Will she wear a sexy red gown to the wedding, or maybe a miniskirt? *I don't care—it's none of my business, I'm moving on,* Astrid tells herself. *Focus on the letter.*

Aunt Maude mentioned the letter was typewritten. She said, *The typewriter is here.* Maybe the letter is in the typewriter case. But no, the case is empty except for a couple of small cleaning brushes.

The little flattop typewriter looks like a miniature grand piano, sleek and beautiful, the L C SMITH & CORONA TYPEWRITERS INC logo imprinted along the bottom front and CORONA MADE IN USA printed in gold type on the back. The decal on the plate above the keyboard reads CORONA STANDARD, indicating the model. It's a shiny machine and remarkably clean. In her mind's eye, she sees her mother a few days after Nina's death, her hair a mess as she hunched over the typewriter, tapping out mysterious notes. Maybe the typing helped her to endure her sorrow.

Astrid puts the typewriter on the desk, feeds paper into the machine, and types a few sentences. *Dear Trent and Leona, go to hell. Dear Aunt Maude, get well. I'm a poet and didn't know it.* The ink on the ribbon is new, the Pica typeface—ten characters per inch—crisp on the paper. She has learned to recognize the elements of a typewriter that give it a fingerprint.

She returns the typewriter to the shelf. *The letter is in a safe place,* Aunt Maude said. But where? If someone broke in, if someone searched for the letter, would they have known where to look?

Aunt Maude is an expert at hiding things. Once, over the Easter break, she hid chocolate eggs all over the house, and she had to show Astrid where she had hidden the last one, in a little hollow safe that looked like a book. But that was long ago. No sign of a book safe now.

Astrid widens her search, checking the cabinets in the living room. Old pens, miniature crystal sculptures, antique carved-wood coasters, Victorian-era tins, worn and faded magazine ads. A nonworking wind-up Swiss pocket watch. Aunt Maude kept everything carefully organized in bins and drawers. But no letter.

In the dining room, the antiques are organized in two vintage teak cabinets with sliding glass doors: rare cobalt tea sets, English ceramics, beautiful crystal and glass goblets and bowls. Worth a fortune, probably, and yet Aunt Maude has no security system. If someone broke in, they weren't looking for valuables, at least not in the usual sense.

Next stop, the upstairs. In Maude's room, the faint scent of lavender lingers in the air. The walls are painted pale green. The bed is made, everything in order. Her bathroom, attached to the master bedroom, is as she left it. Toothbrush and toothpaste on the vanity, a towel over the rack.

On her bedside table is a neat pile of library books. In the drawers, Maude has carefully folded and organized her clothes. Astrid does her best to look for a letter, but she feels as though she is trespassing. A slip of paper in an envelope could be hidden anywhere.

In the room next door, in which her parents and Nina once slept, Astrid finds no obvious hiding place. Maude is using this bedroom as storage for antiques. A queen bed takes up half the room. No letter anywhere.

In Astrid's old room, she stands in the center on the threadbare area rug. All those years ago, she lay in bed gazing up at the textured ceiling and listening to the ocean waves in the distance. Her room at home in Seattle was noisy with a view of other rooftops. The city lights cast a constant ambient glow upon the walls at night—it was never fully dark, but here, the brightness of stars in the black sky promised endless adventures. *With Julian,* she once hoped. Her fourteen-year-old brain, bursting with hormones, fantasized endlessly about him.

The walls have been repainted in an eggshell color, no longer the forest green she remembers. The single bed is made up with a plain white bedspread, a vintage Tiffany lamp and vintage clock on the nightstand. The open closet reveals empty hangers inside. At one time packed with her favorite books, the bookshelves are nearly bare, only an old dictionary remaining next to a timeworn hardcover copy of *Gone with the Wind*.

Astrid runs her fingers across the cover of the novel, a deep, long-buried ache in her chest. Now she remembers reading this book and imagining what she would tell Julian about it, but she never got the chance. She left it here on purpose, a symbol of letting go of her past, her heart, her hopes after Nina died. Aunt Maude never moved the book. In reverence, Astrid leaves the book on the shelf.

She turns on the light in the closet and steps inside, holding her breath. On the wall behind the hangers, she finds the initials she once wrote in permanent marker inside a little heart: *A.J. and J.M.* *Astrid Johansen and Julian Michaels.* Her graffiti was a daring defacement of the wall where nobody could easily see it. Her crush on Julian blinded her. A faint floral scent lingers in the closet, or perhaps it's only a memory of the Avon cologne she wore that last summer.

The day Julian first started talking to her, she wore a touch of that cologne. She sat on a driftwood log on the beach, digging her feet into the sand, the salty wind in her face. She was almost to the end of *Persuasion* when a shadow fell over her.

A young man peered down through aviator sunglasses, in a wrinkled linen shirt and pants, barefoot. The top button had popped off his shirt, and she could picture him unbuttoning and rebuttoning it so many times, the thread had come loose and eventually the button had fallen off. He was cute, like a movie star.

She dropped the book, and it slipped into the sand. He knelt to pick it up in one quick movement and glanced at the cover before handing it back to her.

"Sorry, I didn't mean to pull a ninja on you," he said. Strawberry-blond hair fell over one blue eye.

"It's okay, I get kind of focused," she said.

"Concentration—that's good, it will get you places." He pushed the sunglasses back up on his nose. She'd seen him before, she realized, but not for a couple of years. He'd been a teenager then, and she had not paid much attention.

"I know you," she said. "My aunt Maude was your tutor at the library."

"Yeah, math. I hated math." He squinted at her, as if looking at her for a view into the past. "You're her niece. You, let me see . . ." He touched the top of his head, as if anointing himself with the power of perfect recall. "You used to wear those freaky glasses." He laughed, more of a soft chuckle.

The heat climbed up through her neck to her cheeks. "I was a kid. I was being silly. They were reading glasses."

"Julian Michaels." He held out his hand warmly to take hers, and his touch set her on fire.

She swallowed, her throat dry, the sand seeming to glitter in the heat, the squiggles of air shimmering and everything bright. "Astrid Johansen."

"Pleased to meet you for real. And you were not silly. Any kid who loves to read is not silly. And you're outside in the fresh air. Look all around." He swept his arm to encompass the beauty of the sea, the woods, the sky. "What could be more amazing than this?"

"I know, right? Totally," she said, enraptured by his smile, by his white teeth.

"So, are you here for the summer again or what?" he asked. "I mean, you guys are always here for the summer."

"We don't have anywhere else to go," she said. "Like, no grandparents. A lot of my friends stay with grandparents."

"My grandparents live in New York somewhere."

"My grandparents' train derailed on a trip in India, and they were killed way before I was born. On my mom's side. They were traveling to Darjeeling. You know, where tea comes from?"

He looked at her with a startled expression. "So, your mom's sister . . ."

"Is Aunt Maude. But Aunt Maude is like *way older* than my mom."

"Your mom is beautiful," he said.

Her stomach turned over. She was at once proud and jealous of her mother. "Everyone says that."

"I'll bet they do. You look like her."

"Thanks, I think. But I'm more like my dad, personality-wise."

"Yeah, I guess I can see that. He knows a lot. About butterflies, dragonflies, and frogs. He's a cool guy. Erudite."

She made a mental note to look up the word *erudite* in one of Aunt Maude's dictionaries. "Yeah, he's into nature. He and my uncle Raj used to go out counting birds. My uncle died, too."

"Hell, all those losses suck," Julian said, and he came and sat beside her. He smelled of fig soap and something else sweet and smoky. She wanted to drink him in, and her heartbeat quickened. She became slightly breathless and hoped he didn't notice.

"It's okay," she said. "I don't remember much."

"I don't imagine you would." He pulled a rectangular, brown packet from the pocket of his shirt, extracted a thin brown cigarette, and waved it toward her. "Do you mind? My parents don't like me to smoke up at the house. But these aren't even real cigarettes. They're cloves."

She looked at his profile and knew that she was already in love with him. "I don't mind, but you have to let me try, and then I won't tell."

He was already lighting the cigarette from a match, cupping his hand against the wind. He had long, slender fingers, the kind that could reach an octave on the piano. Glancing at her sidelong, he inhaled and blew the smoke away from her. "Not a chance. You go ahead and tell, but it's a nasty habit, smoking, and I won't get you started. Never start, okay?"

She frowned at him. "You're kidding me, right? I'm not a baby."

"Oh, I know you're not, but I've been trying to quit, so you're already ahead of me."

She sat up straight. "Then quit, right now." She held out her hand.

He looked at her, shook his head again, then stamped out the cigarette on a rock. "You're something else, you know that? You're reading Austen and wanting to smoke. Next, you'll be a connoisseur of whiskey."

She needed to look up the word *connoisseur* as well. *Connoisseur* and *erudite*.

"Yeah, I've had alcohol," she said, a lie. A gust of wind ruffled the open pages of the book. "I'm not a kid."

"Obviously not." He got up and squinted at her. "I'll see you around, Austen Girl."

After that day, they often walked and spoke of literature and his dream of becoming a famous writer someday. His dream came true. The bio in his books mentions that he lives with his wife and son on a "Pacific Northwest island." Aunt Maude said their house is hidden away in the forests of San Juan Island.

Astrid leaves the room and her memories and goes back downstairs. Where else to look for the letter? The cottage, painted to match the house, sits in the back left corner of the property near the tree line.

She pulls on her sneakers and walks out through the lush, overgrown garden. She has not been in the cottage in years. Aunt Maude added electrical outlets, insulated the walls, and furnished the interior with antiques. *Someone could live in here,* Astrid thinks, turning on the light to reveal a high, wood-beamed ceiling. The modest living room is furnished with a drafting table, a soft futon couch by the window, and a plethora of books packed into shelves along one wall. A barrister bookcase with glass doors holds a number of old books.

In his will, Uncle Raj left Aunt Maude a respectable sum of money he'd made from his business ventures around the world, before he retired early. His funds allowed her to renovate the cottage and indulge in her love for antiques, including the original Tiffany lamp on a side table—and a few in the main house—and the old stove in the small kitchenette.

Aunt Maude once spoke of renting out the cottage to families experiencing homelessness. They visited the library to use the bathrooms and the computers. But while the cottage smells clean, nobody appears to be living here. And Astrid finds no letter anywhere. She sits on the couch and looks out the window through the trees, across the flowers and shrubs and back toward the main house. She sees the ghost of Nina, her blonde head bobbing up and down as she runs. She loved to play in the sprinkler and splash around in the kiddie pool that Maude bought for her.

She could have drowned in the kiddie pool, Astrid thinks. *Just as easily as anywhere else.* Aunt Maude drained that little pool every day, after Nina had finished playing in it. But the reflecting pool in the woods remained full of water, fed by an underground pipe from the Michaels house.

Astrid closes her eyes and listens to the birds chittering in the garden. When she opens her eyes, she is looking straight at the bookshelves. On the bottom far left, an old photo album is wedged in between two books. She kneels on the carpet and pulls out the album. The pages are faded and yellowed. Inside are early photographs of her mother and Aunt Maude with their parents in Southern California, back when the two girls were very young.

Aunt Maude has her arms wrapped around Rose on the beach, a sandcastle in front of them. Their mother, Ranu, appears in the background, her long black hair cascading down to her waist. She's wearing a blue one-piece swimsuit and gigantic sunglasses, and she's reading a book. Their father, Calum McCann, must be taking the picture. Aunt Maude said their father often took snapshots of all of them. He was a press photographer, and he and Ranu were in India on business when their train derailed.

All the pictures in the album were taken before that tragedy, before Rose and Maude went to live with their grandparents, Calum's parents, who had immigrated to Los Angeles from Ireland. How often did the girls see Ranu's family? They were all in India. *No wonder my mother felt so lost,* Astrid thinks. *She carried a trauma that went right back to her childhood.*

Rose is still trusting, hopeful, and happy in these pictures. Still young. She is chubby, tanned, and grinning widely, a front tooth missing. In another picture, she's sitting at a table blowing out birthday candles, surrounded by young friends. Maude stands behind her, hands on her shoulders.

In some images, Calum, the grandfather Astrid never knew, is holding Rose tightly and kissing her cheek. She must be barely three years old. How terrible it must have been for such a young girl to lose both parents, before she had even learned to read. And Maude, already twelve years old when Rose was born, became her sister's protector, her surrogate mother until the two of them moved in with their grandparents.

All these images recall a time when Rose and Maude were still part of a complete family, when Rose still trusted what life had to offer. Maude had already enjoyed the benefit of fun, loving parents. Maybe her genetic makeup simply made her more resilient than Astrid's mother, who seemed more brittle, more fragile than Maude. And then Rose endured another terrible loss of her own child.

Astrid flips through many empty pages, but then near the end, new photographs appear of her own mother holding baby Astrid. Once again, Rose looks hopeful and happy—and yet. She does not hold Astrid close to her body. Does not kiss her pudgy cheek and cuddle her. She holds her a little away, as if she fears getting too close.

In other photos, Bjorn carries Astrid on his shoulders, gripping her hands and laughing. Memories come to her of riding on his feet, riding piggyback, sailing with him on Lake Washington in a catamaran he made with his own hands.

When they visited Aunt Maude, he didn't go sailing. The seas were too rough. He disappeared into the woods to count wildlife. He never fully felt at home here in Heron Bay. Bjorn's family all lived in England and Sweden. His brother, a much older sister, distant relatives with whom Astrid has traded letters and telephone calls, still live abroad, but Astrid barely knows them. *Aunt Maude is my closest family,* she thinks.

The album holds no photographs of Nina.

Astrid flips to the last page and draws a sharp breath. Aunt Maude never mentioned saving this photograph of Astrid's wedding. The photographer took several shots in this spot at Point Reyes National Seashore, at the Sea Lion Overlook against a backdrop of misty cliffs.

In his fitted black tuxedo, Trent grins into the camera, his arm around Astrid's waist. She smiles more tentatively in her vintage, short-sleeved wedding dress with a trumpet silhouette and boat neckline. She chose nontraditional white bridal sneakers, barely hidden beneath her floor-length gown. She wanted to walk along the clifftop trail, and in those shoes, without a bridal train, she could.

The photographer took pictures of her and Trent at the overlook, at Drakes Beach, and then running through the famous cypress tree tunnel, a lane overhung with elegant branches. They giggled, breathless and giddy, embracing the moment. Later, at the reception, Leona stood to make a toast, swaying a little. *Here's to the happy couple, may your ups and downs be only in bed,* and *we're all here to celebrate something magical and wondrous and beautiful. Me. But seriously, folks, Astrid is my best friend, and I'm so happy for her.* Then she listed all the reasons she loved Astrid. *She's smart and kind, and I always looked up to her. Plus, she has the coolest job on the planet. She can read your handwriting and tell you if you're a serial killer.* This was entirely untrue, but Leona persisted in the misconception that a handwriting expert could read personality traits in the flourish of a pen. Like reading tea leaves or gazing into a crystal ball. Then she raised her champagne glass in a toast. *To the happy couple, may your marriage last a hundred years longer than mine did.* Leona had been married to a doctor for exactly one year. He'd cheated on their wedding anniversary.

Was Leona ever a true friend? Did Trent ever really love me? Astrid will never know for sure. Did she even understand true love? Or did she feel infatuation, a sense of safety with him? A way out of her past?

She puts the album back on the shelf, wondering why it's out here instead of in the house. Maybe because it's from a time before loss—of marriages, of beloved family members. All those endings would be enough to send anyone running from grief, as Rose did, but Maude stayed. She didn't seem to feel the need to escape. But then, Nina was not her child. Maude did not give birth to her, did not nurse her, did not hold her day after day, night after night. But she sensed her sister's despair. *Losing a child is worse than anything,* she told Astrid once. *Your mother is grieving. This is not about you.*

Astrid unfolds her legs, and as she is getting up, she spots something under the couch, sticking out next to the bookshelf—a pile of black, shiny fabric. She pulls it out and holds it up—it's a nylon camisole with a faint scent of perfume. Size small. Nothing like what Aunt Maude would wear. What is it doing here? Maybe a guest stayed here, but Aunt Maude has more than one guest room in the main house.

Astrid tucks the camisole into her pocket and leaves the cottage. The door was unlocked, but it has a lock and a dead bolt. *Aunt Maude must trust people in this town,* Astrid thinks. She leaves the door unlocked, since she doesn't have the key, and goes back to the house to check the library one more time. If Maude hid the letter, it would probably be there. *I must have missed something.*

After rechecking the filing cabinets and bookshelves, she looks through the desk drawers again. She is going through the top, middle drawer when she spots the corner of something sticking out from the bottom. A hint of manila.

The drawer has a false bottom.

Her heart rate kicks up. She pulls out the drawer, sets it on the desk, and pries off the extra wood panel. Aunt Maude wedged a file folder between the two wood panels making up the bottom of the drawer. The label is dated only a month ago. So recently! The name hastily scrawled across the label, below the date, is **Nina**.

CHAPTER SEVEN

Why would Aunt Maude write the name Nina on a file folder dated only a month ago—and then hide the folder? Inside are clipped newspaper articles following the tragedy of Nina's death. Toddler Drowns in Shallow Pool, the first headline reads.

> A 3-year-old girl died Friday night as the result of drowning in a reflecting pool on the vast acreage owned by Verne and Beatrice Michaels. The child's family was on summer vacation in Heron Bay. Her aunt, Maude Dasgupta, placed a 911 call at 11:06 p.m. The county sheriff, Cillian Burke, responded to the call within minutes at the Dasgupta residence at 19 Overlook Lane, near the Michaels estate.
>
> "The child apparently wandered away from her home and got lost in the woods on the nearby property," Burke said. The child's 14-year-old sister discovered her . . .

Discovered her, as if Nina were an unknown planet, an uncharted island, or a new species of plant growing deep in the forest. Astrid can still see the back of Nina's head beneath the moonlight as she floated facedown in the water, her blonde hair undulating like strangely colored kelp.

I can't go there.

Astrid inhales sharply, lets out her breath in a long exhale. She skips to the next article: Lifesaving measures by EMS personnel failed to save the child. She could not be revived. She was pronounced dead on the scene...

And, farther down: At this time, a cause of death is undetermined... as the sheriff continues the investigation.

Another article mentions suspicion falling briefly on Len Wilkers, a local diver who attended the party at the Michaels home. But in the end, he was never charged, and he dropped out of the news. *Funny, I don't remember his name*, Astrid thinks, but then, she wasn't following the news back then. Her dad took her back to Seattle a few days after the drowning.

The articles grow shorter, quick updates on the investigation, which led nowhere. Nobody was ever charged with a crime. Nina, and everything associated with her death, faded from the public eye, and she became a piece of history. Another tragic accidental drowning.

A tear splashes onto the newspaper article, and Astrid struggles to accept that Nina will always be the age she was, lost in time. The file includes a few condolence cards sent to Aunt Maude afterward from people in town.

In the garden, the trees whisper and sway, leaning in to accuse Astrid. They know that she should have saved Nina, that she should have been watching her. That she let her sister wander away in the night. That she was distracted. She should not have been certain that her parents were home. They weren't.

With trembling hands, Astrid sets aside the articles, and from the bottom of the file folder, she pulls out a faded color photograph. It was taken up at the Michaels estate. She recognizes the mansion in the background, the stone patio, and the white patio tables topped with colorful umbrellas. The photograph appears to have been taken late in the evening, the background aglow with orange sunset, the faces grinning at the camera relaxed and flushed with alcohol. Astrid's mother is raising a glass of red wine. She's beautiful, her hair long and black, her skin rosy, large eyes gazing with longing at something or someone a little to the right of the photographer. She's in that red dress, which means the picture could have been taken the night of Nina's death. Astrid can't remember if her mother wore the same dress on any other night, but Rose made a point of choosing a different outfit every time she went out.

She is sitting between two men. One is a tall, handsome, blond man with a wrinkled white shirt unbuttoned at the top. He looks professorial, raising his wineglass. He's Astrid's father, Bjorn. On her other side is a dark-haired man with ropy muscle. And next to that man . . . Julian Michaels in a white linen shirt. His strawberry-blond hair falls over one eye. He's wearing a roguish grin. At the front of the photograph, slightly disembodied, is a quartz watch attached to a hand. The watch face reads Bulova. A photobomb, an accident. The person is outside the frame of the photograph. A blurry shape flits by in the background, but Astrid can't make out who it is.

She flips the photograph to the back, thinking perhaps the picture is marked with a date. Instead, her aunt handwrote, in a signature flourishing style, words that make Astrid's eyes water. The first word is smudged out, unreadable. But the rest of the sentence is unmistakable: . . . *killed Nina??*

CHAPTER EIGHT

At the end of Oceanfront Street, overlooking a gravel spit and the marina, the police station is nothing like Astrid remembers. Years ago, she and Conor rode bicycles through town all day and stopped here to visit his dad. But the old stucco building has been torn down, replaced by an entirely new one with cedar siding, sleek modern lines, a slanted metal roof, and tinted windows.

She brought the file folder in her shoulder bag, but the reception area is empty. Of course, it's Saturday. She called Conor, and he told her to meet him at the station, but now she wonders what she's doing here. What can he do with a smudged question, with the name missing on the back of an old picture? Aunt Maude often accidentally smears words, even in her letters. The writing looks recent, in the same bright-blue ink used on the file-folder label.

Back at the house, Astrid brought out her equipment from her suitcase: a small handheld microscope, a digital camera, and an illuminated jeweler's magnifier. Through the microscope, she looked at the smudged ink on the back of the photograph but could not distinguish any indented writing. The smooth surface obscured any name that might have been written before the word was smudged out. Different types of ink respond to light differently, reflecting and absorbing it at different frequencies. She couldn't tell simply by looking through the microscope. *I could use my filters, but they're back at the lab,* she thought, frustrated.

Conor comes down the hall in his sheriff's uniform and ushers her into a bland conference room furnished with only an oblong table and plush chairs. They sit across from each other, the vast table between them.

"You're working today," she says.

"The law never sleeps," he says, and winks at her.

She blushes, hastily extracts the file folder, and slides it across the table. "I found this in my aunt's desk. Hidden in the false bottom of a drawer."

He opens the folder, flips through its contents, then gives her a skeptical look. She recognizes the slightly raised left eyebrow, the way his lips turn down.

She turns over the picture, points to the note on the back. "A double question mark, why? The label is dated last month, not seventeen years ago. When she said the letter would change everything about the past, I thought she meant the past in general. Now I'm pretty sure she meant the letter would change everything we believe about what happened to Nina. Someone might've killed her. My aunt used a fountain pen and accidentally smudged the name. I tried, but I can't restore it."

He clasps his hands together on the table. The room is stark, the lights harsh. "And you think the evidence is in this mysterious letter. But did you find this letter? I don't see it here."

"She must have hidden it. Or someone broke in and stole it."

"Isn't that a bit of a stretch? How would she get an incriminating letter seventeen years after your sister's death?"

"Maybe it was already somewhere in the house, hidden away, and she recently found it? Or someone sent it to her?"

He flips the picture over to the front again. "This was taken up at the Michaels house. Verne and Beatrice aren't in the picture, but Julian is. I almost mistook him for his son, Thomas. They look so much alike. Thomas spends a lot of time here with his grandparents. He's sixteen, drives through town in Verne's classic cars sometimes."

She remembers seeing Verne's old vehicles in the multicar garage attached to the mansion on the bluff, a long time ago. Julian used to drive around in them, too. "What about the other man sitting next to my mom? The guy with ropy muscles?"

"That's Len Wilkers."

"The investigation focused on him for a while. I read it in the newspaper clippings."

"He was a diver—still is. He lives on a boat down in Seabank. It's about thirty miles south of here."

"Why was he under suspicion?"

Conor shrugs. "I'd have to check the file."

"Did your dad's interviews implicate anyone else?"

"Not as far as I know."

She points at the picture again. "Someone in the foreground is wearing a Bulova watch. And there's someone in the background, walking by. Blurry."

"Your aunt must've been referring to someone sitting at the table," Conor says. "Someone in focus. If she meant someone who's blurry, why choose this picture? Why not pick a better photograph of the suspect?"

"I have a lot of questions for her, when she wakes up."

Conor puts the picture back in the file folder and slides the whole thing across the table. "This would be a cold case, anyway. The trail left by anyone who might have harmed your sister has long ago gone cold. My dad finally had to accept the coroner's ruling of accidental drowning. He couldn't charge anyone."

"What about the letter? What if I find it?"

"I won't know until I see it. If you do find the letter, try not to touch it with your fingers. Wear gloves or use tweezers. Then bring it to me, and I'll see what I can do."

"I'm going to keep looking for it." She tucks the file back into the bag, slings the strap over her shoulder. What was she thinking? All these connections are fragile threads, hunches, suspicions. Zero evidence.

Back in the car, she sits in the driver's seat as the sun lights the morning. *Coming here was a bad idea,* she thinks. *Why am I even pursuing this?* Because Aunt Maude might've been attacked by an intruder. Because she summoned Astrid to Heron Bay. Because she thought Nina was murdered.

And if she is honest with herself, Astrid thinks perhaps she expected to nail Nina's killer and instantly absolve herself of responsibility. After all, she has felt, all these years, as if she herself has been drowning in guilt.

She is about to start the car when Conor strides out and approaches her.

She rolls down the window.

He pulls a large, thick manila envelope from inside his coat and hands it to her.

"What's this?" she says, looking at the envelope in her hands.

"Be careful with it, okay? I'm going to need it back."

She opens the flap and looks inside. "This is the police file on my sister. Why would you show this to me?"

"There is nothing in here that we would keep confidential."

"I thought you said you can't pursue this."

"I can't, but maybe you'll find something that will help you."

CHAPTER NINE

In the hospital on Saturday afternoon, Astrid sits next to her aunt's bed. The ventilator makes a strange whooshing sound, and the monitors are still beeping. "Can you hear me?" Astrid asks her aunt. No response. "I have the file on Nina. Conor was very generous to share it with me." More whooshing and beeping.

"What do you think I'll find? I'm almost afraid to read it."

Her aunt does not move.

"Trent and Leona are getting married. I don't want to ask where. I hope not at Point Reyes. Can you believe Leona wants me to come to the wedding?" Astrid sighs and looks out the window. "Thank you for visiting me in my new apartment . . . Was it already nine months ago? It was a nice distraction. You kept me sane. Did you know that? Wake up so we can have fun again. We'll drive across the Golden Gate Bridge, visit Muir Woods, and take the BART train into San Francisco. Would you like that?" Astrid wipes a tear from her cheek. She imagines her aunt saying, *I would love that so much.* "Thank you for always being there . . . You never made any promises that everything would be okay." Her aunt simply listened, said, *That is terrible,* or *I hear that you are lonely,* or *I felt lonely, too, after your uncle Raj died.*

Somehow, over the months, as Astrid got used to sleeping alone in the single bed in her apartment, going out now and then for a drink with colleagues, she got over the worst of the pain and sleepless nights. Aunt Maude sent her wonderful novels about love and loss, like *The Seven Husbands of Evelyn Hugo*, *The Boardwalk Bookshop*, *Everything Must Go*, and more.

Astrid squeezes Aunt Maude's hand. "Everything will be okay. You'll get better. And then it will be my turn to bring you books to read. And I'll call you more often . . . I can't call Trent anymore, though . . . He has crossed a line." She breaks into silent sobs, squeezing her aunt's hand too hard. She lets go, fumbles for a crumpled tissue from her purse, and blows her nose.

"She's doing much better," Dr. Sawari's soft voice says behind her. "It doesn't look like it, but she is."

Astrid whips around and smiles. "That's so reassuring. Thank you." She gets up to leave, and on the drive back to Aunt Maude's house, she rolls down the window for fresh air and tells herself she is strong—she will get through any and all surprises.

Seated at the kitchen table, she opens her sister's police file. The report takes up fifty-nine pages, and it even has a table of contents. Investigative summary, interviews, autopsy report . . . Does she really want to open Pandora's box?

She takes a deep breath and skims the 911 dispatch report. Aunt Maude's call was transferred to Fire & Rescue. The operator instructed her on how to perform CPR and rescue breaths, only Nina's body was too far away from the home phone. It was nearly impossible to get a cell phone signal at Aunt Maude's house.

The reflecting pool was shallow at each end, only three feet deep in the middle. But Nina couldn't stand up. The water would've reached the top of her head. How did she get to the center of that pool? Was she lured there, or did she wade in all on her own? Was she chasing the silver ball?

Astrid told the sheriff that she'd seen the ball floating at the other end of the pool. It was Nina's favorite toy. She loved shiny objects. Maybe someone put that ball in the water. Or Nina herself carried it there. But the authorities didn't find it. The ball was gone when they arrived.

The coroner pronounced Nina dead at the scene. Medics transported her body to the morgue for a postmortem examination. The coroner's report indicated no tissue abnormalities and no sign of bruising—only brain edema consistent with drowning.

Astrid sits back, her breathing shallow. It's difficult for her to remember the details from that night, with all the chaos. Astrid's mother was sobbing, the sirens wailed, police lights flashed.

The file contains a transcript of the sheriff's conversation with Astrid's mother. She is described as distraught, frantic, in denial. According to the sheriff, Rose rushed out from the forest trail leading up to the Michaels house, where she had been at the party. Other partygoers did not remember seeing her out on the patio with them during the hour preceding the drowning. *So where were you, Mom?*

Astrid scans the transcripts of interviews with everyone who attended the party. Two witnesses, friends of Julian's, said he stayed there the whole time. He told the police the same thing. The authorities interviewed him at home. If he was there, and her father drove into the city that night, whose heavier footsteps did she hear along with her mother's downstairs, and whom did she see outside? The notes in the file are playing tricks with her memory.

Astrid's mother said that she had been in the bathroom up at the Michaels house for a while, then she went out onto the patio to get some air. She felt woozy. Then she must've returned to Aunt Maude's house.

After Astrid heard two sets of footsteps going up the stairs, and her mother's voice, she'd thought her parents had gone to bed. She'd thought her father was home. The next morning, she knew otherwise. That night, Rose must've returned to the party, but Astrid did not hear footsteps leaving Aunt Maude's house.

Perhaps Rose only said she returned to the party, and she stayed at Aunt Maude's house the whole time. And for some reason, she ran out onto the trail later on, still in her red party dress.

None of this makes any sense.

The sheriff called Astrid's father, Bjorn, at home in Seattle, and he drove back to Heron Bay, where the sheriff interviewed him in the morning. Len Wilkers left the party to smoke pot with some teens in the woods, who corroborated his story. He was under suspicion but never charged. If the sheriff discovered anything more, he took his secrets to the grave. *There must be something here, something that answers the question my aunt asks on the back of the photograph.*

She leaves the file in the library and goes upstairs to the room in which she once slept. That night long ago, in this house, Nina was fast asleep in the little alcove in the room next door. Or so Astrid thought. She looks out the window, unsettled by the memory of what she saw that night, Julian walking into the woods.

The wind has picked up, a bite in the air. Astrid pulls on warm clothes and goes down to the beach. To the west, the sky is ribbed with pink, the reflection rippling unevenly across the sea. She pictures Aunt Maude in better days, striding along the shore, scanning for the unbroken seashells she used to line her walkway, the bits of smooth, worn-down sea glass that once belonged to new bottles, washed up and shattered and smoothed by sand and water. Chitons and shore crabs dwell in the shallows, a great blue heron hunting in a quiet stretch of the bay, its hairlike feathers quivering in the breeze.

Overhead, an osprey calls out, its magnificent wings spread as it rides an updraft. Astrid breathes in the clean scent of the ocean, and her worries evaporate in the wind, in the surf, in the chuckles and calls of the gulls, in the whistles and chattering of the pigeon guillemots in the distance.

The sun is dropping in the sky. In the balmy evening, she doubles back and takes the trail through the woods again, trying different branching offshoots until she reaches the stone garden in a clearing. The statues are crumbling, and most are covered in moss. She can remember the distant, fragmented voices drifting down from the party at the Michaels house that night.

Slowly, she approaches the reflecting pool, her memory filled with its dank, still water, but now the rectangular pool is empty, full of leaves and pine needles and detritus. It looks unremarkable, nothing but a ruin in the majesty of the darkening forest.

Her heart grows numb. She can hear the wind, smell the sea, sense the birds hopping in the underbrush. A giant gray squirrel races along the ground. The pool looks forlorn, neglected, the patio around it overgrown, the stones cracked and worn through by root systems and grass. *The placid present belies the violent past.* People walking through here will see crumbling stone, but Astrid will always see her sister floating facedown—and what happened before that?

Nina must've struggled to come up for air, and before that, she waded innocently into the water, and before that, she wandered into the woods, getting lost, maybe looking for her mommy again. Or following someone else. But whom? Or maybe she simply got lost in the woods, stumbled, and fell into the pool entirely by accident.

CHAPTER TEN

That night seventeen years ago, Astrid dragged Nina out of the pool and laid her on the stone patio. On automatic, not thinking at all, she pinched her sister's nose and breathed into her mouth. In between breaths, she called for help, her voice thin and desperate, swallowed by the forest. Nina's lips felt cold and slippery. Astrid kept up the mouth-to-mouth, turning her head to listen in between. But there was no breath. She had learned to do this in lifeguard training, yet nothing had prepared her for trying to revive her little sister. Why had Nina gone back out? Why hadn't she stayed asleep? Astrid kept up the breaths, but her sister did not respond, did not cough. Her lips turned blue. Her hair clung to her head. Astrid started fast chest compressions, *at least a hundred compressions a minute, if mouth-to-mouth doesn't help.* Still no response, but Astrid's arms began to ache from the exertion.

Faint laughter drifted down from the Michaels mansion in the distance, the sound like cruel cackling. Nina's wet, dirty nightgown clung to her, muddy at the hem with tiny daisies printed all over it. Astrid felt that strange sensation of floating outside her body. She tried to drag her sister to the trail but stumbled and fell in the dirt, sobbing. The statues seemed to be breathing, watching her. She was

Dreaming of Water

still calling for help. She ran back down the trail in the moonlight toward Aunt Maude's house.

She could've run to the Michaels house, to the party full of grown-ups, but instinct sent her to the most familiar place, to Aunt Maude's, screaming for her parents. She shouldn't have left Nina at the reflecting pool, but it couldn't be helped. The porch light drew closer too slowly, no matter how hard Astrid pumped her legs. Her lungs yearned for oxygen, but she kept on running. And then a car door opened, a dome light illuminated in the driveway. Aunt Maude's Honda was parked at an angle. She got out and dashed toward Astrid with uncommon speed, dropping her book bag in the dirt. She wore a beautiful dress of shiny, pale blue. "What's going on?" she yelled.

"Ambulance . . . Nina . . . in the pool . . ." Astrid gasped.

"Oh my God!" Aunt Maude called 911, and before she could protest, Astrid was running back through the woods to the pool. She had to keep trying to revive her sister. Nina was stiff and cold, but Astrid kept up the chest compressions, part of her hovering above the stone garden, a ghost separated from her body, looking down at the rabbit with mossy ears, the bear with its stone paws, the bench, the stone patio. Looking down at herself and Nina. She could see through the trees the lights of Aunt Maude's house. The silver ball still floated in the water.

Then Aunt Maude was there, pulling her away and gasping, "Oh my God, oh my God. Dear God. Honey, go back to the house. I'll take over. Make sure the medics know where to go."

Astrid ran back through the woods, her legs shaking. The sirens grew louder. By the time she reached the driveway, the ambulance lights spun in bright red flashes, the sheriff's car lights flashing, too. Sheriff Burke got out and strode toward her, a big and imposing man, all his gear clanking. "Astrid? Where is Nina?"

"She's in the stone garden!" she yelled, pointing toward the woods. "Hurry!" But she knew that it would do no good, even as the medics sprinted into the woods with their bags and a stretcher, another police car arrived, and people were yelling and gesticulating—bright lights flashed.

After a time—Astrid didn't know how long—the medics emerged from the woods carrying Nina on the stretcher, their faces grim. They transferred her into the back of the ambulance. Aunt Maude followed them, then ran to Astrid and hugged her. The sheriff was asking questions. "Maude, are you all right? Was anyone else here? Did Nina wade in alone? Who found her?"

"Astrid did," Aunt Maude said as the sheriff ushered her and Astrid toward the house. A couple of police officers walked into the woods with yellow tape, shining flashlights, talking into their radios. *Crime scene tape,* Astrid thought, but this was not a crime scene. Nina must've fallen into the pool, or she'd waded in after the silver ball—but the ball was gone now.

Astrid gripped Aunt Maude's hand tightly, and then someone was screaming, a loud, earsplitting screeching. Astrid's mother stumbled out from the trail, still in her red satin dress, holding her delicate high-heeled shoes by the straps. Her feet were bare. She was screaming and running toward the ambulance.

The lights were so bright, and people rushed everywhere—medics and police officers. How were there so many officers in Heron Bay? A sleepy place—not a town where little girls drowned. Aunt Maude kept her arm around Astrid's shoulders and directed her up the porch steps and inside the house. "Go upstairs and change your clothes," Aunt Maude said. "You're cold."

The sheriff stepped into the foyer. "Wait. Hold up."

"She's in shock," Aunt Maude said. "She just found her sister. She's soaked."

"One minute." The sheriff ushered someone into the house, a female police officer with blonde hair tied back. "If you don't mind, Astrid, hold out your arms."

Dreaming of Water

"What is this all about?" Aunt Maude snapped. Astrid's mother wailed and yelled outside.

"May I take pictures of your arms?" the police officer said. "Hold them out."

Astrid held out her arms, not sure why. The officer took photographs from all angles, then said, "Thank you, honey," and stepped back.

"Do not take any more photographs of my niece," Aunt Maude snapped. "She needs a parent with her. Is she a suspect?"

"We're just covering all our bases," the sheriff said. "Astrid, could the nice officer go upstairs with you and keep your wet clothes?"

"Why?" Aunt Maude yelled. "She rescued her sister. How could you?"

He held up his hands. "Maude, I'm with you on this. Just following procedure."

"If she drowned Nina, she would be a psychopath. Do you think she would wade in and try to save her? Look at her!"

"I understand," the sheriff said, although he did not sound fully convinced. "But I'll still need to ask her some questions."

Astrid went upstairs to her room. Aunt Maude and the police officer followed and waited in the hall with the door open. Astrid took off the wet clothes that smelled of dirt and moss and dank water. She could still see her sister's cloudy eyes. The officer put her clothes in an evidence bag.

Then Astrid put on warm, dry clothes and went back downstairs. The officer followed her and went outside. Astrid's mother was still screaming and crying. The sheriff had gone out to talk to her. He came back in. The ambulance doors slammed, and the ambulance drove away—with Nina inside, Astrid was sure. Rose had stopped screaming. She must've gone with Nina. Where was Dad?

Her teeth still chattered. The sheriff was talking to Aunt Maude, asking her questions. "I need to talk to Rose," he said. "I'll go to the hospital."

"Is that necessary?" Maude snapped. "Right now?"

"She said she was at the party and that the child's father is in Seattle."

"Then that's where he is. Why don't you question the people up at the Michaels place? The stone garden is on their property."

"I have a deputy up there now."

Astrid took a deep breath. Every part of her was still shaking. It seemed the grown-ups had forgotten about her, but then the sheriff turned and gave her a friendly, sympathetic look. His eyes softened, kind and gentle like Conor's eyes.

"I'm sorry about your sister, Astrid," he said. "Would you be willing to answer a few questions?"

"No, she wouldn't," Aunt Maude said. "Is she under arrest? She's a minor! You can't interrogate her. And if you do, we need a lawyer."

"I want to find out what happened, that's all."

They all sat in the living room, and while the sheriff's voice remained gentle, his words felt like pointy-tipped spears thrown at Astrid, arcing through the air and piercing her heart. When he asked her why she had gone out looking for Nina, she told the truth. She said she had seen Julian outside. What else could she say? But he would never have hurt Nina. She told the sheriff that she'd heard footsteps, that her mother must have come home to check on Nina. She convinced herself that maybe she hadn't heard the heavier footsteps, since her father must've been well on his way to Seattle by then. She didn't tell anyone about what her mother had said: *Such a likeness . . . I swear.* Maybe it had been a dream, or she had simply imagined her mother's voice. Her throat was too tight, a strangling sensation in her chest. Finally, the sheriff stopped asking questions, and the police left.

Later that night, Astrid lay on top of the covers in bed, a deep pit in her stomach. The female officer had taken her wet clothes. What would the police do with them? Analyze them under a microscope?

She held up her arms in the pale light of the bedside lamp and looked at them. They were clean, no scratches, and there were no scratches on her face. She knew what the cop had been looking for—evidence that Nina had been alive when Astrid had waded into the pool and had fought back. Evidence that Astrid had drowned her very own little sister.

I'm sorry I didn't want to babysit you, Astrid thought, her eyes filling with tears. She could not believe Nina would never laugh again, would never ask for a bubble bath, would never crawl backward down the stairs. Would never ask for Mommy or another story. Would never pout and bang her hands on the piano keys.

A sick, scared feeling filled Astrid's chest, mixing with her anger. *Mom was right—how hard could it be to watch my little sister?* She pressed her eyes shut and tried to clear her mind. But the image of Nina's hair, the way it floated and then clung to her head, would not disappear. It wrapped itself around her heart, her thoughts. Nina's cloudy eyes pleaded with her. She fell asleep that night and dreamed of water rising and lapping around her legs. She waded after her sister, but the ocean swept Nina far out to sea.

◆ ◆ ◆

When Astrid woke in the morning, voices drifted up from downstairs. Dad was talking to Aunt Maude. Footsteps came up the stairs. The door opened to the bedroom next to hers, where her parents slept, then shut again.

Astrid sat up, still in her clothes from the night before, her head fuzzy. Her heart sank into a deep pit. Her head throbbed, and her stomach growled. She didn't know when she had last eaten. She didn't want to ever eat again. The world seemed fragile, the walls made of paper. If the wind rose, everything would blow down. She wanted to become invisible. She wanted to turn back time and stop Nina from running outside.

She could hear her mother crying inconsolably in the room next door, then her father's deep, soothing voice. Then Rose snapped at him. Now and then, Astrid could make out the words. *Where were you? Who was watching her?*

She made fists, hardly daring to move. Her fingernails dug into the palms of her hands. Someone clanked around in the kitchen downstairs, probably Aunt Maude. The voices quieted next door. Footsteps creaked down the hall, and Dad came in, still in his clothes from the previous night—a button-down shirt and lightweight cotton hiking pants. He looked wrinkled, disheveled, as if his whole being needed to be ironed. His eyes were red. Astrid had never seen her father cry.

"I'm sorry, I'm sorry," she said. She sat at the edge of the bed, and her father sat next to her, wrapped his arms around her, and hugged her.

"Oh, my Astrid," he said, and his chest heaved. "It's okay—everything will be okay."

"No, it won't," she said, her voice muffled. "I didn't know she went out."

"I know you didn't know."

Her mother stood in the doorway, her eyes puffy and red. She came in and sat on the other side of Astrid. She smelled of perfume and sweat. She hugged Astrid, and for a moment, Astrid belonged again in this tentative new family of three. But then her mother got up.

"I'm sorry," Astrid whispered.

Her mother did not say anything. She did not tell Astrid it was not her fault, did not soothe her. But Astrid didn't deserve it, she knew. She didn't expect it.

Her mother left the room, and Astrid burst into tears.

Her dad hugged her again. "We have to be strong. Let's go downstairs and have some coffee, okay?"

"I'm not allowed to drink coffee yet," she said.

"There's always a first time. Let's put aside the rules for today."

Downstairs, they both sat at the kitchen table and drank their coffee black. The liquid tasted hot and bitter. He didn't ask her any questions. He merely stared out at the forest, his eyes brimming with tears.

Aunt Maude was bustling around, loading and unloading the dishwasher, wiping the counters. The grown-ups seemed broken to Astrid, and she felt broken, too. She hated herself for all the times she had wanted Nina to die. Like the time Nina had spilled cereal all over Astrid's homework. Or the time she had climbed onto the piano stool and got chocolate fingerprints all over the sheet music for Bach inventions.

Aunt Maude rummaged in the refrigerator, started throwing away old food in the garbage can under the sink.

Dad looked at Astrid. "We have to take care of a few things this morning. Your mom and I will be going to the hospital. Will you be all right here with Aunt Maude? We need to make some arrangements."

You mean you're going to the morgue, Astrid didn't say. *You're arranging to bury or cremate Nina.* She couldn't ask which. She squeezed her eyes shut, the coffee like acid in her stomach. She knew what happened to bodies when the ambulance took them away. When someone died, they went into a freezer drawer. She couldn't bear to have her sister be gone there, in a drawer.

The floor creaked. She turned to see her mother standing in the doorway, her body swaying a little. Her face was white. "Is Nina back? Nina—where is Nina?"

Aunt Maude gave Dad a look. He gave her the look right back. Astrid knew already that something was wrong with her mother, who had only the day before played in the kiddie pool with Nina. Had gathered seashells with her, done finger paints like they were the best of friends. Rose had clapped her hands and praised Nina for banging tunelessly on the piano. *She'll be a concert pianist,* she had exclaimed. Astrid had just played her Mozart concerto perfectly for the first time, and her mother had not seemed to notice. The previous night, Rose had smoothed down that red satin dress and had cuddled Nina. *Mommy's going out for a little while.* And then, later, her impatience with Astrid: *How hard is it to babysit your sister for a couple of hours?*

Aunt Maude went to the door and hugged her sister. Rose burst into terrible, deep, racking sobs. Her sorrow filled the whole house. Astrid couldn't stand it. She thought she should've died instead of Nina. Aunt Maude steered Rose out of the room. "Let's go up and get dressed," she said in the hall.

Astrid stared at the coffee in her mug. Dad had put toast on her plate, but she thought she could not possibly eat. Her father got up.

"I'd better get ready to go," he said. "Eat your toast. You need food."

Astrid nodded, but when he left the kitchen, she kept staring at her plate. His footsteps creaked upstairs. Aunt Maude did not come back into the kitchen, but Astrid could hear activity in the library down the hall—books being moved around, file drawers opening and shutting.

She peered out the window. Tears slipped down her cheeks. Nina's little inflatable kiddie pool sat forlornly in the backyard among all the beautiful, colorful flowers that kept on growing. Her parents soon left, the car rumbling away. She went down the hall and peered into the library. Aunt Maude sat at her desk at the typewriter, but she wasn't typing. She was staring out the window.

"Mr. Michaels gave me this typewriter many years ago. Did you know that?" she said without turning around. "I'll have to go down to the repair shop for a new ink ribbon. It's going dry." She wiped a tear from the corner of her eye.

Astrid went up to the desk and took her aunt's hand. "It's okay, Aunt Maude."

Aunt Maude squeezed Astrid's hand, then let go. "This will be it, won't it? No more summers with you all."

Astrid didn't know what else to say. It hadn't occurred to her that she and her parents might not ever return to Heron Bay. She couldn't think of much of anything. It was all she could do to put one foot in front of the other, to keep on breathing.

"Remember that I love you," Aunt Maude said.

Astrid and her parents stayed in Heron Bay a few more days. Her mother often walked through the garden and stood motionless for a while before coming back inside. Sometimes she hunched over the typewriter in Aunt Maude's library, typing on a sheet of white stationery. Astrid didn't dare interrupt her and instead spent a lot of time in the lush back garden. All around her, the flowers grew up and the birds sang. She could see the ghost of Nina running inside the house, calling for her mommy, as she had done only a week earlier.

She had cut her hand on a shard of sea glass. She had wandered down to the beach when nobody was looking. They'd all been eating dinner, and Nina took off without anyone noticing. Mom and Dad had spirited Nina into the downstairs bathroom to clean her hand. Mom had yelled at Dad, accusing him of not paying attention. He had replied, *Last I heard, she had two parents.*

Mom had said icily, *And an older sister.*

When it was time to go back to the city, Astrid's mother wanted to stay. She said she couldn't leave Nina.

The way my mom is acting—it's all because of me, Astrid thought. *Does she even know Nina is dead?* She was all packed, waiting for Dad to finish getting ready. She joined Aunt Maude in the kitchen. The room smelled of blueberry muffins, the berries from the hundred-year-old blueberry bushes in the garden. The aroma made Astrid's mouth water. Her aunt had harvested the blueberries the previous summer, picked buckets of them to store in the freezer.

Every time Astrid and her family visited, Maude made muffins to celebrate, but this time, the muffins were not a celebration. They were a goodbye. The kitchen countertops gleamed, and a hummingbird buzzed up to the feeder outside the window. Spilled water droplets reflected sunlight on the table.

Neither Astrid nor Aunt Maude spoke. Sometimes, there was nothing to say. They ate muffins in silence. When the suitcases were downstairs, and Astrid and her dad were ready to leave, Aunt Maude hugged Astrid for a long time. Rose hugged Bjorn and Astrid briefly and then retreated into the house. Astrid and her father left and returned home. How many days passed? Not days, weeks.

When she returned to the city, Rose took to her bed. She downed sedatives, antidepressants, and other pills. She and Astrid's father argued more often.

Nina's room, the nursery, was left as it was, as if she would come back at any moment. The original crib was still pushed up against the wall next to the little chest of drawers, her stroller, the old baby monitor. Her washed pants and onesies and little sweaters and boots and bibs and socks and shoes were all arranged with inordinate neatness. And all the toys remained as well.

Bjorn had wanted to donate nearly everything to charity, but Rose had screamed and dragged the donation bags back upstairs, accusing him of erasing her child. He'd tried to reason with her, hugging her and telling her they had to let go.

Yet Nina seemed to grow larger, more present in death than she had been in life. And Astrid grew even more ephemeral. The more she tried to be seen, the less her mother saw her. She had wanted her parents to stop expecting so much of her. She'd wanted to be free to go out with her friends, to not constantly be doing chores and keeping her room clean and dressing appropriately and babysitting her little sister.

She got her wish. She came home late, and nobody cared. Her dad was often gone. Her mother didn't bother to scold her. Astrid dressed in skimpy tube tops and left the house to meet her friends, and her mother didn't comment. When Astrid started skipping school and the teacher called her parents for a conference, her father went but not her mother. Rose didn't even make an excuse.

Dad told the teacher that his wife didn't feel well. Not feeling well became a way of life for Rose. Astrid found herself seeking some structure, some boundary, but it never came. Rose seemed to resent Astrid, to feel affronted by the very existence of her living daughter. To blame Astrid in an unspoken way.

Astrid kept to herself, staying after school at the library more often than before. She didn't want to go home to the faint alcohol smell lingering in the air or to her mother sprawled out on the couch, unconscious. At times, Astrid dumped out a few of the antianxiety or sleeping pills, whatever was in the cabinet, to keep her mother from mixing drugs and alcohol or taking too many pills and ending up in the ER.

The library became Astrid's sanctuary. She loved the order, the quiet, the smell of books. The anonymity. Books reminded her of Aunt Maude, the stacks like the library in the house in Heron Bay. Astrid read about the meaning of dreams, trying to understand why she often dreamed of wading into the reflecting pool, water rising around her legs. She often woke gasping for air, drenched in sweat. Sometimes, she sensed Nina nearby in the shadows, as if the little girl wanted to speak but could not find the words.

The librarian was eager to help Astrid, no matter what she wanted to read. Her parents never paid attention. They were both too caught up in their own worlds. Her father would sometimes suddenly notice her and ask how she was doing in school. She said she was doing fine.

She had to be fine because her parents certainly weren't.

One afternoon, she stayed at the library as long as she could, reading books about the history of handwriting until she ran out of snacks and began to feel faint. She walked home, hoping her mother had sobered up. In the kitchen, she grabbed an apple and crackers and tiptoed upstairs to hide in her room. The walk-in closet door squeaked in her parents' bedroom next door. Her mother yelled, drunk again and shouting.

"We lost our daughter, in case you forgot."

"Let's not get into this," Bjorn said. "You're always looking for someone to blame."

"Isn't there? Isn't there someone to blame?"

I'm to blame, Astrid thought. She was less of a daughter than Nina had been, maybe not a daughter at all.

"The investigation is over," Bjorn said.

"How could she just . . . walk into that water?"

"You have to stop doing this to yourself."

Astrid closed her eyes and tried to conjure Nina from the dead to make her mother happy, but she realized that she had forgotten what her little sister looked like. Her features were fuzzy, her voice distant.

Astrid's mother fell into that bereft, inconsolable crying, full of gasps. "Did you ever even love her?"

"Of course I loved her. You can't grieve by blaming people, Rose. Be sad, but don't blame me."

"What are you doing? Where are you going?"

"I need to take some time to think. I can't stay here."

"What about your home? What about us? Your other daughter?"

Astrid flinched. *Your* other daughter. Not *our*.

"Don't turn this around on me, Rose. You can barely hold yourself together. When I get home, Astrid has opened the mail and set aside the bills. You don't even bother."

"You're exaggerating. Everything is fine. The bills get paid, don't they?"

"Our fourteen-year-old daughter shouldn't be the one monitoring everything."

"Well, she should monitor something, shouldn't she?"

A stony silence followed. *I'll spend my whole life making up for this,* Astrid thought. She tried to make sure nothing else was forgotten or overlooked, but it was never enough for her mother.

"Don't blame Astrid, either." His tone was flat and tired, not angry.

Wire hangers clattered in the walk-in closet in her parents' room. Her father's heavy footsteps creaked across the wooden floor, back and forth to his suitcase. *Maybe I could go with him,* Astrid thought. But who would take care of her mother? Who would take off her shoes and cover her with a blanket when she passed out on the couch? Answer calls and fudge for her?

Dad was leaving, and he deserved to try to be happy, and nothing was happy here anymore. They had gone to family therapy, but it hadn't helped.

She quietly shut her door. Her mother's muffled voice rose to a high pitch of desperation and accusation, growing more caustic and insulting, never once admitting that she was scared but instead driving her husband further away with every shouted word.

Astrid hardly dared to breathe as footsteps stomped down the hall, her father's suitcase squeaking on wheels. He clopped down the stairs, her mother yelling after him that he was quitting and abandoning his family.

Astrid couldn't move as her mother ran outside, yelling after him; then Astrid tiptoed downstairs with her pack and out the back door and pretended to come back in. She didn't want her mother to know she'd been eavesdropping, that she had been in her room the whole time. Her mother would berate her, demand to know what she'd heard, might even seize the opportunity to blame Astrid for something more, for sneaking around, perhaps.

Her father came home two weeks later, and then they started to move—first to Eastern Washington for a year, then to California. They kept running, trying to escape the past, but changes of scenery didn't help.

They fell apart piece by piece, the three of them. Astrid's parents fought more and more often. Astrid often hid at the library. Her dad spent more time in the woods, counting butterflies and owls. Her mother ended up in rehab, and when she was released, she began speaking of moving even farther away, to South America, to Ireland, to northern Canada. Sometimes, Astrid caught her mother staring at her quizzically, as if trying to see someone else.

In the end, after the divorce, Astrid's mother left the country, traveling through Europe with one boyfriend and then another. It was never clear what she did for work—art, interior decorating—but she managed to attach herself to successful men who supported her. Somehow, she made her way, and Astrid wondered if Rose had finally managed to outrun her grief.

But Astrid never sloughed off the weight of guilt. She dreamed of rising tides lapping at her ankles, pulling her under. She dreamed of running in the woods, calling for Nina but never finding her.

CHAPTER ELEVEN

Astrid gathers up the police file on Nina and drives into town, parking at the beach, where her cell phone signal comes in strong. Then she calls her father on FaceTime. Since he moved to the woods with his second wife, who is also a naturalist, he and Astrid hardly ever talk. She doesn't expect him to answer, but he does. He is still handsome, although his face is weathered by time and grief. He still wears those small, studious spectacles. His prominent nose nearly fills her iPhone screen, the hollows of his face accentuated by the lamplight next to his desk. His computer monitor flickers in the background, a full wall of textbooks behind him, all about ecology, the environment, and more esoteric subjects, such as the reproductive life of the tree snail and the rise and fall of fungi in the temperate rain forests. Dappled light falls on his graying hair—wild, wispy, and still mixed with blond strands.

"Astrid—to what do I owe this pleasure?"

She tells him everything, from finding the photograph to combing through the police file. She tells him about Aunt Maude hitting her head, ending up in the hospital. He makes the appropriate sympathetic sounds.

Astrid holds up the photograph she found in the file on Nina. "You're right here," she says, pointing at him. "I'm assuming it was taken the night Nina died."

Her father sits back, blinks, and scratches at the stubble on his chin. "Wow, a blast from the past. Yeah, I remember someone taking that picture—"

"Who? With whose camera?"

"Hell, I don't remember. I was a little sloshed."

"And yet you drove back to Seattle. I heard Mom come home with someone. I wanted to believe it was you, but I knew better. I fudged when the sheriff asked me questions. I didn't want you and Mom to get in trouble." But did she really want to protect her parents—or protect herself from their anger?

He laughs nervously. "We did nothing wrong. I suppose you've already discussed all this with your mother?"

Your mother. He distances himself from Rose. She is not his ex-wife, someone with whom he shared a home for many years. She is now only Astrid's mother.

"You know Mom doesn't *discuss* anything to do with Nina anymore. It's like the past doesn't exist. She believed Nina's spirit stayed with her, she couldn't leave this place for the longest time, but then . . . poof, gone, just like that. She erased the past. But yes, I'm bringing it up, because I need to know what really happened that night."

His face grows pale. He sits even farther back. "I thought we put all of this to rest." *To rest*, as if Nina's death would ever lie still.

"Somebody was with Mom that night. Who the hell was with her?"

"A phantom, Casanova, Batman, the Pink Panther? My guess is as good as yours, Astrid. Your mother was always a mystery to me."

"You really have no idea what she was up to."

"She never admitted to anything, Astrid."

"Tell me why you went back to the city."

Her father rubs the stubble on his chin and glances out the window. Then he looks at Astrid, regret in his eyes. "Your mom and I had a fight."

"I could tell. About what?"

He scratches harder at his chin. "It was years ago. Nina is gone. What's the point of all this?"

"I've been living in the shadow of Nina my whole damned life. I've made a mess of everything, my marriage, my friendships—"

"Your mother was flirting with other men," he blurts.

She swallows, suddenly silent, stunned. "With whom?"

"Everyone. Just about."

"Len Wilkers? Verne Michaels? Julian Michaels?"

"Whoa, Len Wilkers. Another name from the past. Yeah, he spent time with your mother. She went out on his boat with him."

"How did you know?"

"They were discreet, but I saw them once. I took a trail down through the woods to the old marina, on the other side of town, and they were setting sail. I recognized your mother's hat. She'd taken off that morning with her beach bag."

"Did you confront her when she got home?"

"She said I was seeing things."

"How long was this going on? Did it start before she got pregnant?"

"Only your mother has the answer to that question." His face droops, as if he has aged ten years since the beginning of the conversation.

Astrid tries to wrap her mind around the possibility that her mother had an actual affair. Perhaps she did nothing but flirt. Perhaps she merely wanted to escape her family for a while.

"Bjorn, who's that?" His wife, Reenie, sounds robust, her voice musical in the background.

"I'll be right there," he says, and Astrid can feel her father slipping away.

"Dad," she says. "You drove to the city and left me with Nina and my wayward mother!" The anger tightens her throat. She didn't feel betrayed by him back then. She felt responsible, but now a sliver of resentment lodges between her ribs.

"I had no reason to believe anything would go wrong. Accidents happen. Let it rest. It wasn't your fault." He throws out the words as if tossing garbage into a can.

"But was it yours?" She is startled by her own question.

A curtain closes over his face. "You need to leave that place. It does no good to rehash the past. The sheriff turned over every stone."

"I'm turning them over again, Dad."

"You'll find nothing new about what happened to Nina."

After they hang up, Astrid seethes with new anger—or old anger, perhaps, that she did not allow herself to feel before now. Her father won't take responsibility for anything that happened that night. He should've been there for his kids. He should not have gone to the city. Was he planning to stay in Seattle, and only Nina's death brought him back to Heron Bay?

Her mother was fragile, but she was also an adult with responsibilities. Yet she left her life and everything in it, including her second daughter. She flirted with other men, and who knows what else Rose was up to back then?

I'm going to find out, Astrid thinks. She dials the number for her mother's cell phone in Italy.

CHAPTER TWELVE

Her mother's voice sounds tinny over the phone. "Len Wilkers. A name from another life. That was eons ago." Rose yawns as if the conversation is already boring her.

"Dad said you used to go boating with him."

"That's ridiculous. Why are you talking to your father about all this?"

"Then where did you go when you left for the whole day?"

"I never left you for that long. I might've gone shopping, and sometimes I needed some time alone. I went for walks."

With your packed beach bag? Astrid thinks. "Did you know Len Wilkers was in the woods the night Nina drowned?"

Another yawn, shuffling closer to the phone. "Do you know what time it is here?"

Of course—Astrid forgot. Whenever she mentions Nina, her mother pretends not to hear. "Did you know he was under suspicion? Did you suspect him, too?"

"I'm not getting much sleep these days."

"Mom."

"Oh, Astrid. How am I to remember? He did ask me to go out on his boat. I think the poor man had a crush on me. But I didn't actually go. Has he done something? Did he hurt Aunt Maude?"

"Maybe. And he might've hurt Nina. I've got the police file on her—"

"Why do you have that? Why would the police give up such a thing?"

To you is what Rose doesn't say. "I'm investigating some new leads," Astrid says, deliberately vague.

Her mother's voice skims along the frozen surface of a lake. "I'm concerned about you. It's not good to dwell on the past. You should go home, try to straighten out your life in the Bay Area."

Should, straighten, dwell, not good. Astrid never realized how judgmental her mother has always been. She laughs to herself, sitting back in the car and shaking her head at nobody. "You don't really know what's going on in my life."

"I know you left a perfectly good marriage."

Perfectly good. Astrid bites her lip to keep from spouting an acerbic reply. "You weren't there." *And didn't you ruin your own "perfectly good" marriage?*

"Your behavior is troubling—you should see someone."

"My behavior!" Astrid takes a deep breath. There it is, another *should*. *You're not going to get to me, Mom,* she thinks, forcing herself to let out her breath slowly. "This photograph from the party has you in it, and Dad. And Len Wilkers. Maude thinks one of you killed Nina."

Her mother laughs in that tinkling, musical way that attracts people. "Maude was always eccentric, but now she has gone off the deep end. I asked the doctor if she could've suffered a stroke. It could've been the reason she fell."

"She didn't have a stroke." Rose spoke to the doctor? Without telling Astrid? Who is driving back and forth to the hospital, sitting by Aunt Maude's bedside?

"She always *did* have fanciful ideas. Magic and fairies and all that—she put ideas into the heads of you children. I wasn't sure that was such a good idea."

Astrid imagines her mother as a little girl, orphaned, wandering through a silent forest. Her loneliness forces her to grow up too quickly, no longer able to see the fairies and gnomes and butterflies. All the magic has fled her world. Now she is grown, hollow inside but believing she has all the answers. "I don't think this is a fanciful idea," Astrid says carefully.

"Is there a good psychiatrist in your area? You know, psychiatrists are properly trained to understand these things. They can also dispense medications. And they're *physicians*."

Astrid holds the phone away from her ear. The therapist who helped Astrid the most these last couple of years was a social worker, not a doctor, but he understood her deep need to be seen and heard. *Humans have simple needs,* he said. *We want to be understood, and we want our lives to mean something.* He didn't have to be a physician to know this. "Mom, you don't have to tell me if there was anything going on between you and Len Wilkers. It's none of my business. I'm only trying to get to the bottom of what happened to Nina, for my own peace of mind."

Her mother snorts derisively into the phone. "Well, we all know what happened to Nina, don't we?"

I can't even believe you're saying this, Astrid thinks, clenching her teeth. But another tip from her past therapist, *always be kind and polite,* plays in her mind, and she wants to live up to that standard. "Yes, we do," she says, wanting to scream, *Have you forgotten that I found her while you were traipsing around in your tight red dress, holding your spiked heels in your hand?* "Who was with you when you stopped back at home to check on Nina that night?"

"I'm not sure what you're referring to." Her mother now sounds stone cold. As if she is on the stand in court, responding to a hostile attorney on cross-examination.

"That's right, I forgot. You didn't even come home. You were at the party the whole time. I was imagining things. I heard you say, 'Such a likeness . . . I swear.' I heard your footsteps. And someone else's, too."

There's a click on the line, crackling, and then a dial tone blaring in Astrid's ear.

CHAPTER THIRTEEN

Astrid throws her phone on the passenger seat, whacks the palms of her hands on the steering wheel. "Why do I keep doing this? Why do I keep banging my head against the wall?" She should know by now that there is a steel barrier in her mother's mind, a shield. *I'm not responsible for what happened to my mother, for the person she became.* But perhaps it would've been best not to agitate Rose, disturb her fragile mental equilibrium. Why would she deny going out on Len Wilkers's boat? *She won't admit to an affair.* In Rose's mind, she never transgressed. She was a perfect wife, perfect mother.

Astrid pulls out onto the road, turns on the radio, and opens the window, singing along loudly to the new Red Hot Chili Peppers song on the radio, from their first new album in years. The cool air helps to cleanse her mind, to whisk away the conversation she just tried to have with her mother. *This pattern is nothing new, I should know that by now,* she tells herself.

Trent used to remind her that her mother would not change. *Why do you bother?* he often said when she railed against Rose after a difficult long-distance conversation. *Talk to my mother instead.* His mother reacted with sympathy and stability, because she was a normal mother, a caring one, but Astrid hasn't spoken to her in a few months now. As the marriage slowly dissolved, so did Astrid's relationships with Trent's family. He was the thread connecting her to them. She did try calling his mother a few times after the breakup, but invariably, his name popped up, and with it, Leona's name, too. And each time, a festering wound opened in Astrid's heart. What does his mother think of his engagement? Leona met his family on a few occasions when she attended events as Astrid's best friend. *I hope it's all horribly awkward,* Astrid thinks venomously. *I hope they all make Leona uncomfortable.*

Back at Aunt Maude's house, she goes into the kitchen for a glass of water and glimpses Livie striding through the back garden toward the house, head down, watching each step on the paving stones. What on earth is she doing there? Astrid opens the door and waves. "Livie, hello!"

Livie looks up, her cheeks suddenly flushed. "Astrid! Sorry—I was just checking the garden. Ms. Dasgupta likes me to do the weeding. It's getting kind of overgrown out here."

Astrid steps back to let Livie into the kitchen. "Under the circumstances, I'm sure the weed police will show leniency."

Livie laughs nervously. "I had a nightmare that the plants came to life and overtook the whole house."

"In my professional opinion as interpreter of dreams, seems like you're feeling overwhelmed."

"You're right. I guess I'm worried about Mrs. D." Livie walks down the hall and stands awkwardly outside the library, playing with the tiny silver cross on her necklace.

"My aunt means a lot to you," Astrid says.

Livie gestures in the general direction of town. "I live with my parents down the road . . . I'm saving up to move out. I like coming here . . . to get out of the house. It only takes like five minutes to get here on my bike. But I walked this time. I needed to get some air."

"Come by anytime. Weed the garden to your heart's content. I won't complain."

"Thanks. Uh, I should go." Livie looks around, her face still flushed and a little sweaty. Then she gestures into the library. "I think I left a book here. It was due a week ago. Could I look?"

"Oh, go ahead." Astrid goes into the bathroom in the hall, washes her face, and tries to compose herself. *What now, Aunt Maude? It was a mistake to talk to my parents.* She can hear some thudding against the wall between the bathroom and the library. Livie is making a lot of noise in that room. Astrid tiptoes out of the bathroom, leaving the door open, and peers into the library. Livie is surreptitiously checking between books, under them, under the typewriter. She glances up toward the doorway just as Astrid steps back out of sight, holding her breath. A drawer slides open in her aunt's desk, then shuts, then another one opens and shuts.

Astrid tiptoes back to the bathroom, runs the water, and flushes, then shuts the bathroom door loudly before returning to the library. "Did you find what you were looking for?"

Livie stands at the desk, her face red. "I guess it's not here . . ."

"What are you really looking for?" Astrid says.

"A book, I told you." Livie glances out the window with an anxious expression.

"Have you been in the cottage lately?" Astrid says, walking into the library.

"What? No, why?"

"Could you have left something in there?"

"What did you find?" Livie says, breathless. She brushes past Astrid and heads for the front door.

"Wait right there. I'll be back." Astrid dashes into the guest room, brings back the skimpy camisole. "Someone left this in the cottage. Is it yours?"

Livie plays with the cross on her necklace and shakes her head vigorously, but her gaze stays on the camisole.

"This isn't what you're looking for," Astrid says.

"No, no—I've never seen it before. I'll see you later." Livie dashes out the front door and down the steps.

"Wait!" Astrid calls out. "What's the title of your missing library book?"

But Livie is already jogging down the driveway. She picks up her pace. Either Astrid spoke too softly, or Livie pretended not to hear.

That was strange, Astrid thinks. *Why was she really here? Why would she pretend the camisole isn't hers? It obviously is.* She takes the flimsy garment into the guest room, drapes it over the chair. How similar it looks to a lacy negligee Trent gave her for her birthday two years ago. *Come to bed in only this,* he said, and she did.

She clicks through the contacts on her phone, stops at his information, her finger hovering over the "Delete" button. *Trent Hoffman.* Soon, Leona Kemp will become *Leona Hoffman* or *Leona Kemp-Hoffman.* She once said to Astrid, "I'm a liberated woman, but I want to take my next husband's name. Does that sound too old fashioned?"

"No, not at all," Astrid had said. "I took Trent's name." But now she has reclaimed her given name, *Johansen.* She can't bear to think of Trent taking Leona's hand, sliding a ring onto her finger. *Don't think about it,* Astrid tells herself.

It's Saturday night—always date night when she and Trent were married. They reserved this evening once a week to turn off all electronic devices and pay attention to each other. They walked in Golden Gate Park, along Haight-Ashbury, or they took the BART train into Berkeley and wandered the campus, hand in hand. Before the pandemic hit, they loved to attend plays or the movies or to simply wander into a bookstore. She took their oneness for granted, believing they would always be together.

She takes the carved wooden Kashmiri box off the dresser and opens the top, the hinge a little stiff. Inside, she has kept the best moments of her marriage—a love note Trent wrote to her on Valentine's Day. *I will love you my whole life. You and no other.* She thought the sentiment was so romantic until he told her he'd stolen it from the movie *Braveheart*. A printed wedding photo, her favorite, in which she and Trent are both in motion, slightly blurry. She's lifting her right foot, holding up her gown, revealing the bridal sneaker. She's about to run, but Trent holds her arm and kisses her cheek. They're both smiling.

She kept two movie ticket stubs for a showing of *Roman Holiday* at the local indie theater, two tickets for *Hamilton* at the Orpheum

Theater. A vintage mechanical watch from the 1940s that he gave her for her birthday two years ago. The watch broke, but she can't bear to part with it. The time is always two fifteen.

She pulls out a small velvet box and takes out the simple carved gold wedding band that Trent slipped onto her finger while reciting the vows they'd written themselves. *I take you, Astrid Johansen, to be my beloved wife . . . to treasure you, to be at your side in sorrow and in joy . . . and to love and cherish you always . . .* She slides the ring onto her finger, and she feels the weight of all it once meant. She removes the ring, her heart heavy, and places it back in its box. The wooden box holds the secret she kept, but she can't bear to look at it a moment longer. She closes the box and tucks it back into her suitcase.

In bed, she tries to read a paperback mystery she bought in the airport, but her mind wanders. She tries to picture her apartment in Vallejo, but the details grow fuzzy and distant, as if she doesn't really live in that small, cluttered space on the upstairs floor of a house. Sometimes, she can hear the downstairs tenants arguing, a young couple headed for divorce, she is sure. Their tense voices remind her of her own marriage near the end. After the separation from Trent, she couldn't afford her own place anywhere near the Pacifica house, and of course she moved out. He'd bought the place long before she met him.

The rents were lowest in Vallejo, northeast of San Francisco, and so she moved into the house on a busy street. She had to shut down her little office in the city and find another one closer to her new home. The modern office building in San Ramon offered many affordable vacancies—essentially one-room cubicles for one to two people. She set up all her equipment in a small, bland space with bright overhead lights. The commute to work is thirty minutes each way in Bay Area traffic. She passes the time by listening to audiobooks or music, but mainly she spaces out, trapped in her day-to-day life. She loves her work, but the rest of her life feels dried out like the climate around her—overcrowded and yet ultimately lonely.

Here, although she is alone and heartbroken in this house, she feels a little more at home. She didn't realize how much she had missed the cool air off the sea, the lush greenery, the character of this house. The gardens. The quiet, the bright stars at night.

Nina's thick file folder sits on the dresser, and strangely, Astrid finds herself thinking of Conor, of his smile and his kindness. He didn't have to give her the file. He didn't have to do anything, but he wanted to help. He always did, even seventeen years ago.

It's like no time has really passed, she thinks. *And Nina might have been murdered.* What are her parents hiding? Why don't they want her here? They could not possibly have drowned Nina. And what if Aunt Maude doesn't wake up? Why was she afraid? And where is the damn letter?

Outside, an owl hoots in the distance. The room feels warm. Astrid opens the window to let in the breeze through the screen. Leaves rustle in the garden; then she hears a crunching, like footfalls. Her heartbeat taps in her throat. *It must be a deer or a raccoon,* she thinks. She peers out into the not-quite darkness. The shadowy shapes of shrubs and trees sway against the sky. In the waning light of dusk, she can barely make out, on an open stretch of lawn at the edge of the forest, the distinct outline of a man.

CHAPTER FOURTEEN

The lights on the sheriff's car are still flashing in the driveway while Conor searches the property. He arrived quickly. As he stands at the entrance to the forest, shining his flashlight into the woods, he looks almost like the shape of the man she saw there. She buttons up her sweater, the chill penetrating her bones. The image of the man lingers in her mind—a silhouette, arms at his sides, motionless and facing the house, as if he were mocking her, trying to scare her. He certainly wasn't hiding. He stood out against the sky. He wanted to be visible.

At first, in shock, she grabbed her car keys. But then she couldn't bring herself to run outside. The man could ambush her before she ever reached her car. She crosses her arms over her chest, her teeth chattering. After she called Conor from the landline, she looked out the window again, and the man was gone. But he could still be out there watching her, laughing at her. Maybe she ought to cut her losses and return to California, but how can she run away again? And if the man is trying to intimidate her, she can't give in.

Conor traipses back to the driveway, turns off the lights in his vehicle, and comes up onto the porch. "Where did you say you saw the man, exactly?"

She points toward the wooded trail leading into the forest. "He was there. I could see his shape."

"Did you recognize who it was?"

"Just a shape. Maybe your height. I couldn't see his face."
"You sure it was a man?"
"No, it was the Sasquatch."
"Broad shoulders, narrow? Height?"
"Just a normal Sasquatch. Regular height."
"Clothing?"
"Do Sasquatches wear clothes?"
"Come on, Astrid."
"Pants, a hooded sweatshirt. Loose fitting. Yes, hooded."

Conor looks toward the woods, now cloaked in darkness. "Could it have been a tree?"

"Are trees shaped like men?"

"Sometimes, depending on the light."

"I know what I saw." She pulls at a thread on her sweater, her teeth still chattering. With the porch light on, she feels exposed, as if she is being watched.

"I had to ask. That stretch of woods is public property. Anyone can walk through those trails."

"Can't you check the woods?"

"I can't stop anyone from walking through there. If someone steps onto your property, that's another story, but I don't have the resources to post an officer here to watch for trespassers."

"I didn't ask you to do that." She gestures toward the woods. "But that guy was watching me. Taunting me. Trying to scare me. He wasn't just some person out for a walk."

"I believe you." He heads up the porch steps. "I'll check inside."

"Why? He didn't climb in through a window."

"To give you peace of mind, so you can get some sleep."

"Fun way to spend a Saturday night. I doubt I'll sleep ever again." She follows him inside and up the stairs. She stays behind him as he searches the rooms.

He lingers in her old bedroom. "Remember when we used to play Boggle in here? And Scrabble? You always beat the hell out of me with all those big words."

"You weren't a big reader," Astrid says. Back then, she and Conor lay on the bed to play games, never once thinking about what it meant for a teenage boy and girl to be up in her room. Or maybe he thought about it—she didn't. And nobody ever stopped them.

"My vocabulary has improved a bit since then," Conor says. "Thanks to you."

"Me? What did I do?"

He shrugs. "I wanted to impress you. I started reading the damn dictionary."

"I had no idea."

"Now you know."

She follows him back down and through the rooms on the first floor. "You don't still read the dictionary, do you?"

"I look up words online." He laughs, steps into the living room, goes to the front window. "We used to sit out on the porch and eat chocolate bars."

"Aunt Maude had a swinging chair!" she says, standing beside him. He smells of a minty soap. The swinging chair is gone.

"And we played records." He goes to the vintage stereo system still sitting next to the couch.

"We danced to *Saturday Night Fever!*" She remembers mimicking John Travolta's disco dancing.

Conor kneels to open the cabinet under the record player. "They're still here, all the records. Your aunt doesn't throw anything away."

"But she's hyperorganized. And she's really good at hiding things. I looked everywhere but I can't find the letter. Yet."

He stands again. His knees crack. "Maybe she slipped it into a record sleeve."

"You know, it's entirely possible," she says, nodding slowly. After Conor leaves, she'll check every record sleeve in the house. "She could've slipped it between the pages of a book, too. I haven't checked every single book in the library."

He gives her a long look. "You're serious about this letter. You think it really exists."

"You told me yourself that my aunt was not confused."

"Right," he says, heading for the front door. "You were always pretty determined. Keep me posted, okay?"

"Thanks for coming by," she says.

He opens the front door. "Lock up after me."

"I will."

He walks down the steps, then turns to face her. "How come you never wanted to slow dance with me?"

"Excuse me?" His question takes her by surprise.

"When we danced, it was fun. But you wouldn't dance the slow dances."

She presses her hand against the doorjamb, her face heating. "I don't really remember—"

"You were obsessed with Julian Michaels, like every other girl in town."

"I'm sorry," she says, looking down at the welcome mat. "I didn't mean to be rude. I was young and immature. I was socially inept."

"Don't worry, so was I."

"I'm sorry seventeen years later, if that helps." She stands there awkwardly, shivering in the cool night.

"Ah hell, I wasn't fishing for an apology. I was curious, is all."

"I can't answer for my fourteen-year-old self."

"I wouldn't expect you to." He points at his face. "You don't wear glasses."

"No, why? I don't need glasses to see strange men standing in the yard."

"No, I mean . . . you used to wear these huge glasses. When you read to your sister."

"I forgot about those glasses. They didn't help me see any better." She can feel her blush deepening. "I guess they made me feel studious. Important."

"Those glasses didn't even have lenses in the frames," he says, and they both laugh.

She smiles at him. "I can't believe you remember all that."

"Why wouldn't I? You used to read the same book to Nina every time. A yellow book . . . *Curious George*. You were so patient with her. She would say, 'Again,' and you read it again."

Astrid bites her lip, gazing off toward the moonlit water. "I wasn't patient. You're not remembering it right."

"No, I am. You were the best big sister—"

"Stop. Conor, please." She steps back over the threshold, into the foyer. "I was not a good big sister, believe me." The pressure of grief is too much, even now, after all these years. She can still remember Nina climbing onto the armchair next to her, turning the pages with her little fingers.

He comes back up the steps. "Guilt does that to you, makes you think you did everything wrong, even when you did things right." He leans down close to her face, and for a moment, she expects him to kiss her.

"What do you know about guilt?" she snaps, stepping back.

His expression sours. "I've had my share . . . Like almost killing my wife a month after I got back from Afghanistan. I had a nightmare. Woke up and hit her."

Astrid flinches. "You didn't do that on purpose, did you?"

"I thought she was someone else. An intruder. She was pretty understanding, but her coworkers weren't. She showed up at her job with a black eye and a bruised cheek. They told her to leave me."

"You didn't know what you were doing," Astrid says.

"That was the only time I ever raised my hand to a woman. Good night, Astrid." He turns, races down the steps, and returns to his car.

What just happened? Astrid thinks, watching the lights of the sheriff's car disappear around the bend. He was about to share something with her, a kiss or an intimate thought, and she instinctively pushed him away. *What do you know about guilt?*

Inside, she locks the doors and windows and pulls down the blinds in the guest room. How the hell is she supposed to sleep? She lies in bed watching the door, expecting the silhouette of a man to show up at any moment. Eventually, she nods off but sleeps shallowly, drifting in and out, startled by every unusual sound—a branch crackling in the woods, the creaking of the house settling, even the sound of a boat horn in the distance.

In the morning, she begins to think she did imagine the shape of a man at the edge of the woods. A tall, narrow rhododendron bush near the entrance to the trail could look humanlike from a distance, in a certain light.

She makes coffee and returns to the library to look for the Wi-Fi password. Finally, she finds the information taped to the bottom of her aunt's computer keyboard. At the kitchen table, she powers up her laptop and signs on to the internet. She catches up on email, inquiries about her services, and she responds to clients, promising them reports next week. The cursor hovers above the icon for the Facebook app. She considers not logging in—she shouldn't. But she does, clicking through the usual notifications for birthdays, events, and her colleagues and acquaintances playing with their children, dogs, and cats or traveling to stunning, far-off climes. Everyone in the world has a wonderful life, so much better than hers.

She is no longer friends with Trent or Leona, but she can't help clicking on Leona's page. The profile picture shows Leona and Trent cheek to cheek. Leona's face is round, radiant, and happy. Astrid's stomach turns over. The background picture looks familiar—a spectacular bluff at Point Reyes National Seashore. The caption reads, Wedding plans! We couldn't wait any longer.

Dreaming of Water

The comments are all enthusiastic. OMG, you're getting married so soon? And He's so hot, and Leona, you rock! And Congratulations to the happy couple, you must be thrilled!

"Vomit!" Astrid says aloud, the bile rising in her throat. "The happy couple, really?" She clicks a link at the bottom of the caption, all while telling herself not to do it. A website pops up titled TRENT AND LEONA FOREVER, showing stylish photographs of wedding invitations, a bridal gown on a hanger, and a gold necklace in a bowl against the background image of a beach at sunset.

Astrid closes the window, logs out of social media, and turns off her computer. Her muscles tense up, her breathing shallow. Her eyes are stinging. *I already knew all this,* she tells herself. *I didn't need to see it.* But what really irks her is that Trent and Leona chose Point Reyes National Seashore for their upcoming ceremony—in only three weeks! A late-September wedding. Why couldn't they have picked any other place? San Francisco offers many beautiful venues. Point Reyes belonged to Astrid and Trent. *But nothing belongs to us anymore,* she reminds herself. *Nothing is sacred.*

She pulls on her shoes and opens the front door, preparing to go out to the mailbox at the curb for the Sunday Seattle newspaper, to which her aunt has subscribed faithfully for years. A folded slip of paper falls to the welcome mat. It must've been wedged inside the doorjamb. She pulls it out—a flyer for a solicitor, she suspects. But who would've stopped by in the night? When she unfolds the paper, her heart nearly stops. It's a handwritten note in pen, a jagged cursive script slanting a little to the right and clearly legible.

Go home. You don't belong here.

CHAPTER FIFTEEN

After Nina drowned, Astrid felt like she no longer belonged in Heron Bay. She had ruined everything good about being here, and yet, mornings still came, seeping in through the curtains. The surf rose and fell as if nothing had changed. In the distance, the ferry foghorn blew.

On the third day, before she and her dad returned to Seattle, Astrid felt numb inside. Her parents were out again. She lay on top of the bedcovers in her clothes. The future would go on forever and ever without Nina in it. That was the thing, she thought, that happened when people died. Life went on. Like when that girl at school, Sara, had died in a car accident. Astrid had seen Sara every day. Sometimes they'd sat together at lunch. They'd been friends, but not close. They'd never hung out together on weekends.

Then suddenly, Sara's seat in the classroom was empty, and over the loudspeaker, the principal announced two minutes of silence. The family held a private memorial service. Sara's short obituary showed up in the newspaper. And then she faded away. She would never pass by Astrid in the hall again, would never grow up to become a veterinarian. She'd rescued a succession of animals. She would never share her desserts at lunch again. The kids at school whispered about her and her family, and Astrid thought about how sad her parents and her older brother must be. He kept coming to school—he was a senior about to go to college. His face looked pale and blank. Nobody wanted to approach him. Nobody knew what to say.

Astrid wished she had spoken to him. Now everyone would be whispering about *her* family, pitying them. Pitying her. She didn't want to ever go back to school again. She didn't want to go anywhere. She would stay in her room forever.

"Why don't you get some air?" Aunt Maude said, peeking into her room. "No sense moping around. Why don't you go to the beach?"

Astrid sat up, thinking maybe the sheriff would come soon to arrest her. She felt guilty enough to go to jail. But she got ready to go out for a walk. The house felt oppressive, the air inside like concrete in her lungs. She put on her sneakers and dashed outside, inhaling the sea breeze, as if she had just broken the surface after holding her breath underwater.

At the end of the driveway, she turned to gaze up at her aunt's house. She tried to memorize the way it looked—the porch, the stained-glass windows, the lush garden. As she walked down to the beach, her heart made of stone, the day denied that anything terrible had happened. The sun refused to hide. It shone down in all its glory, warming the land and reflected in brilliant diamonds off the surface of the sea. In the distance, a cargo ship stood motionless against the horizon. The sky was too blue. A heron hunted in the shallows, unaware and uncaring about the death of a little girl. Everything went on.

Astrid felt like a ghost walking through the waking world. A deep survival instinct kept her from wading into the surf and plunging headlong into the depths. She wanted to live, and she felt ashamed by her need to go on breathing. A part of her even welcomed the warmth of the sun and the calls of the birds—the life all around her. She lost herself in that life as she trudged along, not bothering to shake the sand out of her running shoes.

She walked and walked and walked. The receding tide uncovered crabs, rocks, and anemones. She had often walked this beach, full of excitement and anticipation every summer for as long as she could remember, from the time she was five through her mom's second pregnancy, through the birth of Nina and every summer since then.

Once, they had even come out for spring break, two months before Nina's birth. Astrid's mother had slept most of the time, while her father had taken off on wildlife hikes, sometimes all day. And then her mother had driven off in the car on her own, never saying where she was going. Sometimes she was gone all day, too.

Astrid's parents often fought in hushed voices in their room, and once, during that spring trip, Astrid had overheard her mother confiding in Aunt Maude. *Bjorn doesn't want another child. He doesn't even want to be here with us.*

Aunt Maude had reassured her. *You need to talk to him. He loves you.*

But did he? Astrid felt now, in her heart, that her family would finally break into a million tiny pieces like grains of sand on the beach.

She passed around the bend toward the bottom of the cliff below the Michaels mansion. The long wooden dock floated in the water off a distant cove, a yacht bobbing next to it. A man stood on the dock, untying the boat. He waved at her, and she waved back, although she could not tell who he was.

She stopped at the stone steps, where she and Julian had often sat and talked. She loved his clove cigarettes, but now the thought of the sweet smell made her sick to her stomach. She missed Nina with a deep, unfathomable ache. She missed her sister's soft hair, her laughter, her baby-powder smell, the way she hugged Astrid with pudgy arms around her neck.

She had walked quite a distance. When she turned to head back, the yacht was gliding away from the dock. She passed a gathering of teens smoking in a cove. She averted her gaze and picked up her pace.

"Hey!" a boy called out.

She kept walking.

"Hey, you!" Out of the corner of her eye, she could see a skinny boy sprinting toward her from the cove. She'd seen him before, maybe at a beach party, but couldn't remember his name.

She turned toward him, waved tentatively, and kept walking, adrenaline rushing through her.

"Aren't you that kid's sister?" the boy yelled. "The kid who drowned?"

Panic spiked inside her. She picked up her pace, but the boy fell into step beside her. He was smoking, the acrid fumes making her cough. "I heard you found her?"

"Where did you hear that?" she snapped. She did not like this kid. He was blowing smoke in her face.

"Word gets around. So, I heard you hated her. Did you drown her?"

She bit her lip to keep from crying and broke into a sprint. The kid was following her.

"Hey! Leave her alone!" someone yelled, running toward them. She hadn't seen him coming, Conor. He wore long Bermuda shorts and a T-shirt, his short hair sticking straight up in the wind.

"Whatever," the kid said, a smirk on his face. He backed off a bit, but he was muttering under his breath. He was not ready to leave her alone.

Conor fell into step beside her. He had been following her all summer. But they were friends, nothing more. "Don't listen to kids like that," he said. "They're immature."

"I know." But she thought of Conor as immature compared to Julian. Conor was already fifteen, but he seemed like twelve. He still made fart jokes. He didn't read Jane Austen or Nabokov.

The smoking kid followed them, yelling, "Hey, killer! Kill-er! Kill-er!"

She tried to tune out the bully, but his voice cut through her mind and her heart.

Conor took her hand, and she let him. She forgot, for a moment, that she didn't like him that way. This time, she needed his support. "It'll be okay," he told her. "Hang in there."

But the bully caught up to them, and he shoved Conor. "You in love with a killer? Maybe she'll drown you next!"

Conor turned and shoved the bully, sending him stumbling backward.

"Conor!" Astrid yelled, but he was already on top of the bully, punching him in the face, and all she could see was blood flying, the boy gurgling, and she was shouting at Conor to stop, tugging his sleeve, pulling him away. He stumbled backward, panting, his fist covered in blood. She held on to his arm. "Stop, stop," she said as the bully staggered to his feet, holding his bloody nose. Then he turned and ran away.

CHAPTER SIXTEEN

"You might as well move in," Astrid says to Conor as he walks up the driveway, pulling up his pants. He had parked at the curb.

"Show me the note," he says, frowning.

She hands him the note. "I didn't know what it was. It has my fingerprints all over it."

"Doesn't matter," he says. "We don't have the resources to fingerprint everything."

"Not even a note like that? It's a threat!"

"It's not nice. But it's not clearly a threat."

"'You don't belong here'? 'Go home'?"

"Where did you find this?"

"In the door! Who would've done this? Who wants me gone? Why? The same guy who stood in the yard, staring at me? How can anyone know why I'm here?"

"I was in the Heron Bay Café an hour ago," he says, folding the note. "I overheard Livie telling her friend that you're looking into your sister's drowning from seventeen years ago. People heard. I heard."

Astrid presses her hand to her forehead. "Are you kidding me? I didn't tell her about the file or the photograph. But maybe she inferred something, or maybe Aunt Maude confided in her—"

"I have no idea. Livie is harmless, but she talks."

"You think someone doesn't want me to look into Nina's death?" She paces back and forth on the porch.

"Towns like ours, we don't like to be associated with tragedies. For a long time, this place was all about a little girl drowning in a shallow pool belonging to rich people who don't even live here year-round. People don't want strangers coming in and dredging up the past."

Astrid sits on the porch, her body heavy with fatigue. She rubs her forehead and looks up at him. "So now I'm a stranger stirring up trouble. I didn't come here to threaten anyone or . . . bring up a tragedy." Part of her wants to run from this place again and never come back. But Aunt Maude is still unconscious, and someone might have made her that way.

"Whether you want to or not, you're revisiting Nina's death."

"Someone is trying to scare me. Not very subtle."

He sits next to her on the porch. "You don't have to stay here and pursue this. It might not be safe for you."

"What, now you, too? If there's anything that would make me stay here, it's someone trying to scare me off. It makes me even more certain that my aunt was onto something."

He gets up, rests a hand on her shoulder. "I don't want you to get hurt."

"What about the note? Can you look into it?"

"Not much I can do. It's not a direct threat to your life. There's no video surveillance, and like I said, fingerprinting is expensive. We only do it if there's a credible threat."

"Wow, I'm so glad I called the helpful police!"

"I'm sorry, Astrid. But you could still do something about this. You analyze handwriting, don't you?"

"I would need more samples for comparison."

"Wish I could magically make another sample appear, but . . ."

"Don't you think it's strange that I saw someone standing out there, and then someone left me a hostile note? Someone's stalking me, and you can't do anything." She tries to tamp down the desperation boiling up inside her.

"Stalking is tricky. If I had unlimited resources, I'd have someone here watching your property, but you weren't attacked, nobody broke the law, nobody threatened to kill you, and my resources are stretched to the limit as it is."

She snatches the note back from him. "I suppose it was coincidence that my aunt fell and hit her head in her library. That some guy was staring at me, that someone is telling me to leave. Everything. Coincidence. Yay. I appreciate all your help." She can't help the sarcastic tone in her voice.

"If you're going to stay, maybe go to the Heron Bay Hotel."

"I won't let anyone scare me out of Aunt Maude's house!"

"It would be temporary. We have many getaways here. It's a tourist town in summer."

"This is a getaway," she says, pointing down at the ground. "Right here."

"You could stay with me," he blurts, then looks toward the water, squinting, shoves his hands into his pockets. "I mean, you know, my parents had a guest room. Big house."

"With you?" Astrid blinks at him, then smiles. "That's the sweetest thing I've heard since I've been here."

"I'm not kidding."

"Thank you for your kindness, but no."

"All right," he says, rocking back on his heels, then forward. "At least have dinner with me. Or lunch. Sometime. I mean, when you have time."

"Are you asking me on a date?"

"Old friends," he says. "We could catch up, put aside all this . . . for a little while."

She looks up at him, trying to imagine a date with him. He's kind, and he has become a good-looking man, haunted, but handsome. But he'll soon find out that she is unreliable and haunted, too. "That might be nice," she says diplomatically. "Can I think about it?"

"Yeah, sure, think about it." He turns and once again strides back to his car, and she realizes that he is always walking away.

Back inside, she puts the Sunday newspaper on her aunt's desk and places the note beneath her handheld microscope. The paper is unremarkable, cotton résumé paper available at any office-supply shop. The blue ink shows striations, indicating the use of a ballpoint pen. The writing seems natural, the downstrokes heavier than the upstrokes, the note written in cursive, dashed off without any deliberate attempt to alter the style of the writing. Whoever wrote it didn't think that she might try to examine the details—or didn't care. But the pressure of the pen on the paper, harder than normal, indicates frustration or anger. Who would be so angry at her? She hasn't threatened anyone.

She sits at her aunt's desk, looking out at the forest. Conor's voice plays in her mind. *At least have dinner with me. Or lunch . . . old friends.* She is hardly dating material. Can't he see she's a mess? Pursuing a phantom letter, a possible killer, a long shot while her aunt lies unconscious in the hospital? While Astrid lurks on her ex–best friend's Facebook page? *But I could go out with Conor, no obligations, just as old friends, like he said.*

Astrid goes to the hall bathroom, examines her face in the mirror. She hasn't seen herself as a possible date in many months, not since a colleague set her up with another forensic document examiner, a perfectly nice, stable man with a receding hairline, a formidable intellect, and a habit of licking his lips. Although she barely listened to him at dinner, he tried to kiss her when he dropped her home. She made an excuse and ran inside, bursting into tears. But now—what does Conor see in her, with the dark circles beneath her eyes, the vertical lines on her forehead, between her eyebrows? Her unkempt hair? Her baggy sweatpants and house slippers? But still, it would be nice to put all this searching and wondering and worrying aside for a short time . . . maybe.

Someone knocks on the front door, and as Astrid is going to answer, she finds Livie already standing in the front hall in a flowing paisley shirt, leggings, and black ballet slippers.

Astrid presses her hand to her chest. "How the hell did you get in?"

"You told me to come back anytime to do the weeding, and I thought I would catch up on the bills. The heating bill is coming up due."

"You can't sneak up on me like that. You can't just come in!" *Livie's acting so strangely,* Astrid thinks.

"I didn't mean to sneak. I thought . . . I always walk in." Livie produces a ring of keys from her pocket, including a car key. "Mrs. D gave me this whole set. I run errands for her."

"My aunt trusts you an awful lot, but I don't."

Livie's face reddens. "I've known Mrs. D since we moved here. I was five."

Astrid holds out her hand. "I'd like the keys back if you don't mind."

Livie's face drops with disappointment, but she hands Astrid the keys, then turns on her heel and heads to the door.

"Wait!" Astrid runs after her. "The sheriff said he overheard you gossiping about me at the café."

Livie stops at the door, her hand on the knob. "I don't gossip—I was just . . . talking to my friends."

"What do you know about why I'm here?" Astrid snaps. She can't help her tone of voice.

Livie yanks open the door. "You think someone killed your sister. So did Mrs. D." She turns to look at Astrid.

"How do you know that? I never told you. Not once."

"Mrs. D had the file out on her desk . . . last week." Livie's gaze slips past Astrid toward the library. "And I heard her talking to you on the phone once about a letter. I was cleaning up the guest room for you to stay in . . . She said you were coming to help her."

"You just put two and two together," Astrid says in disbelief.

"Yeah, pretty much."

"Why don't I believe you?"

"You don't have to believe me, but it's the truth."

"Did you write me a note?"

Livie looks at her blankly. "No, I didn't. Why?"

"Do you know who was standing in the yard in the dark, watching the house?"

"I don't know what you're talking about. I have to go." Livie steps out onto the porch and races down the steps. Astrid watches her pedal away on her bicycle, hair flying. Maybe she's just a teenager jumping to conclusions. Or maybe she knows something more. Either way, she was presumptuous, walking right in. Astrid feels shaken, unsettled. She looks at the keys in her hand, including the key to Aunt Maude's Honda. Livie had them all this time. Aunt Maude's words pop up from the voice mail she left Friday morning. *I meant to tell you about the key . . .*

Did she mean a key among the ones Livie kept?

Astrid goes back into the library. A stack of books has been moved from the desk onto the computer table, as if Livie set them aside. Astrid closes the desk drawer. Livie might've been looking for something earlier. The letter? But why?

Astrid searches the rooms in the house, sliding the keys into the door locks, but they don't fit anywhere. Only the main key fits the front and back doors. *What did you want me to do with this, Aunt Maude?* The bathrooms have simple push-button locks that engage from the inside.

The library.

She looks around in her aunt's library. *The barrister's bookshelves.* The glass case opens with a keyhole lock. What if the letter is in that case? Why didn't she think of it before? One of the keys turns easily in the lock and opens the case. She checks through all the books inside, but she doesn't find a letter.

Of course it wouldn't be this easy.

She goes out to the cottage and tries the keys in the open door. After much jiggling and finagling, one of them works. But the key must be almost stripped, or the lock is worn.

Another smaller key opens the barrister bookcase inside the cottage. She checks through all the books in the case but finds no letter. *Now what, Aunt Maude?*

She leaves the door to the cottage unlocked as usual. If she locks the door, the key might not work next time. She makes a mental note to call a locksmith.

Back in the house, she opens the piano bench, brings out the sheet music for Bach inventions, sits on the bench, and starts to play. The piano is slightly out of tune, but the tone is still robust and wonderful. As her fingers fly—and sometimes stumble—across the keys, she feels her heart beginning to calm. One key is touchy, vibrating. The B-flat key above middle C. Aunt Maude always kept her piano perfectly in tune. What if, when she said, *I meant to tell you about the key* . . . she meant a piano key? What about the thud at the end of Aunt Maude's last voice mail message?

Astrid lifts the lid of the piano to look inside. Nothing unusual. Just the piano out of tune.

I'll never find the letter, Astrid thinks. What if there is no letter? She goes upstairs to check her aunt's room again. This time, she checks inside the pillowcases, between the mattresses. Checks for a possible false bottom in one of the dresser drawers. Nothing.

Next, she checks the room in which her parents once slept. The dusty antiques cluttered in a corner, the bed pushed up against the wall, the alcove all seem arrested in time, lost in the past.

In the room in which she once slept, she checks the desk drawers again, then sits on the bed and runs her hand across the bedspread. The mattress seems narrow, the room small, but seventeen years ago, she relished this beautiful space with its angled view of the forest and the sea. She picks up the book *Gone with the Wind*. She read it to the end that summer. She discussed the story with Aunt Maude, said that it seemed unfinished. Aunt Maude told her that war changed the characters, they did what they could to survive. Especially Scarlett. Aunt Maude thought it was too late for Rhett and Scarlett, but Astrid fantasized that they would get back together.

Except that some broken things can't be fixed.

Astrid opens the book and flips through the pages. The back of the book, inside the cloth cover, feels thick, and something slips out—a folded sheet of paper. Aunt Maude said, *The letter is in a safe place.* Inside the back cover, Astrid finds not one but three flattened, faded, folded letters.

CHAPTER SEVENTEEN

Hardly able to breathe, Astrid unfolds the letters. She has already marred the paper with her fingerprints, but then, so has Aunt Maude. It's too late to wear vinyl gloves, for all the good they might do. Each letter is a single page, typewritten on a manual typewriter but signed by hand in ink. She begins to read the first letter:

> My Love,
> The house was empty this morning. I watched everyone leave. A side door was open. I slipped inside and looked for evidence of you . . . I could hardly believe what I'd found. I needed to know for sure. If I hadn't found out about your betrayal, you wouldn't have ever told me.
>   Perhaps you're no longer attracted to me. Giving birth wasn't something I planned. Not once, but twice. Do you know what it does to your body? You become damaged. You're only a receptacle. You're never the way you were before. Maybe you think of me as broken. Maybe I am. You know what I've found. Maybe I'll do something you don't expect.
>   *Your Rose Petal*

The body of the letter is typed, but the signature is handwritten and signed *Your Rose Petal*. The nickname Astrid's father gave to her mother. He thought of her as fragile, beautiful, like a flower. A rose. Astrid barely remembers her mother's writing. This looks like hers. She can't hold the letter steady. *I'll have to compare the signature to others before I form an opinion,* she tells herself, trying to remain objective. Aunt Maude kept other notes and postcards from Rose downstairs in the library.

Rose typed these letters to Astrid's father, Bjorn, it seems.

But how can this be? Did Astrid's father have the affair, not her mother? What if Aunt Maude was referring to entirely different letters, not these?

These are the letters, they have to be, Astrid tells herself. In a fit of jealousy, her mother broke into a neighbor's home. Or is she lying? Would she really do something so bold? Would she break the law? Or was she only imagining her husband's affair with a neighbor? Was it Beatrice Michaels? No other neighbors live close by.

Astrid leans back in Aunt Maude's office chair and closes her eyes. She takes deep, steady breaths. *Don't lose it. Keep your cool.* She opens her eyes and considers the letter again. Rose says she never wanted to give birth, that having two children changed her body, made her less attractive. Astrid thinks back to what her mother said to Aunt Maude all those years ago. *Bjorn doesn't want another child.* And what did she mean by *Maybe I'll do something you don't expect?*

The second letter reads:

> My Love,
> The party was magical. I felt we might find our way back to the beginning, but then, I saw you push the hair back behind her ear. You touched her earring.
>
> And then you were gone. You said you would return, but I had to go looking for you. I had to elude Julian. He would've come after me. I made an excuse.

I followed the trail to the stone garden. The silver rubber ball bounced to the center of the pool. Our daughter was there in her white fairy-tale nightgown. She waded in after the ball. Did I throw the ball into the water? Probably. She was there. And you were leaving me forever.

The next thing I knew, she was floating in the water. And then she wasn't in the water anymore. She floated into the woods, and I ran after her. I knew she would lead me to you, that you weren't going to leave me forever. I know what you think of me, but someday you will understand that you drove me to this. It's all because of my love for you and for our daughter.

I drowned her.

Your Rose Petal

Astrid's eyes begin to water, the text blurring on the page. She drops the letter on the desk and begins to tremble, hyperventilating. She gets up, gasping for breath, and paces on the creaky wooden floor, forcing herself to inhale deeply and count to eight on the exhale. *This can't be real.* Someone faked these letters as a practical joke, to play a trick on Aunt Maude.

My mother is confessing to murder. Astrid's hands close into fists. She grits her teeth, nearly biting her tongue. Her mother, Rose, admits to drowning her own child—*her own flesh and blood, the little girl she claimed to love so much.*

Or at least, she confesses to letting her drown and not saving her. *I drowned her . . . Did I throw the ball into the water? Probably.*

Astrid collapses into the chair and doubles over, her stomach cramping. *I won't believe this. I can't.* No wonder Aunt Maude wouldn't reveal the contents of the letters. No wonder she didn't send them or email them. No wonder she wanted Astrid to come to Heron Bay in person. *My mother must've been fantasizing. Yes, she imagined everything.* This gives Astrid a temporary flood of relief. *Don't jump to conclusions.*

I know my own mother. She's not a killer. She loved Nina. Fragmented images flit through her mind, of her mother dressing Nina, brushing her hair, kissing her cheek, reading to her. Running after her on the beach to keep her from toddling straight into the water. Nearly losing her mind when Nina cut her hand on a shard of sea glass. Yelling at Astrid, *How hard is it to babysit your sister for a couple of hours?*

No, it's impossible—Rose would not drown her own child. She couldn't have. Did Aunt Maude tell her about the letters? Most likely not. Astrid needed to arrive to authenticate the letters first. Perhaps Maude desperately wanted to believe that her own sister did not drown Nina. *I want to believe the same thing,* Astrid thinks.

She stands next to the desk, shivering, and reaches for the third letter, then stops. *I'm not sure I can read it—what kind of hell is this?* Finally, she takes another deep breath and unfolds the letter:

> My Love,
> She is here with me. Sometimes, I speak to her. People give me peculiar looks. But I tell you, our daughter never left us. I told Dr. Garwood. You said she is a preeminent psychiatrist, the best one here. But she asks me annoying questions about my thoughts and sleep patterns. She checked off boxes and concluded that I'm clinically depressed and . . . She stopped short of calling me delusional. She suggested medication. She said she was worried about me. Can you imagine?
> I pretended to agree, and then I left.
> For supper, I made your favorite casserole with vegetables directly from Maude's garden. I cannot bring myself to tell her what I see. She would send me back to Dr. Garwood, but I'm not going.
> Our daughter was there with us, sitting in her own little chair, kicking her legs, licking chocolate frosting off her fingers, and then she was gone. I followed her

into the woods, and she seemed to know I was there. And I saw all the iridescent colors of the rainbow reflected in that pool. It was another sign from her. She wanted me to find her.

I took off my shoes and waded in. The bottom was slimy. The water rippled, greenish blue in the light. I looked up and saw her in the woods. Then she was gone again.

But I glimpsed her this morning in the distance when I walked to the sea. Then the neighbors came to gather seashells. They looked at me with suspicion. What do they think they know?

Your Rose Petal

Astrid wipes away tears, but they keep sliding down her cheeks. Numbness spreads through her, as if she has been standing in a freezer for hours. The letter falls from her hand and flutters to the desk. A piece of paper, so seemingly innocuous, but the words have just socked her in the gut. She can't catch her breath. *Nothing is what I thought it was, nothing at all.* Her whole life, everything she believed, lies shattered on the floor. *I thought my mother loved Nina best.* Did Rose love her youngest daughter, or did she overcompensate, treating Nina with care because, underneath, she hated her?

No, my mother did not hate Nina. She must've been delusional, despondent, mentally ill. Yes, that would explain Rose's behavior, her deranged words in the letters. She wasn't herself. Astrid pictures her mother on the trail that night, barefoot, holding her high-heeled shoes by thin straps. Screaming in grief. The next day, she swayed in the doorway, asked to see Nina. Rose didn't believe her daughter was gone. And then . . . Astrid's father must've made an appointment for Rose to see the psychiatrist, Dr. Garwood. Here in Heron Bay? Astrid never knew. The adults conducted secret lives behind closed doors.

Think about this, be logical, Astrid tells herself. She grabs a tissue from a Kleenex box and wipes her face. *My mother is not a killer.* But how well does Astrid even know Rose anymore? Were her feelings of guilt so strong that she lost touch with reality?

Astrid shivers, suddenly feeling very alone and frightened. Like a child again, a child without a mother. *My mother left me long before she lost her mind. She did love Nina the most, couldn't survive losing her.* Rose must've typed the last two letters when she was grieving so deeply, she noticed nothing else around her. She stood out in the garden, staring into the woods for hours. She sank into a fantasy world.

But why would she kill her own child? To spite her husband? Punish him for an affair? Or maybe she only imagined drowning Nina—and none of her confession is true. *I can't handle this on my own,* Astrid thinks, walking out into the hall. Her stomach hurts, her head is swimming. She picks up the landline, begins to dial Trent's number. She hears his voice: *There's something I need to tell you . . . engaged.* He didn't say the wedding would be coming up so soon. No, she can't call him, can't—she goes to the guest room, finds Conor's business card, dials his number instead. She can hardly speak, her voice breaking on the phone. "I found the letters," she tells him through her tears. "My mother confesses to drowning my little sister."

CHAPTER EIGHTEEN

Ten minutes later, a silver truck parks in the driveway. Conor gets out in jeans and a T-shirt. He must be off duty. When she lets him in, he has a bewildered look on his face. "You look like hell. What's going on? Where are these letters?"

She wipes her face again and leads him into the library. He reads the letters in silence while she stands by the window, looking out at the woods in which her mother stood so often after Nina's death. "I can't believe this," Astrid says.

"Okay," Conor says, letting out his breath. "Remember what I said before? Don't jump to the worst-case scenario? I say don't jump to conclusions. Here, sit." He pulls out the chair, and Astrid sits, staring at the folded letters on the desk.

"I can't believe it . . . my own mother."

"Let's be objective," Conor says, sitting on the side of the desk. "You have skills. Let's use them, okay? Come on. What would you do first?"

Astrid blinks, tries to gather her thoughts. "I would look at the paper and ink."

"Okay, let's do that."

She gets up and takes a deep breath. Conor watches as she examines the paper through her magnifier and takes measurements. "It's deckle-edge, eight and a half by twelve inches, bearing a faint watermark, made in Italy," she says.

"What does that even mean?" Conor stands too close, giving off that smell of mint soap.

"I have to do some research."

He nods, waiting patiently while she powers up her computer. Her internet research quickly informs her that the paper has been handmade for a few centuries, that it is easily available in the United States. "Dead end," she says. "Nothing special here. My mom loved this kind of paper."

"What about the ink?" he says.

"I need my equipment, like my VSC—"

"Speak in English, please."

"My video spectral comparator . . . It would help me figure out whether or not ink was added or removed from the signatures, or if there's other faded writing beneath the visible signatures. But everything's back at the lab . . ."

"Now we're talking, though. Can you tell if the same person signed all three letters?"

Her head is beginning to hurt, a faint throbbing at her temples. "No, I can't tell . . . The ink on all three letters appears the same, but I can't tell how each signature responds to filtered light. I would need to take the letters—"

"To the lab, okay." He runs his fingers through his hair. "What can you tell with what you have here?"

She looks at him. "Thank you for being here," she says. "I'm sure you have other places to be—"

"No, I don't. This is my day off."

"Yes, you do."

"Okay, I was going to play baseball, but this is way more important. Go on, talk to me."

"All right. The ink is smooth, not striated, which means the writer . . . did not use a ballpoint pen. But I can't tell you what kind of pen was used. Possibly a fountain pen. Looks like the same pen was used to sign all three letters, but I can't know that for sure."

"No, no, of course not."

She gestures toward the door. "Can I . . . get you a cup of coffee or tea? A glass of water?"

"You know what? I'll get two glasses of water. You sit tight, keep analyzing."

He disappears into the kitchen, and she finds the sounds of clanking cups and the running of water to be comforting. She looks down at her trembling hands. *Pull yourself together. Set aside your emotions,* she tells herself, but her thoughts stray back to the reflecting pool, to her sister's pale face, her lips turning blue. Her mother's words. *I drowned her.*

Conor returns with two glasses of water and pulls up another chair from the corner of the room. He dusts off the cushion and sits, a glass in his hands. "What about the chemical composition of the ink?"

"I can't tell you much," she says. "I could send the letters to an ink chemist—"

"Could the letters be copies? Photocopies, doctored?"

She uses the handheld microscope to examine the letters. "They're typewritten, but they're not copies," she says. "There's no pixelation, no dots."

"All right, what does that tell us?" he says.

"Just that they're real letters."

"They're not dated. Could they have been typed recently?"

"I don't think so . . . I think they were folded into envelopes, like someone was going to send them or *did* send them, but the envelopes are missing." She hovers over the microscope, examining the magnified folds of the letters. Then she looks up at Conor. "The paper was folded *after* the letters were typed. Just like I thought. The contours of the ink don't follow the folds, you see." She unfolds a letter and shows him the creases. "They were triple-folded and then folded right to left. There are no staple marks, no grease marks, no pinholes."

"So, the letters were typed and then folded."

"Yes," she says, her lips trembling. "My mother—I can't believe . . ."

He grabs her hand, his fingers warm and firm. "Keep it together. You're strong." She hears his voice from seventeen years ago, when he showed up to defend her on the beach. She squeezes his hand, looks into his eyes.

"Thank you," she says. "I never thanked you."

"For what?" He lets go of her hand.

For punching that bully who called me a killer. "For . . . keeping me focused."

"That's my job, to keep you on track. Consider the evidence."

"Right, the evidence." She grabs another tissue and wipes her nose, then flexes her fingers and takes a deep breath. "The paper could've been manufactured anytime in the last several years, but based on the content of the letters, it seems they were likely typed around the time of Nina's death."

"Whoa, wait." Conor holds up his hands. "How do you know this?"

"The coincidences are too great. The reflecting pool, the nightgown, Julian's name mentioned, the party next door. No doubt my mother typed these letters seventeen years ago, here in Heron Bay, probably here in the library, at Aunt Maude's desk, at her typewriter." She stops to catch her breath.

"But you need to be reasonably sure," Conor says. "Isn't that why your aunt called you here?"

"Yes, yes. You're right." Astrid opens the filing cabinet and pulls out the file full of postcards from her mother. She compares the writing to the signatures on the letters. The trouble is, Rose never signed her postcards "Rose Petal," although she did sometimes sign them "Rose."

"Well?" Conor says, hovering over Astrid's shoulder.

"The signatures seem to match her writing here and here." She points to a couple of unsigned postcards. "Her actual signature was just 'Rose.' Similar . . . but later, her signature is messier, bigger and loopier. She was drinking . . . she became an alcoholic. The signatures are similar, but the words 'Rose Petal' on the letters are written more deliberately."

"What does that mean?"

"It means the letters are carefully written," Astrid says. "One person's handwriting can vary considerably over time. And nobody else knew my mother's nickname. She reserved it for my dad." She draws a deep, shuddering breath.

Conor frowns. "What next?"

"You don't need to stay—"

"I want to," he says. "I want to see what you do."

"All right." She takes photographs of the signatures on the postcards, connects her computer to her aunt's laser printer and prints out enlarged images of the signatures. She tapes them to the wall, since her aunt does not have a bulletin board, and measures the height ratios (small to capital letters), the spacing, the pushes and pulls and pressure of the ink at different points in the curves of the letters. "She lifts her pen between the *o* and the *s* on the letters and on most of the postcards. It's pretty clear that my mother most likely typed the letters."

"You can't say for sure."

"We never say for sure. We have professional opinions, and we say 'most likely.' I don't have other examples of her signature exactly as written, 'Rose Petal,' but . . ."

"Could you get samples?" Conor asks.

"Maybe from my dad. But I'd be bringing him into this . . ."

"You might have to," Conor says.

"You know, on a few of the unsigned postcards, the general handwriting is remarkably similar to the signatures on the letters," she says. "That's another factor suggesting that she did author those letters." In

Astrid's mind, this is better proof that her mother typed and signed the letters, but such a comparison would not hold up in court.

Not that she will ever go to court with these findings. Would she implicate her own mother? Was Aunt Maude about to implicate her own sister? It doesn't make sense. Why would Aunt Maude try so hard to keep the letters a secret, and why did she seem nervous, if her own sister authored these letters? A sister who never wants to return, who spends her life flitting around Europe? Astrid keeps these thoughts to herself.

She and Conor are both looking at the typewriter. He nods slightly and brings the typewriter off the shelf. He sets it next to the letters on the desk and stands back.

Ideally, Astrid would use the same paper to retype the letters, but her aunt's résumé paper, on a shelf beneath the printer, will have to do. She retypes all three letters, trying to set the margins and spacing as they are in the original letters.

"The typeface is the same, standard Pica, ten characters per inch," she says. "The typebars on the *a* and the *f* subtly hit the paper twice, leaving a faint echo, and the bottom loop on the *g* is flattened. The *i* is out of alignment, sitting below the line formed along the bottom of most of the other letters."

"The similarities are astounding," Conor says.

"Except for a couple of differences," she says, hardly able to breathe. "The *h* key is slightly broken in the original letters, the serif missing on the right tail of the letter, see? But *h* prints normally on this typewriter."

"So, this isn't the typewriter," Conor says.

"Wait, hang on." Astrid checks through the filing cabinets. Her aunt kept meticulous records, retaining nearly all her receipts. There it is, a manila file folder marked TYPEWRITER MAINTENANCE AND REPAIR. The receipts come from Heron Bay Office Machines downtown. Periodic repairs and cleaning were performed on this machine every year or so over the past fifteen years. She checks to make sure

Dreaming of Water

the serial number noted on the repair slip is the same as the unique serial number imprinted on the inside of the typewriter's ribbon cover.

"About ten years ago, the *h* type slug was replaced," she says, waving the receipt. "It's the top part of the typebar that puts print on paper." She uses the flashlight on her phone to examine the typebars in the type-basket. Conor peers over her shoulder again, and she can smell the toothpaste on his breath. Did he brush his teeth before coming over here? Or chew gum? Was he worried she might smell his breath?

"The *h* slug appears to have been recently soldered onto the typebar," he says. "The color of the seams is a little darker than it is on the other keys."

"You're correct," she says, her breathing shallow again. "I don't want this to be true—"

"It's looking a lot more like your mom typed these letters," he says, stepping away from her.

She paces the room, alternating between rage and disbelief, her hands in fists. She focuses on her breathing.

"You okay?" he says.

She shakes her head. "No, no, I'm not okay." She is wearing a path into the threadbare carpet. "My mother . . . she let me live with this guilt . . . all the while . . ."

"Unless your mother imagined everything down to the last detail," Conor says.

"Yes, yes, I keep looping back to that possibility . . ."

They both look at the signatures taped to the wall above the printer—the only free space—and her microscope attached to her computer, her notes and the letters on the desk. The typewriter, the retyped letters. "Have I been at this all day?"

"Almost," Conor says.

"I need to try calling my mother." But when she calls from the landline, she's dumped into voice mail. "I knew it was too good to be true," she mutters to herself. "Mom, it's Astrid. Give me a call. This is important." Then she hangs up.

Conor's standing in the doorway to the library, leaning against the doorjamb. "You need to get away from here for a while. Let's go for a bite. I know a good place. I promise to bring you back before you turn into a pumpkin."

CHAPTER NINETEEN

In the guest room, Astrid realizes she didn't bring any fancy dinner clothes, at least nothing suitable for a date. Only this is not a date—it's a temporary escape from the shock of what she has just discovered. While Conor waits in the foyer, she quickly changes into a black low-neck blouse and a floral cardigan, then pulls on a pair of gray slacks and black flats. She brushes her hair, applies a touch of lipstick and eyeliner, puts on a pair of gold hoop earrings. Now she's presentable.

"You look nice," Conor says when she joins him in the hall. He holds the front door open for her.

She steps outside. "You don't need to compliment me. I had to change . . . I looked like I just tumbled out of bed."

"I'm sure that wouldn't be so bad," he says, leading her to his truck.

She feels a strange flutter in her chest, a quick image coming to her of waking next to Conor. *Don't go there—now is not the time. Maybe never.*

Again, he opens the car door for her, and she remembers he was always like this, chivalrous but not patronizing. He offered his help, stood up for her. She feels a little awkward, but it's nice to sit back in the passenger seat and relax. The truck smells faintly of aftershave, and he's casual about leaving his life lying around—a pair of sunglasses and a battered box of tissues on the console. "How about Thai food?" he says.

"Perfect," she says, although in truth, she can't imagine eating much of anything. After reading the letters, she has lost her appetite. He drives through town, down along Oceanfront Street, and he doesn't try to make conversation. The restaurant, Green Curry, is on the second floor of an old building on the waterfront side, at the top of a narrow staircase. The small dining room, painted in green and gold, seats maybe twenty people. The place feels familiar, from its tall windows to the narrow outdoor deck. Only a few other patrons are here this early—it's almost five o'clock. The waiter shows them to an outdoor table.

"Are you cold?" Conor says, pulling out her chair.

"No, it's good, private," she says, wrapping her cardigan around her as she sits. Out on the water, cormorants ride the waves, and in the distance, the ferry glides in from the islands.

The waiter brings the menus, and she hides behind hers and tries to focus on the starters—garlic green beans, spring rolls, tofu edamame.

Conor's phone buzzes in his pocket, but he doesn't answer. The waiter comes to light a flame in a glass candleholder on the table. The angle of light brings out the contours of Conor's face—he has grown into a man of character. *But I'm not on a date,* she reminds herself, focusing instead on the ferryboat.

"What are you going to tell your mom?" he asks, sipping his water.

She can feel him looking at her, but she focuses on the menu. *Tom Kha—coconut soup, house green salad, pad thai.* "She needs to tell me the truth. If she ever calls me back."

"How likely is that?"

"To be honest, I feel like I don't know my mother anymore. Maybe I never did." She watches a family of four, parents and two little boys, situating themselves at a table just inside the window. A little boy presses his tongue to the glass, and Astrid smiles. His mother pulls him away, scolding him.

"I never knew my mother, either," Conor says. "After the divorce, she started wearing makeup and dressing up and going on dates. And she went back to school to become a paleontologist. It was like she slept through her marriage to my dad, and when she'd finally had enough, she woke up."

"Enough of what?" Astrid says, sipping her ice water.

"He didn't sleep around. But he was married to his work. He was a distant kind of guy. Not too emotional."

"And she got sick of that."

"I'm guessing. She never told me, just said, 'Your father and I are separating, but we both still love you.'"

"My dad told me something similar," she says.

The waiter returns, and Astrid orders the pad thai.

"Make that two," Conor says. "And a Thai iced tea. For you?"

"Water is fine," she says. "Thanks."

The waiter takes their menus, and Conor leans across the table and lowers his voice, as another couple has taken the table right behind him. "Do you remember this place? It used to be called the Bay Diner. We came here for the french fries."

Astrid looks around and gasps. "I thought it was familiar!"

"The owner died. New owners opened the Thai place."

"Wow, first time I've remembered the Bay Diner. Those were big fat french fries!"

"I brought dates here in high school," Conor says.

"It's a romantic place," she replies, avoiding his gaze. "Do you still bring women here?"

"Not in a while," he says. "I can't believe you're not seeing anyone."

"They're getting married, Trent and Leona."

"Oh hell, I'm sorry."

"Yeah, well, I guess it was coming. I should start, you know . . . getting out there again."

"We can count this as Date Number One, if you like," he says.

She's about to reply, but the waiter returns with a glass of Thai iced tea. "Anything else to drink?" he asks. "Wine, beer?"

"I'll stick with water," she says, raising her glass and smiling at the waiter. He nods and walks off. She looks at Conor. "I need my wits about me when my mother calls to confess to murder."

"I'm really sorry about this," he says. "I was hoping to distract you."

She unfolds the cloth napkin on her lap. "Would you prosecute her, if you thought she was guilty?"

He sips his Thai iced tea. "Not on the basis of a letter."

"Right, right . . . that's a relief. So, you think she could've made up everything?"

"She'd just lost a child. That is huge. Maybe she felt guilty about *not* being there for Nina."

"I can't wrap my own mind around any of this. She typed 'I drowned her.'"

The couple at the next table looks over at them, then back at each other.

Conor lowers his voice. "Maybe she believes she did. It doesn't mean she actually did."

Astrid twirls her fork between finger and thumb. "What I don't get is . . . why would someone write me a note, telling me to get out of town—and stand at the edge of the garden trying to scare me? If this is all about my mother confessing to drowning my sister? She's in Italy!"

Conor puts his own napkin in his lap. "Okay, maybe your mom typed those letters to someone else, not to your dad. Maybe some other man is involved."

The wind picks up, and Astrid's hair blows into her eyes. Goose bumps rise on her skin. The waiter arrives with two plates of pad thai, then nods and moves off.

She leans across the table. "You think she was having an affair? I have to look at those letters again, but it's pretty clear to me that she's talking to my dad, her husband. I mean, breaking in to find 'evidence of you,' betrayal, the whole thing."

"You're right. It does seem that way." Conor glances at the next table, then keeps his voice low. "Livie gossips. We already know that . . .

Maude probably told someone about the letters, maybe not in so many words, but . . . Many people in this town wanted to sweep the whole thing under the rug. And now you're here . . ." He digs into the pad thai.

Astrid stares at her plate of food, her stomach queasy. "Okay, so someone wants me to leave. But who knocked out my aunt? Why would anyone here care about my mother typing a letter to my father?"

"My guess is as good as yours." Conor shovels food into his mouth, completely unselfconscious.

Astrid cuts the noodles, daintily wraps them around her fork. Takes a bite. *I'm hungry,* she realizes. *How long has it been since I've eaten?* Maybe not since breakfast.

"My dad called my mother Rose Petal. It was a specific nickname he gave her. She took to signing her letters and cards that way, but only to him."

"And how did the letters arrive in Maude's possession?"

"Maybe she recently found them in the house when she was tidying her library. My mother must've left them in a book. Or somewhere hidden."

"But why did Maude find them now and not, say, two years ago? Or three years ago?"

"My aunt has a lot of books in her collection, in case you didn't notice. Like thousands. It could've been in there . . . and she just pulled out the book a couple of weeks ago."

Conor nods, half his plate of food now gone. He waves his fork around. "Why would your mother do something so terrible, drowning your sister, and then stay here in town? Why not leave?"

Astrid chews her pad thai—it's bursting with flavors of lemongrass and peanut sauce. "I think . . . my mother didn't realize what she'd done until afterward. Like she was in a fugue state, confused. She mentions breaking into the neighbor's house—the Michaels house? And she accuses my father of an affair. With Beatrice? But the tone of her letters is like a dream."

Conor points the fork at her. "The question is why, Astrid. Motive. Why would your mother drown her own child?"

"She says my dad was going to leave her. He left that night. Maybe he was going to leave us all for good." *He left a few times after that,* she thinks. *But my mother finally cut the ties.*

"She wanted to punish your dad by killing her own child?"

"No, no . . . but she was distraught. She went looking for my dad. She says so in the letter. She thought Nina was still running in the woods even after she was already in the water. She may not even remember the truth. She mentions Dr. Garwood, a psychiatrist?"

"Yeah, I know of her," Conor says, nodding. "One of my deputies went to see her, after he witnessed a shooting a few years ago. She might be retired now, though."

"I have to talk to her."

"She won't be able to share what she knows about your mother. She'll be constrained by privacy laws."

"But she might be able to shed some light on the letters, about whether they're real or . . . imaginings."

"Give your mother some time to call you back." Conor sips the last of his iced tea.

On impulse, Astrid reaches out to grasp his hand, and he squeezes back, smiling at her. "Thank you for being here," she says. "It's nice to come out here and look at the water. To have someone to talk to about all this."

"Hey, the pleasure is all mine," he says, holding her hand a moment longer before letting go.

Another couple comes out onto the deck, clad in sweaters, and passes their table, the woman's belly bulging. *She's about to pop,* Astrid thinks. As the couple takes their seats, the woman adjusts her distance from the table, trying to make herself comfortable. And as the woman pushes back her long black hair and opens the menu, Astrid sees the profile picture of Trent and Leona in her mind, and the Facebook announcement of the wedding date. Leona looked radiant, *glowing.*

And in the comments section, she'd typed, *We couldn't wait any longer.* Astrid nearly chokes on her noodles.

"Dessert?" Conor asks from a distance, as if he's talking to her from the other side of the universe. "They have fried bananas and ice cream."

"Um, no, I'm fine," Astrid says. She's no longer hungry. She might throw up. "I'm sorry to be such a party pooper, but if you don't mind, I'd like to go home."

"Yeah, sure, no problem." Conor summons the waiter and insists on paying the check. On the drive home, he stares straight ahead, his face unreadable.

"It's not you," Astrid says. "It was the couple at the table beside us . . . the woman made me realize that Leona is pregnant. My ex-husband's new fiancée."

"Wow, lightning speed," Conor says. "You're still sweet on him, huh?"

"What, no—I mean, I was the one who moved out."

"Yeah, but love doesn't just disappear."

"No, I suppose not." Does she still love Trent? She never posed the question to herself. "It's not that I still love him. He wanted kids. More than anything."

"Oh, I get it." Conor nods knowingly, tapping his fingers on the steering wheel. "He wanted kids, and you didn't?"

"Sort of—you could put it that way."

"You mean you couldn't have kids? Sorry, I don't mean to pry."

"No, I can, as far as I know . . . but we didn't."

"Okay, none of my business."

Back at Aunt Maude's house, he walks her to the door. "Thank you for dinner," she says. She gestures back behind her. "I should . . . try my mother again. And try to get in touch with Dr. Garwood."

Conor nods, backing down the steps. "Call me if you need me," he says in a clipped voice, then jogs back to his car. She wants to go after him, explain to him that she's damaged goods, but instead, she goes back into the house and shuts the door. In the guest room, she opens the carved wooden box again. Her wedding band glints in the light. She can't bring herself to sell it or give it away. Trent gazed into her eyes so adoringly when he slipped the ring onto her finger, promising to love and cherish her always. *What a load of horseshit,* she thinks now, blazing with anger.

Right after the wedding ceremony, he became someone different. Someone obsessed. It began on their wedding night. *Let's make a baby,* he announced. *All I want is a family.* He chose the room in the house that would become a nursery. He wanted at least one boy and one girl. He talked about all the places they would go as a family, all the fun they would have.

And she understood. She knew why he wanted children, although she could not find the same burning need in her own heart. He came from a big, happy family of three sisters and two brothers and loving parents who nurtured their children, who never put themselves first, who seemed to overflow with love. Many relatives visited for holidays, converging from different cities in California. Nobody seemed to have moved far away. Every time she and Trent visited his parents in San Rafael, his mom and dad hugged and kissed and asked each other if the other one needed any help. They told stories about their time together in the Peace Corps in Africa. His father ran a charity for educating women in the Gambia; his mother was a social worker. Astrid basked in the warmth of their normalcy. But she never truly belonged with them.

After what had happened to Nina, she didn't belong anywhere, and she didn't trust herself to care for a child. *After all,* Astrid thought, *I would be a terrible mother.* But she acquiesced. She feared disappointing Trent, although she had no intention of trying to raise a family. Month after month for nearly three years, she pretended to know when she was ovulating. She pretended to have doctor's appointments that came to nothing. Trent began to suggest fertility treatments, and she stalled. She hated the disappointment in his eyes when she said she had her period again. She wondered if he loved her anymore or the idea of her as a mother.

"Would you stay with me if we could never have children?" she asked.

"We still have many options," he said.

"What if I don't want kids at all?" she had burst out one night, trembling with anxiety. She was so afraid of losing him, she hadn't been able to say it before that moment.

He looked at her blankly, as if her words had not penetrated. He didn't know about her dreams of pulling Nina out of the water, of the ocean rising around her. She found herself trapped in nightmares in which she ran through the night, following the urgent cries of an infant. A baby could drown in a sink, in a bathtub, in a puddle. Astrid could not trust herself to protect a child. Oh, she thought of telling Trent. She wanted to . . . But now it doesn't matter. He has his pregnant fiancée, everything he always wanted.

She takes out the tickets and ring box and other mementos and sets them aside. On the bottom of the carved wooden box lies the secret she kept. Trent never had any idea—at least, not until he rummaged in her drawers, looking for his favorite socks that might've been mixed in with hers in the laundry. If he hadn't done that, maybe he never would've known. But he found them in her underwear drawer—the birth control pills she had been taking throughout the entire marriage.

CHAPTER TWENTY

Monday morning, Rose laughs on the phone, a curiously lighthearted sound that echoes over the landline in Aunt Maude's hallway. "I didn't sit around typing letters and not sending them. I know I went through a phase of writing to your dad, though. It was a terrible time for all of us."

For all of us. This is the first time Astrid's mother has acknowledged that anyone else could have suffered from the loss of Nina.

"I'm sorry to bring it all up again, but . . ." *You thought you killed Nina,* Astrid doesn't say. *And Aunt Maude might've believed you.*

"There's nothing to bring up," Rose exclaims. "Your father had all the letters . . . I'd be surprised if he hung on to them, though. He liked to get rid of things." She says that last part with bitterness, even now.

"Ciao, bella!" a man calls out in the background, and he rattles on in Italian.

"Hold on, would you, Astrid? Luigi!" Rose covers the phone and speaks in Italian with an accent and tone that Astrid does not recognize— louder than normal, a little abrasive but also bouncing with joy. *My mother truly has a new life,* she thinks, wondering if it's painful for Rose to talk to her at all.

"Sorry," her mother says, coming back on the line. "We've got a big family dinner tonight. I'll need to go soon."

Family dinner? Of course, Rose has a new family now, one in which tragedy didn't happen. Children didn't die. Luigi's family. "These letters are . . . unusual," Astrid says. "They have to do with what happened to Nina. And you and Dad."

"I didn't leave any letters at Maude's house. I would know if I did. Where did you say you found them? Inside a book? How strange."

"To be honest, these letters are disturbing. You mention seeing Nina . . . afterward."

"After what? I'm worried about you. I should've insisted you see another therapist, but your father didn't want to force you."

You're not worried about me at all, Astrid thinks. "I'm okay, Mom."

"You're not married anymore, though, are you?"

Neither are you, Astrid wants to say, but she is not going to engage in this conversation. "I'm just trying to get to the bottom of this—"

"It's in the past. Contrary to popular opinion, I do remember everything about that time. But I've chosen to move forward."

Chosen. No, you didn't choose to move forward, Astrid thinks. *You ran away. But so did I. I ran and never came back.* "This is what you typed . . . 'I slipped inside and looked for evidence of you.' I'm assuming you mean Dad. You mention his betrayal. You talk about not planning to give birth . . . You signed the letters 'Rose Petal.' You mentioned speaking to Nina . . . that she never left. That Nina came back and ate chocolate frosting . . . and you waded into the reflecting pool . . . and—"

"Stop," her mother says, an edge to her tone. "I'm not sure what you're playing at, but I don't want to hear any more."

"Did you break into the Michaels house? Did you suspect Dad of having an affair with Beatrice?"

"Honey—you need to talk to someone. I always thought there was something off about you, after what happened."

"About *me*?" *Off.* Rose is calling her own child *off.*

"You always had a problem with Nina, and that's okay. You were entitled. But this . . . I'm not sure what sort of story you made up or why—"

"I didn't make this up!"

"I'm terribly concerned about Maude, too. That should be the focus here."

"Then why aren't you here? She's your sister!"

Rose falls silent, the way she always does when Astrid becomes upset. Rose goes quiet and still, as if she is the calm one and Astrid is overreacting. *My frustration is normal,* Astrid reminds herself.

"I spoke with her doctor today," Rose says.

"You called the *hospital?*" Astrid bites her lip, forces herself to calm down.

"She's my *sister.* She's doing well. Her vital signs are good. She's not going to die."

I knew that, but she is still in the hospital, and if you love her . . . But Astrid understands now that, for her mother, decisions are not based on love, on being there for anyone but herself—and possibly for Luigi and his family. But if she couldn't bear her own pain or to be present for her daughter and sister, how is she truly there for Luigi?

Astrid feels suddenly sorry for him. She doubts her mother is truly capable of loving him selflessly. She didn't leave because she was strong and focused on the future, on *moving forward.* She left because she was too fragile to stay. And maybe her fragility made her believe she had killed her own child.

I'm stronger than I thought, Astrid thinks. *Stronger because I am here, facing all this without running away. Not this time.* "Mom, in the letter you say you drowned Nina—and—"

"I'm sorry, Astrid. I can't listen to another word of this. Goodbye." There's a click on the line, then the buzz of a distant dial tone.

Astrid hangs up. This is the second time her mother has hung up on her in a matter of days. She feels as if she has been punched in the stomach, but the sensation quickly passes. Her mother long ago stopped wielding the power to make her feel pummeled for very long. What did she expect? That her mother would confess?

She takes her cell phone out into the garden, focuses her breathing. Of course her mother denied typing those letters. Denied an affair.

Denied all her transgressions and dark thoughts. What else could she do to maintain the life she now leads?

Astrid walks down the driveway until she catches a faint signal on her cell phone. She looks up at the house and sees the ghost of her mother hunched over the typewriter, composing a series of confessional letters, imagining that she saw Nina in the woods, and then . . . her guilt and her downward spiral. And perhaps a patchy loss of memory.

Astrid calls her father on FaceTime again and reads the letters aloud.

He sits back, blinking as if someone has slapped him. Tears slip down his cheeks. "I didn't know any of this."

"Did you know about Dr. Garwood?"

"Rose was sometimes depressed even before Nina died. Maude recommended Dr. Garwood, but I didn't know your mother actually went. I had no idea she felt so guilty. Maybe that was why she kept seeing the ghost of Nina."

"We knew she was grieving. I didn't really understand. I was too young. She stopped talking to me. It was like I didn't exist. She still says she didn't type these letters."

"Were they there all this time?"

"She must've typed them to you and then hidden them instead of sending them. They were folded into the back of a book."

Her father breaks into silent sobs, his shoulders shaking. "If I'd known, maybe I could have helped her."

"Do you still have any of the other letters Mom typed to you back then?"

"Uh, no, Astrid. I didn't keep them. None at all."

Her mother's words echo in her mind. *He liked to get rid of things.* "I'm not even going to ask you about an affair, about whom Mom saw you with . . ."

"She must've been hallucinating."

"That night, you went back to the city. Did you go to meet your lover?"

"Your mother was the one with a possible lover! But she turned it on me, always suspicious. She was drinking too much at the party. We fought, and . . ."

"Were you going to leave her for the other woman? Who was it, Beatrice?"

"Beatrice Michaels? Oh, God no."

"Where else would she break in to 'find evidence' of you? No other neighbors live close by. Maude's right on the edge of the water."

"That must've all been in your mother's mind. I don't know about any break-in. But at the party, she begged me not to leave her. She said she loved me. She wanted to erase our problems and start again."

"And she erased Nina."

"Nina drowned by accident. It's not complicated. I was angry, your mom and I fought. I went back to the city. She didn't believe that I would really leave her . . . but I left." There is something in her father's eyes, as if a part of him has broken away. "Then I got the call from the sheriff. Your mother was too distraught to talk. I drove back. I got there early the next morning. You were asleep." He holds up his hands in defeat.

"No, there's more. I can feel it, Dad. What are you not telling me?"

He looks away and wipes his eyes. "Nothing else."

"Don't hang up on me this time. I don't believe you! Dad, come on!"

He heaves a deep sigh and peers into his iPhone, squinting, as if he's looking at Astrid across a galaxy. "I thought you might have figured this out on your own . . . I was convinced that Nina was not my daughter."

CHAPTER TWENTY-ONE

Astrid nearly drops the phone. It never crossed her mind that Nina might have been her half sister, the product of an affair. Or maybe the idea was simmering in her subconscious mind. "What exactly made you think Nina wasn't yours?"

"The timing, for one thing," her father says. "When your mother got pregnant, we hadn't been sleeping together too often. I mean, we did, but . . . we were in a rough patch."

Astrid winces. "Spare me the details. What else? Nina looked like you, Dad."

He runs his fingers through his hair. "She had a habit of taking off, running toward the water. I was scared of water as a kid. You were a careful child, but Nina had a reckless streak. She liked to be upside down, wanted me to throw her in the air. She was fixated on shiny objects."

"But she could've inherited all those traits from relatives. Or Mom!"

"She could roll her tongue. I could never do that. And her nose. It was like a little button. Neither of her parents has a button nose."

"That's it? Her nose, her habits?"

"Her taste in food," Astrid's father goes on. "Neither your mother nor I—nor you—ever had much of a sweet tooth. Sugar was like a magnet for Nina. She ate sugar cubes like she was inhaling oxygen."

"Wow, Dad, just wow." Astrid looks up at the clouds skittering across the sky, an elegant blue heron soaring overhead, its massive wings outstretched. She tries to remember every habit of Nina's in light of different parentage. She grips her phone so tightly, she's afraid it might break. "What did Mom say when you confronted her?"

"She insisted Nina was my daughter. She denied having an affair. Open and shut."

"And did you believe her?"

"Did I have a choice? Your mother despised me for asking the question. She insisted Nina was exactly like me."

"I thought the same thing, Dad. Nothing about Nina ever gave me pause."

"But you weren't looking for anomalies. You were a kid."

"You never discussed it with Mom after that?"

"Again, there was no point." True to form, her father glances at his watch, sets his jaw. He has already taken too much time away from work to indulge her strange imaginings.

When she hangs up, she thinks that her parents, although divorced and living opposite kinds of lives, are still similar to one another. Caught up in their own insular worlds, unable—or unwilling—to look back in time to understand the past and how it created the present.

In the living room, she scans the photographs on the mantel. Nina shared Bjorn's blue eyes, his blond hair, his lithe physique. The soft oval shape of her face came from Rose. If someone else fathered Nina, his features and personality traits hid somewhere out of sight. Did someone lead her along a trail to the reflecting pool and drown her that night? If so, why? And what is the connection to Rose's possible affair, or Bjorn's? The questions hover in the air, the answers elusive.

Downstairs, Astrid reads the letters again in the library, then looks through Aunt Maude's address book in her desk. She does not find contact information for Dr. Garwood, so she calls information for the number and leaves a short message, asking the doctor to call back regarding letters connected to a drowning.

Aunt Maude does have the telephone number for Verne and Beatrice Michaels. When Astrid calls the number, a mellifluous woman's voice answers right away. "Astrid, I've been meaning to come by with a quiche," Beatrice says softly. "We heard what happened to Maude. You must be lonely rattling around in that house all by yourself."

"I'd like to talk to you about something I found," Astrid says. "I could come up there or . . . you could come over."

A moment of silence follows, then: "Oh, what did you find?"

"I'd rather tell you in person."

"Of course, where are my manners? We'll be enjoying breakfast out on the patio tomorrow morning. You must join us. Around nine?"

"I'm not sure—"

"Nonsense, I won't take no for an answer. I look forward to seeing you. Thomas will be delighted to meet you, and Verne would love to see you again as well."

Astrid hangs up, wondering if any member of the Michaels family would actually "love" to see her, or any member of her family, again. But somehow, Beatrice made her believe it to be true.

◆ ◆ ◆

Tuesday morning dawns crisp and sunny. Astrid dresses in casual walking clothes and takes the beach route to the Michaels mansion. On the way, her cell phone gets a signal, and a voice mail pops up from Conor. "You okay? I've been thinking about you. Um, the letters. They're a shock. Let me know if you want any help. Investigating and whatnot. And it sucks about your ex. But . . . if the guy really gave a shit about you, he wouldn't have cared about the whole kid thing. He would've cared about being with you."

A jet roars overhead, perhaps headed to the private runway on the island, and in the distance, a ferry foghorn blares. She listens to the message twice more. *He would've cared about being with you.* His words warm her heart, but Conor doesn't know about the birth control pills, doesn't know that she lied, that she pretended to want children. That she felt defective in some way, still does. Like only half a person.

She stops at the bottom of the stone staircase cut into the hillside, at least three hundred steps rising from the sand to the Michaelses' stone patio. She and Julian sat on these steps to talk and flirt, but now the stones are crumbling, weeds poking through the cracks. In a hundred years, the shoreline will have eroded, and these steps will be gone.

The climb goes on forever, and at the top, she stops to catch her breath. She has walked through an invisible portal into the world of the rich. Perhaps Verne and Beatrice retreated to Heron Bay to escape the visibility of their other lives. Here, they could hide out far from the upper-class milieu in Seattle, far from fundraisers for the poor or some cause or another to make them feel less guilty about their privilege and wealth.

Or maybe they just welcomed the relief of relaxing on a wooded bluff overlooking the sea, in their spacious rooms. As Astrid remembers, the living room opens onto this patio with its surrounding stone wall, which is low enough to afford visitors a sweeping view of the ocean. The interior of the house reminded her of a museum full of breakable objects: handblown original Chihuly glass, crystal goblets, ceramic sculptures. The living room could've doubled as an antiquarian library with a full wet bar near the sliding glass doors to the terrace.

Beatrice Michaels strides across the patio. She hasn't changed much, except for the slight effects of time and age weathering her around the edges. She's slightly stiffer in her movements, her blonde hair threaded with silver. But she is just as beautiful as ever in a white linen shirt, robin's egg–blue linen pants, and white sandals. The gold rings on her fingers glint in the slanted morning sunlight, and everything is radiant—her oversize, fashionable sunglasses, her earrings, her skin. "I was worried you wouldn't come!" She gives Astrid a cologne-scented hug.

"How could I miss the opportunity of a lifetime?" Astrid smiles, feeling suddenly awkward.

"My, you've grown up," Verne Michaels says in a booming voice. She forgot how his voice traveled as if broadcast through a bullhorn. He emerges from the house and marches over to shake her hand fervently. She'd forgotten how tall he was. He bested even her father in height—and everyone else at the party. But with age, he has become a little stooped, and his gray eyes have faded. His hair has bleached itself to pure white, no trace of whatever color it was before—perhaps brown, she thinks, but she can't remember. His face is still full of warmth and kindness. No wonder he was so successful in business and politics. He is handsome in a personable way, a man with whom you play golf, watch a baseball game, share stories over glasses of whiskey at the bar.

"We're hopeful for your aunt's full recovery," he says, pulling out a chair for her. He sits in his own chair.

"Thank you," she says. On the table is a feast, orange juice in a pitcher, a plate of steaming scones, another plate of boiled eggs and toast.

"Juice?" Beatrice says, lifting the pitcher.

"Thanks, yes," Astrid says awkwardly. Beatrice expertly pours a glass, the perfect host.

"The eggs are from a friend's happy hens here in town," Beatrice says.

"I'll stick with a scone," Astrid says, smiling.

"Would you see what's keeping Thomas?" Beatrice says to Verne. Her delicate brows draw together. She glances back toward the second floor of their vast mansion, hidden away from prying eyes.

Verne gets up abruptly, and Beatrice smiles at Astrid. "Thomas is our grandson. Julian's son. He's starting the eleventh grade next week."

"Time flies," Astrid says. "Is he also in love with literature?"

"He's more of a scientist," Beatrice says in a clipped voice, searching Astrid's face. "He's much more practical than his father." Does she know how much time Astrid spent with Julian, discussing *impractical* subjects like the classics?

Verne is striding back into the house.

As Astrid sips the orange juice, she finds her hand unsteady. It's strange to be back here after all these years, on the patio where she stared longingly at Julian, the patio from which they escaped to chat away from grown-ups.

"What is it that you've found?" Beatrice says, leaning toward Astrid.

"Letters that my mother typed to my father but never sent—after Nina's death."

Beatrice's arched brows rise. "I see."

"The letters are a bit . . . alarming. The things she says in them, about Nina." She doesn't say that her mother has denied typing the letters, that she hung up on her own daughter. That she seems to have confessed to murder.

Beatrice puts her fork down on her plate and dabs at her lips. "How can I help you with this?"

"Did you visit my mother again at Aunt Maude's after my dad and I left for Seattle? I'm wondering how she was . . . if she seemed okay."

"You're a woman of many questions," Beatrice says, keeping her composure. But when she puts the napkin back in her lap, it slips off and floats to the patio. She reaches down to pick it up. "And many answers are called for, no doubt. Have you spoken with your mother? It's what I would do. Speak with Rose."

Astrid cuts her scone with a knife. "I did a little, but it was a bad connection—she's traveling right now." Her lie sounds silly even to her. Her cheeks heat up.

"Maude often worried about Rose. About her state of mind."

"Back then, or now?"

"Well, both then *and* now." Beatrice smooths the napkin in her lap. "I did try to be there for your mother. I saw her . . . outside sometimes." She looks off toward the sea.

"Even before we left, she had started typing on Aunt Maude's typewriter."

"Yes, the typewriter Verne gave to Maude. He has many of them . . . well, he *used* to have many, but he's sold most of them."

"Sometimes my mother went outside and wandered. Did you see her?"

"Yes, yes . . . She seemed to be looking for someone or talking to someone," Beatrice says, her brows furrowing. "But I never saw anyone with her."

A chill creeps into Astrid's bones. "Do you know if she saw a psychiatrist?"

"If she did, she kept such a thing private."

"Of course," Astrid says.

"Grief is a difficult thing, you see." Beatrice's eyebrows draw together. Then she looks toward the house, her face brightening like the sun emerging from behind a cloud. "There he is now. Thomas, come and meet Astrid! She's Maude's niece."

Verne strides out and sits in his chair again. A young man follows, tall and lanky, his strawberryblond hair a mess, and yet he looks like the height of fashion, as if he has stepped out of the pages of a magazine. "I was figuring out a calculus equation, Nana," he says, kissing the top of her head. "I'm getting a head start on my classes."

She looks up at him, beaming. "I knew you were up to something good. My grandson enjoys math and biology."

"And physics," he says.

She squeezes his arm. "Sit and eat. You never eat enough."

"I eat all the time, Nana." But he sits and piles up his plate.

Astrid cannot stop staring. Thomas is a young Julian with minor differences. His nose is softer, his features, too. He has higher cheekbones, his eyes a more piercing blue. He must take after his mother in some ways.

He smiles at Astrid, that same disarming smile that Julian once had. "Hello, Astrid. I've heard a lot about you." He reaches across the table to take her hand.

"You have! I can't imagine what!" she says.

He holds the ends of her fingers with only his finger and thumb and bows forward slightly, the way a man might have done a hundred years ago. Then he lets go and slathers jam on his toast. "I play duets with Mrs. Dasgupta sometimes," he says, lifting an egg to his lips as if about to shove the whole thing into his mouth. But one warning look from his grandmother, and he takes a bite off the top, restraining himself. "I hear you play piano as well. Your aunt told me about you—you're in some of the photos in the house."

"Not often lately," Astrid says. "I'd like to get back to it."

"When she's better, we'll all play together," he says.

"He's wonderful," Beatrice says, patting his arm.

"Oh, I wouldn't go that far," Verne says gruffly. "In his grandmother's eyes, he can do no wrong."

Beatrice huffs at Verne. "Sometimes I play piano with him as well. Thomas is very good. He spends a lot of time with us."

"I'd love to hear a performance," Astrid says.

Verne refills her glass of orange juice. "Beatrice says you've got some questions to ask us?"

Astrid sits back and takes a deep breath. "Somebody is trying to scare me away from here, I think. Drive me out of town."

"Well, that's terrible." Verne clears his throat, forks up a slice of egg into his mouth. "What has been going on?"

Beatrice looks at Astrid and raises her eyebrows.

"I saw a man standing in silhouette at the edge of the yard, and someone wrote me this note." She slides the note across the table. *And I'm trying to figure out the connection to the letters,* she doesn't say.

They all read the note. Verne frowns and shakes his head. "What's gotten into this town? Did you report this?"

"Yes, of course. To the sheriff."

"And what are the police going to do?" Beatrice asks.

"Have you noticed anything strange lately?" Astrid asks. "Anyone walking through the woods?"

They all look at each other. "We have a security system," Verne says. "Nothing has registered on it. We have cameras. We would've seen someone."

"How far can your cameras see?" Astrid asks.

"Just to the edge of the woods here," Verne says.

"So, you wouldn't necessarily know if someone walked onto my aunt's property."

Beatrice makes a slight *tsk* sound. "I suggested to Maude that she install a security system. But she is trusting of people."

"Maybe too trusting." Astrid dabs at her face with a napkin. "May I . . . use the restroom? Too much coffee this morning."

"You remember where it is," Beatrice says. "Down the hall past the living room."

Astrid gets up and hurries inside, glad to be away from the palpable tension at breakfast. An undercurrent of unspoken words runs beneath that table. The living room is as she remembers it, only bigger—antiquarian books along one wall, a wet bar along the other, sculptures and chandeliers. And along the entire wall spanning the hallway, a long glass case displays priceless antiques, from swords and armor to ancient pottery and old guns. *It's like the Wild West,* she thinks, stopping to admire a bulky, black desktop typewriter from the late 1800s. Those old machines weighed thirty pounds or more. The typewriter in her aunt's library is a portable, weighing about twelve pounds.

The spacious bathroom belongs in a palace. She hardly dares to touch the ornate fixtures. She takes her time, gathering herself. *Nothing here except a rich family,* she thinks, gazing at her tired reflection in the mirror. She washes her hands, steps out into the hall just as Livie scuttles by, a feather duster in hand. She's in jeans and a T-shirt, wearing vinyl gloves, her hair tied back. "Livie!" Astrid calls out.

Livie turns and smiles, her cheeks spotted with pink. "What are you doing here?"

"I should ask you the same question."

Livie pushes a stray strand of hair behind her ear. "I help out here, too. It's my job. I vacuum, dust, sweep . . . Mrs. D isn't my only customer."

"No, of course not," Astrid says, flustered. "I'm just here for breakfast."

"Well, have fun. I'd better get back to it." Livie turns and hurries away.

She shows up everywhere, Astrid thinks.

When she returns to the breakfast table, Verne is cutting a scone. He puts his knife down and looks at Astrid with regret in his eyes. "I was just telling Beatrice. We feel responsible for what happened to your sister. We never had any idea—"

"The pool was shallow," Astrid says. "I'm sorry about the way my mother acted."

Verne holds up his hand, then rests it on the table. "Never apologize for a grieving mother."

"You're right—but you were only trying to be helpful."

Beatrice clears her throat, dabs at her lips with the napkin again. "It's truly all right," she says softly. "Your mother was like the sister I never had. I was an only child."

Verne coughs and clears his throat.

"Whoa, family drama," Thomas says. "This was all before I was born, right?"

"And lucky for you," Beatrice says. She turns to Verne. "Astrid has found a few typewritten letters from that time period. From her mother to her father afterward."

He looks up at Astrid, his face suddenly tense, horizontal lines deepening on his forehead. "Letters? Is this something we can help you with? Aren't they private between your parents?"

"Yes, and I'd like to keep them that way," Astrid says. "But I'm wondering . . . did my mother leave early from the party? Did she seem upset?"

Verne and Beatrice trade a look that Astrid cannot interpret. "We told the detectives everything," Verne says. "I don't recall what was going on with your mother that night."

Beatrice folds her napkin and places it on her empty plate. Astrid did not even see her finish her food. "Rose was always the life of the party. That night, she felt a little ill. She spent some time in the bathroom, as I recall."

This matches what my mother told the police, Astrid thinks. "And then what happened? I remember her coming home and talking to someone. It couldn't have been my father. He came back so much later—early the next morning. He was in Seattle."

Verne slices into his scone with gusto. "We can't possibly know who was with your mother at Maude's place, since we were here in this house. Probably best to ask your mother?"

"I did. She didn't even admit to coming back to my aunt's house."

"Wait, wait," Thomas says, holding up his hands. "All of this is going over my head. I know something terrible happened here a year before I was born. It was *your* sister who drowned?"

"Yes," Astrid says quickly, not wanting to rehash the details.

"Your parents were already engaged, dear," Beatrice says to Thomas. She looks at Astrid. "Lillian and Julian were engaged at the university and were soon married."

Julian was in love with someone else, flirting with me, Astrid thinks. Or maybe he was never interested in her, not in that way. How could he have been? He was already twenty-two. She had been deluded into believing he cared about her.

"Your mother did leave the party a while after your father drove your sister back to the house," Verne says quietly.

"We didn't notice that she came back," Beatrice says. "But she might have."

"So, nobody really knows where my mother was." Astrid stands abruptly, scraping back her chair. "Did anything else strange happen? Did anyone ever . . . break into your house back then?"

Verne and Beatrice trade yet another look. He shakes his head a little. Beatrice sighs and looks at Astrid. Thomas is watching all of them, shoving food into his mouth. "We didn't want to tell you," Beatrice says.

"Tell me what?" Astrid sits down again.

Beatrice reaches for her glass of juice but does not lift it to her lips. She merely holds on to it. "It's all in the past, and we understand what happens with grief. We never pressed any charges, you see."

"Against whom?" Astrid nearly shouts.

Verne shakes his head. "Beatrice, don't."

"We caught your mother on camera," Beatrice says, ignoring him. "She broke into the house when we weren't here. She seemed to think something was going on . . . between your father and me."

Verne shakes his head, giving her an angry look. "Beatrice. Please."

Thomas cringes a bit, focuses hard on his plate.

"Verne, she needs to know," Beatrice says softly. She gives Astrid a sad smile. "Nothing went on between me and your father. Verne can attest to that. And your father could, too, if you speak with him. But your mother had other ideas. Other . . . fantasies. I tried to be nice to her."

"I remember you came over after Nina died . . . You brought us a big gift basket," Astrid says. "I appreciated it, even if she didn't."

"Well, she broke in here looking for who knows what. As far as we could tell, nothing was stolen. Nothing at all. So, we erased the videotape. We decided to let it go."

CHAPTER TWENTY-TWO

Two days after Nina drowned, Astrid woke to the sound of voices downstairs in Aunt Maude's house. She quickly got dressed and tiptoed down the hall.

A woman's voice drifted up from the living room. "I know what you're going through."

Astrid crept down the stairs and stood in the hallway, out of sight. She recognized the voice—smooth, caring, beautifully modulated. It was Mrs. Michaels, Julian's mother. "We've suffered losses like yours. It's unbearable."

How could anyone know? Astrid thought. *How could anything be worse than this?*

"Thank you," Astrid's mother said, her voice thick with tears. "I didn't know that." Only Astrid could detect the slight reproach in her tone.

"Well, not our daughter, but our niece," Mrs. Michaels said softly. "We were very close to her. It was as if she was ours. She . . . stayed with us quite a bit."

"I'm very sorry," Astrid's mother said, her voice insincere.

"Yes, yes, she was about Nina's age. No, a little older. Her name was Flora. Well, losing a niece is different from losing a *daughter*, of course, but—"

"That must have been difficult," Astrid's mother said flatly.

"Oh dear, I didn't mean to go on. It's just—we all want to be here for you. If there's anything else we can do—"

"That garden with the pool," Astrid's mother said. "And all that stone. And all that water."

"The garden has been there for years," Beatrice said a little defensively. "Accidents happen. Why, when Julian was little, he went all the way down to the beach and waded right into the water. He couldn't have been older than three. A Good Samaritan snatched him up and brought him home. I was absolutely beside myself. What a terrible mother I thought I was!"

Another silence. Astrid heard a tissue being pulled from a box. Her mother blew her nose.

"I didn't mean . . . ," Beatrice began. "If we had known."

"Of course, if you had known," Astrid's mother said tonelessly.

Aunt Maude would have offered snacks and drinks, but she had gone to work. Astrid's father was upstairs, rearranging the contents of his suitcase. She had seen him through the open door, folding his shirts. He didn't like company—he kept to himself and hid when he got the chance.

Astrid lingered in the hallway, and then she went into the living room. Mrs. Michaels had come alone. She wore a turquoise pantsuit. Astrid always thought Mrs. Michaels looked like a movie star, her hair shiny blonde and done up perfectly. Her angular face had no imperfections, nothing out of place. She and Julian had the same eyes, bright blue and expressive, only Mrs. Michaels must've been wearing fake eyelashes. She wore an unusually muted shade of lipstick, her jewelry toned down, too. Her nails were manicured. Instead of her big, bright shoes—*expensive*, Astrid's mother said—she wore black flats. On the coffee table sat a large basket full of food and candy: apples, pears, boxes of chocolates and coffee, butterscotch popcorn.

"Wow," Astrid said before she could stop herself. Her mother and Mrs. Michaels turned to face her, and she thought they could not be more different from one another. Mrs. Michaels smiled warmly but with sadness and sympathy in her eyes, gazing directly at Astrid and holding out her hands. She seemed to exist in a beam of sunlight.

Astrid's mother smiled wanly, everything about her ephemeral, although she, too, looked beautiful in a different way. A lost way. Her hair fell in waves, and she had put on a yellow sundress, sandals, and a touch of lipstick. Rose looked like herself on the outside, if slightly disheveled, but she stared off with a dull expression in her eyes.

"Astrid, come and sit down," her mother said, patting the couch next to her, but Astrid averted her gaze and took the hands of Mrs. Michaels, whose fingers were warm and firm, anchoring her in the real world.

Mrs. Michaels squeezed Astrid's hands and let go, and Astrid sat in the chair next to her, still not looking at her mother. "My dear Astrid," Mrs. Michaels said. "It's terrible, what you've been through."

Astrid looked down at her hands in her lap and said nothing.

"How are you holding up? It must have been so hard for you, not being able to save your sister. I heard you tried hard to revive her."

Stop bringing it up, Astrid thought in desperation. She looked over at her mother, who wore no expression, but Astrid could feel the accusation.

"It must've been a horrible shock for you," Mrs. Michaels went on. "I wouldn't blame you for not being okay at all."

Astrid focused hard on not crying, on keeping herself together. "It was hard—"

"Are you seeing a counselor?" Mrs. Michaels said, her arched brows drawing together. She swung her gaze from Astrid to her mother. "Is she talking to someone? I imagine she needs someone to talk to."

Astrid's mother took a deep breath and blinked, as if she had just woken from a long sleep. A look of concern crossed her face, almost motherly. "Yes, she does. We'll take her to someone—"

"It must've been truly awful for her to carry such a weight. To feel as though you were responsible."

"Oh, she wasn't, she knows that," Astrid's mother said dismissively, but her words seemed to have been plucked out of the air. She did not mean them. She had not asked Astrid how she was doing, had not told her it was an accident, had not reassured her at all.

"I know someone in town," Mrs. Michaels said. "And really, if there's anything else we can do. We all loved little Nina. We're in shock."

"You're in shock," Astrid's mother said, her face flat. "As if you couldn't have seen this coming. As if you couldn't have prevented it."

Astrid gripped her hands together in her lap. Mrs. Michaels sat back, as if she had been slapped. "The reflecting pool was shallow. We had it drained, just in case."

"A bit late." Astrid's mother laughed hollowly.

"Children can drown in a puddle." Mrs. Michaels got up and gathered her purse.

Don't leave, Astrid thought, but she stood up, too.

Astrid's mother stood, her face pale, her expression distant. "But there was no puddle. There was only the pool."

"And the entire ocean." Mrs. Michaels patted her hair, gripped her purse.

"But Nina didn't drown in the ocean," Astrid's mother said.

Mrs. Michaels turned pale. "You're not—you don't really think . . . You were not paying attention. *You* . . . were working on your fifth glass of pinot noir."

"How would you know what I was drinking?" Astrid's mother said quietly. "You were too busy flirting with every man at the party. Isn't that your MO?"

Mrs. Michaels's face shifted from pale to deep red. Rose eyed the floral vase on the table next to the couch, and Astrid felt, suddenly, that her mother might pick it up and hurl it at Mrs. Michaels. But Rose stood very still, resting her hand on the back of the couch.

"I, for one, work hard to care for our guests," Mrs. Michaels said. "And you made it an art to take advantage of our generosity."

"Generosity?" Rose said, following Astrid and Mrs. Michaels out into the hallway. "Is that what you call it? You think that bringing over a food basket could ever make up for your neglect?"

Astrid stepped back into the doorway to the living room. She could feel herself disappearing again. Mrs. Michaels no longer wore a look of sympathy. Her blue eyes had turned to ice. "Let's not get into the subject of neglect."

"What's that supposed to mean?" Rose was nearly shouting now. She waved her arm up toward the house on the hill. "You fly onto a private runway on your Learjet, and you do whatever you want. Stomp all over other people, indulge every whim. A stone garden with a reflecting pool, really? What was it for? A mirror for you? How much time did you ever spend in that garden? You and your kind. Pompous, indulgent—"

"Stop." Mrs. Michaels held up her hand like a cop at an intersection and closed her eyes.

To Astrid's surprise, her mother stopped speaking. Mrs. Michaels opened her eyes. "I'm going to pretend I didn't hear that. I'm going to chalk this up to grief. We are not ourselves when we grieve. I know this in a way you may never understand. I will forgive you for your rudeness. I only wanted to help."

Astrid's mother lunged for the door, flung it open, and shouted, "Get out!"

"I can see it was a mistake to come here," Mrs. Michaels said, stepping outside. She descended the steps and strode toward her black Mercedes parked in the driveway.

"Oh, wait!" Astrid's mother said. "Take your charity with you! Good riddance!" She turned and swished past Astrid as if she weren't even there, picked up the basket of food, and hauled it out onto the porch. She lumbered down the steps, weighed down by her cargo, and threw the basket, but it was heavy and didn't go far before crashing to the sidewalk, the contents spilling out. The apples rolled along the stone pavers into the grass. Bananas, oranges, and bags of nuts scattered everywhere.

Mrs. Michaels ignored the mess, got into the car, and gunned it out of the driveway at top speed. Astrid's mother stood in the yard, and then she burst into tears and crumpled to her knees in the grass.

Astrid stood in the doorway, unable to bear the abject misery on her mother's face. She could feel the tears stinging her eyes. And although she found Rose frightening, she couldn't help but run down into the garden and wrap her arms around her mother to comfort her, and that was how Aunt Maude found them when she arrived home a few minutes later.

CHAPTER TWENTY-THREE

Astrid leaves the Michaels house unsettled—no, worse, confused. Beatrice and Verne never pressed charges, but they knew her mother had broken into their house, looking for evidence of her husband's imagined affair. Beatrice denied having an affair with Astrid's father. Verne did not dispute her claim. So why would Rose break in? The videotape has long ago been erased. And Astrid's mother has denied everything. Why is everyone so obtuse?

Dr. Garwood has called back and agreed to talk. Astrid mentioned that her flight leaves on Friday, only three days away—if Aunt Maude wakes by then. *I may have to reschedule everything,* she thinks on the drive through town. Her life and work have fallen into disarray.

The psychiatrist lives in a cedar rambler on a hill in the historic district uptown. Her garden is a riot of purple hydrangeas beneath the shade of a tall western red cedar tree. Astrid parks in the driveway, tucks the bundle of letters into her coat pocket. Two tiny white dogs yap in the window as she approaches the front door. The day is warm, the sun bright.

The white lace curtains rustle, and Dr. Garwood opens the door before Astrid even knocks. She is in a white wool turtleneck and slacks and white slippers to match her hair. The faint smells of dog and cinnamon potpourri emanate from inside. Soft jazz music plays in a back room. Dr. Garwood tucks one pooch beneath her arm; the other one chases its tail in the hallway, suddenly uninterested in Astrid.

"I apologize for my fierce watchdogs," Dr. Garwood says, stepping back. "You must be Astrid. Come on in."

Astrid steps inside. "Thank you for seeing me at short notice."

"Let's go and sit out on the patio." Dr. Garwood leads Astrid through a spacious living room. She puts the dog down and opens a sliding glass door to the patio, which is enclosed by a cedar privacy fence, hydrangeas planted along the inside perimeter. An ornate iron table sits in the center, surrounded by chairs, an umbrella flapping on top. Before stepping out, she grabs a sun hat from a hook by the door. Puts it on. The dogs scrabble away down the hall, called by a man with a gravelly voice at the other end of the house, perhaps her husband.

"May I offer you a drink? Tea, coffee, lemonade?"

"I'm fine," Astrid says. "Thanks, though. I appreciate you agreeing to talk to me."

"When the pandemic began, I reduced my schedule, started conducting sessions from home, on FaceTime and Zoom," Dr. Garwood says, pulling out a chair for Astrid, who sits on a surprisingly soft cushion. "It was time for partial retirement. I can't bring myself to go back to the office. I hope you don't mind meeting me here at home."

"No, of course not!"

"Good." She sits across from Astrid. The hat shades her face. Her glasses have darkened in the UV light. "It's terrible what happened to your sister—you were quite young, weren't you?"

"I was barely fourteen. But it all stayed with me."

"Your aunt is in the hospital as well, I hear. After a fall? I hope she'll be all right."

"Thank you. So do I."

"I saw Maude at the library over the years." She rests her elbows on the arms of the patio chair, makes a steeple with her fingers. "But you're here about your mother. She mentioned me in a letter to your father."

"Many years ago."

"I saw many clients back then. In some ways, they all blend together."

Astrid takes the letter of confession from her pocket and slides it across the table. "My mother believed she was responsible for my little sister's death. She hid these letters—my aunt must've found them. My mother mentions my father's betrayal and breaking into a house. It was the Michaels estate."

Dr. Garwood's penciled eyebrows shoot up, but she does not look surprised. "I know the Michaels family. Julian is an author—"

"He's only mentioned in the second letter, the one in which she all but confesses to drowning my sister. In the third letter, she mentions seeing you, which is why I'm here. I wonder if you believe what she writes is the truth."

Dr. Garwood reaches for the letter and reads it. Then she puts the paper down again. "This is rather . . . an interesting letter. It certainly raises a lot of questions."

"Is it a confession? Maybe you can't tell me, since my mother is still alive. She never admitted to anything. Not even to me after I found these letters. She claimed not to have written them."

A car goes by in the distance, birds chirping in the trees. "In this letter, your mother seems deeply troubled, but . . ."

"Hallucinating? Making things up?"

"Perhaps. Letters are strange. We never know if what's in them is real."

"I can't imagine my mother killing Nina. She seemed to . . . love her so much."

"And what about you? Did you love Nina so much?"

Astrid shifts in her chair. "I did—but I suppose I was also jealous of her."

"That's natural. Who wouldn't be?" Dr. Garwood frowns. She's holding back.

"Could the confession be designed to cover for someone else? Someone has been trying to scare me. Leaving notes, standing in the garden—"

Dr. Garwood's eyes widen. "That's awful. You've reported these things?"

"Of course. No leads."

"You think this person was connected to your mother—"

"And knows that I'm dredging things up again."

She looks thoughtful. "I see."

"She mentions you in the letter. What did you think was going on with her at the time?"

The slight downturn of her lips becomes a full-fledged frown. "I can't help you."

"Okay, I understand. I just thought . . . since she told you her secrets and you had a relationship, that you might be able to shed some light . . ."

"No, you don't understand. This is not about HIPAA or privacy." Dr. Garwood pushes up her glasses and adjusts her hat. "I'm saying, I never saw your mother for an appointment. I've never even met her."

CHAPTER TWENTY-FOUR

Astrid drives back through town in a daze. In the letters, her mother complains about Dr. Garwood asking her too many questions. Did Rose lie, or did the therapist lie? And what reason would Dr. Garwood have for denying she'd ever met Astrid's mother? *Someone is lying,* but who? Rose has the greatest reason to dissemble, unless . . .

Unless Rose started seeing Dr. Garwood before Nina's death. Perhaps the psychiatrist had ample warning of what Astrid's mother might do, that she might hurt her own daughter, that she was unhinged. *And yet Dr. Garwood did nothing.* She didn't contact the authorities, didn't ring an alarm bell. Maybe she didn't take the warning signs seriously. But this is all speculation.

Could Dr. Garwood be trying to scare Astrid away? No, that's ridiculous. Astrid pulls over to the curb to gather herself. *I'm losing it.* Her suspicions are running amok. Everything is a gray area. If Dr. Garwood saw her mother, there would be records, checks, payments—but her father didn't know if her mother had actually gone to see Dr. Garwood. Aunt Maude would know, but she is still unconscious. She persists in a coma, although she is breathing on her own.

Astrid pulls out into the road, makes a U-turn, and heads for the hospital again. Aunt Maude has been moved out of intensive care and into a regular room, a quiet space with a window overlooking the ocean. A feeding tube still protrudes from her nose. Astrid sits next to the bed and holds her aunt's cool, papery hand. Eyes closed, her face relaxed, Aunt Maude breathes deeply, as though she is merely asleep. Any moment now, she might open her eyes and smile. Is she dreaming, aware of the world around her, or is she merely absent?

"What am I missing?" Astrid says aloud. "Aunt Maude, I wish you would wake up. I have so many questions. I think you know something I don't know. About the letters, about Dr. Garwood."

Her aunt's breathing doesn't change, but she shifts a little. The monitor beeps along in time with her heartbeats.

"Someone is not telling the truth. Or maybe everyone. My dad, my mother, the Michaels family—but why would they lie? And about what? Why would Dr. Garwood lie?"

Aunt Maude's heartbeats are steady and slow.

"Look at me, talking to myself. I had a scary mother growing up— and I made a mess of my marriage to Trent. Leona betrayed me, but first, I betrayed Trent . . . and now, I'm thinking about Conor. I like him. He's a nice man. A good friend . . . I wish you could answer. What would you tell me to do?" She gets up and paces, trying to clear the clouds from her mind. She looks out the window at the ocean. In the distance, a barge passes slowly against the horizon. She crosses her arms over her chest, turns to face Aunt Maude again. She sees her aunt the way she once was, vibrant and full of knowledge.

"You would tell me to do my research," Astrid says. "To broaden my horizons. If I don't have an answer, I should get more information. Thank you, Aunt Maude." She kisses her aunt's cool forehead and rushes out to the car. On the drive back, just past the library, she makes another U-turn on impulse and pulls into the parking lot. She remembers walking to this lovely stucco building many times, a backpack strapped over her shoulders. Often, she returned to Aunt Maude's with the pack full of books.

Inside the library, the wood floors gleam, high ceilings allowing the air to circulate. The smells of old books always promised adventure and escape into fantastic literary worlds. Astrid obtains a library card at the main desk, and when she mentions her aunt's name, the librarian, whose name tag reads WILLA, pats Astrid's arm and clucks with sympathy. "We all heard," Willa says, pushing a strand of straight blonde hair behind her ear, revealing a simple gold stud earring. "We've been visiting her. Reading to her."

"That is so kind of you," Astrid says, tears coming to her eyes again. What is wrong with her? Her emotions keep rising unbidden. She points to the row of computers. "I'm just going to—"

"You go right ahead, dear, and let me know if you need any help."

The connection is fast here. Astrid follows up on a few emails, then clicks on Google. It's not difficult to find an abundance of praise for Dr. Deborah Garwood, who earned her medical degree in New York and completed her psychiatric residency at Dartmouth. Her list of credentials boggles the mind, her reviews are stellar, and yet Dr. Garwood, the person, remains opaque. The internet offers no clues to her true character. She does, however, have a Facebook account. Her profile picture shows her with a tanned man, probably her husband, on a ski slope. Her background image shows a family photo with various relatives of different ages, all dressed in parkas in a ski lodge. Nothing unusual at all.

Astrid logs off and listens to the soft shuffles of footsteps, pages turning, the clicking of keyboards, the clearing of throats. She takes in the view of the willow and vine maple trees on the library grounds. A chickadee alights on a branch, then takes off. Mottled sunlight plays on the wood floor, clouds passing overhead, the sky bright blue through the skylights. The library always calmed her, an escape from the unhappiness at home when she was young. An escape from her sadness and confusion now as well. The library feels like a place out of time, removed from the troubles of the world.

If Dr. Garwood is telling the truth—and why would she lie?—then it's seeming more likely that Astrid's mother, Rose, was hallucinating, imagining that she saw Nina in the woods, fabricating her discussion with her psychiatrist. This is reassuring to Astrid—*my mother is likely not a killer, just a deluded soul.* In which case, Nina drowned by accident, unless someone else was responsible, someone not mentioned in Rose's letters.

She didn't lie about breaking into the Michaels house. Most likely, she mixed fact and fiction, reality and fantasy. But what is the truth, and what came entirely from her mind? Could the letters hint at the real perpetrator, and that person is trying to scare Astrid out of town?

As she heads for the exit, she hears Willa call out, "Did you find what you were looking for?"

"Yes and no," Astrid says, giving Willa a quick smile.

"Oh, hang on! I have something for you." Willa disappears into a back room for a moment, then comes around the counter and hands Astrid a red hardcover book, a Royal Collector's Edition of *Gone with the Wind*.

"This is beautiful," Astrid says.

"Maude was saving this to give to you. It came in a box of donated books. She said you loved *Gone with the Wind*, but you had only a tattered copy."

"That's right. My aunt told me she oversaw the donations."

"She loved—*loves*—looking through all the books. Keeps her busy in her retirement, you know. She'd better hurry up and get well. The boxes are stacking up."

"So, her job is to find books to add to the library collection? How do you choose which books to keep?"

Willa laughs. "If the publication date is recent and the book is in good shape, it's likely to end up on our shelves. We save other books for our Friends of the Library book sales."

"I noticed my aunt had some boxes at home in her library."

"They must be books we're not keeping. Maybe she plans to recycle them or donate them to charity. Oh, and the book in your hand came in a box with her name on it!"

"Why would someone put her name on a box of book donations?"

Willa shrugs, waving at someone across the room. "We all know each other around here. It's no secret that she processes the donations."

"Does that happen often? Someone writes her name on a box?"

Willa frowns, pushes her hair behind her ear again. "That was pretty much the only time. She opened the box here and looked through the books. There were classics and the book you're holding now and some newer titles."

"I see—well, thank you for the book," Astrid says, heading for the door.

"Are you sure I can't help you find something?" Willa calls after her.

"No, I'm good. I've got everything I need."

Back in the car, Astrid opens the hardcover copy of *Gone with the Wind*, half expecting to find another letter hidden inside. But the book yields nothing between its pages.

By ten o'clock, lying in bed, she is unable to sleep. She sees Verne and Beatrice Michaels leaning forward to tell her about her mother's break-in, and the note: *Go home. You don't belong here* . . . She sees Aunt Maude lying unconscious in the hospital, her secrets sleeping with her. And she sees her mother typing her fantasy world on an old typewriter, then denying years later that she ever wrote the letters.

Astrid gets up for a glass of water from the kitchen, not bothering to turn on the light. A small night-light glows in the electrical outlet on the wall above the kitchen counter. A half moon illuminates the room in shapes and shadows. A light flashes in the woods. No, in the garden. There it is again. A fast reflection. Now it's gone.

She peers out the window, barely discerning the outlines of shrubs and trees and, at an angle at the back corner of the garden, the cottage. *The cottage.* The flash of light seemed to come from there. A small blip like a flashlight beam or a phone screen.

She rushes back to the guest room, heart pounding, and checks her iPhone. It's only 10:15 p.m. She goes to the hall phone and calls Conor again. She gets his voice mail and feels a twinge. Where is he? Out on a call? *Maybe out on a date. On Tuesday night, though?* Maybe he's ignoring her. She didn't call him back after he left the nice message. "Thank you for checking on me," she says. "I saw a light in the cottage—it might be nothing. I shouldn't . . . well, I'm going out there to look." She can imagine Conor's response. *Don't do anything risky. Wait for me.*

She grabs a flashlight from the shelf by the back door, pulls on her garden shoes, and steps outside into the cool night air. She doesn't turn on the flashlight but follows the stone path out to the cottage by the half light of the moon. She seems to float above the ground, surrounded by tiny twitters and rustles in the woods. *What if it's the man I saw standing there, looking at me? What if it's him?*

Again, a faint light appears in the cottage window, then disappears. As she approaches, crouching down, voices drift toward her. The window is open—she can hear through the screen. Shuffling inside, whispers. She goes to the door, places her hand on the knob. Steps back. Maybe she should knock. *That's ridiculous! This is Aunt Maude's property.* She flings open the door, flips on the light switch.

"Who's here? You're trespassing!" she shouts in her most authoritative voice.

"Oh shit!" a male voice says.

"Omigod!" a female voice says.

There's a great scrambling and shuffling. The futon lies open, turned into a bed, and Livie scrambles to pull up the covers over her naked breasts. The man who has tumbled out of bed, pulling on his boxer shorts, is not a man but a teenage boy, Thomas.

CHAPTER TWENTY-FIVE

Thomas raises his hands, as if Astrid is holding him up at gunpoint. "Hey, sorry, we're not stealing anything!" He's gangly, his skin pale, and he's starting to grow a little hair on his chest.

"We didn't mean to trespass," Livie says. She pulls a T-shirt on over her head. He throws her a pair of black panties. She scrambles underneath the covers.

Astrid sits in the armchair next to the futon and rubs her hands down her face. "You two scared the crap out of me. I thought it was a burglar."

"I'm so sorry," Livie says, her face red. She gets out of bed and pulls on her jeans. She and Thomas were under a sheet and a blanket that they must have pulled out of the closet. "We'll get out of here."

"Wait," Astrid says. "You two have come here before, haven't you?"

Thomas is pulling on his jeans. He looks at Livie, who resembles a frightened rabbit.

"Uh . . . ," she says.

"The camisole," Astrid says. "You were looking for it the other day. It *did* belong to you. But you were too embarrassed to claim it, right?"

Livie's blush deepens. "I'm so sorry. It's just—"

"Was there ever a library book?"

Livie purses her lips and looks toward the window.

"I understand," Astrid says. "You two can't get it on anywhere else. Not even up at the mansion?" She nods toward the Michaels house.

"Don't tell my grandma," Thomas says, turning white. "Please."

"That depends," Astrid says. "You're a minor. You're sixteen."

"Almost seventeen."

"And I'm nineteen," Livie says. "We didn't do anything. I don't want to lose my job."

Astrid eyes the condom package on the side table. Not yet opened, and a candle on the table not yet lit. "At least you're using protection. But you're too young, Thomas."

"Don't tell my grandparents!" Thomas sits on the edge of the bed, pulling on a black T-shirt. "Or my parents."

"If I don't, you should," Astrid says.

Livie sits next to Thomas, her hair still tucked into her T-shirt. She grabs his hand. "We're in love. We're going to tell everyone ourselves."

"So, nobody knows?" Astrid reaches around them and pulls the blanket off the bed. She'll have to wash the sheets, too. Who knows how many times the futon has been used in this fashion?

"My mom doesn't care," Thomas says, sudden stiffness to his demeanor. He pulls his hand out of Livie's grip.

"She doesn't even know about us," Livie says.

"She's on a plane in France. She's a flight attendant," Thomas says.

"And your dad?" Astrid says.

He shrugs. "Writing his book at home. He's happy I'm not there. He needs to, you know, *write*. Don't tell, please?" He gives Astrid a pleading look.

"Look, you two are . . . Livie, you're beyond the age when an adult has any say over what you do. But Thomas . . ."

"I'm not robbing the cradle," Livie says. "Thomas knows more than me about a lot of things. He's going to be a physicist. We'll live together as soon as he turns eighteen."

"I can't disappoint Nana," he says firmly. "Don't tell her, please."

Livie reaches for his hand again. "She wants him to marry some rich girl. She keeps trying to set him up. One is like, going to inherit a big software company. Another one is like—"

"None of that stuff even matters," Thomas says, kissing Livie's cheek. "Nana is going to leave me her estate. I don't need to marry a rich girl." He squeezes Livie's hand.

"I'm scared of her," Livie says.

"My grandma isn't scary. She wants the best for me, but she doesn't understand about us." Thomas glances at his cell phone. "Shit—it's time for her meds."

"Whose meds?" Astrid says.

"My grandma. She takes meds for her heart."

"She can't take them herself?" Astrid asks.

He pulls a hoodie over his head. "Yeah, but I help her keep track of everything. Grandpa has been going back to the city for work—"

"I thought he was retired."

"He's still on the boards of charities and stuff. I take care of her. My dad doesn't help, and she doesn't have any other family. She was like, an only child."

"Thomas, you don't have to do everything she says," Livie says, reaching back to free her hair from her T-shirt. "She is pretty sharp. She does take care of herself."

"Yeah, but she needs me."

Livie rolls her eyes. "Omigod. Seriously?"

"She's fragile," Thomas says.

"But your grandpa is there!"

"Yeah, right—he doesn't pay attention to her."

"Thomas, were you standing in the woods a couple of nights ago in that hoodie?" Astrid asks, pointing in the direction of the trail to the woods.

"Hell no."

"Just making sure, since you're both out here sneaking around."

"We didn't mean to sneak," Livie says sheepishly.

Astrid gets up. "I won't say anything if you don't do this again, but I'm going to start locking the cottage."

"Oh man," Thomas says, his shoulders slumping.

Livie gives Astrid a pleading look. "Are you going to tell Mrs. D when she wakes up?"

"We'll cross that bridge when we come to it," Astrid says.

A car rumbles up the road and turns up Aunt Maude's driveway, the headlight beams brightening the house and garden.

"Shit, shit," Thomas says, smoothing down his hair. "That's my grandma."

Livie's eyes widen. "How does she know where we are?"

Someone's calling from the front garden. "Thomas! Are you out here?"

Astrid opens the door and looks toward the front yard.

A flashlight beam is coming toward them. "Thomas, honey?"

He scrambles out the door. "I have to get out of here."

They are all out on the little stoop when Beatrice strides right up to them in jeans and a sweater, both fashionable and well fitted. "Oh my," she says, breathless. "Well, Thomas."

"Nana, what are you doing here?" He runs to her and takes her arm. "You're not supposed to exert yourself."

She pats his cheek. "I fell asleep reading a book and had a terrible dream that you'd left me."

"I'm not gone. See, I'm here visiting Astrid!" He speaks with false cheer. "We're going to play duets, right?"

"In the night?" Beatrice says.

"Hi, Mrs. Michaels." Livie gives a small wave, then steps down and sidles onto the stone path. "I need to get going."

"Hello, Livie," Beatrice says briskly.

"Nana, you should be at home," Thomas says, fussing with her sweater. "You're cold. I'll drive."

"I'm fine," she says mildly. "I know what's been going on. You think I don't take evening walks anymore? Last week, I saw lights in the cottage. You were gone. And you were gone again this evening. I wasn't born yesterday."

Livie stops in the trail. "Sorry, Mrs. Michaels."

"I didn't expect anything different from you." Beatrice gives Astrid an apologetic smile. "You will forgive my grandson and his friend, won't you?"

"Of course," Astrid says. "I was a teenager once."

Livie slips away toward the side of the house, where she must have parked her bicycle. Beatrice strides around the other side of the house toward her car. "Come on, Thomas. I'll be driving."

Thomas lingers, watching his grandmother disappear into the shadows; then he sprints back toward Astrid. "Livie and I . . . We were in the cottage last night, too."

"I'm not surprised." Astrid crosses her arms over her chest.

He glances toward the driveway, then lowers his voice. "I didn't want to say anything in front of Livie. I didn't want to scare her . . . but you know the man you said you saw in the woods?"

"Do you know who it is?" Astrid's heart skips a few beats.

"No, but . . . I saw something. It could be nothing. A boat."

"We live near the water. There are boats everywhere."

"Thomas!" Beatrice calls out. "Are you coming?"

"Be right there, Nana!" Thomas glances back toward the driveway, then steps closer to Astrid. "The boat came in close to our dock. My grandpa used to tie his yacht there. I've seen that same boat three days in a row. It prowls around for a while. There's a guy on it . . . looks like he's using binoculars to scan the shore."

Astrid shivers and glances toward the woods. "Did you notice anything else about the boat? The name of it? Color? Type of boat? Can you describe the man?"

Thomas shakes his head. "He looked about average. I couldn't see the name of the boat from far away . . . It was white, with a cabin . . . not too big and not too small. I'm not an expert. But I thought it was pretty creepy."

CHAPTER TWENTY-SIX

Astrid dreams of the letters fluttering into the air. She's on a swaying boat, and the letters fly out into the ocean. She's about to dive in after them, but a man stands in her way. She can't see his face in the darkness. *You don't belong here!* he booms. She screams, and no sound comes out. He steps into the light, and she nearly collapses with relief. It's only Trent. She has so much to tell him. *I'm sorry I lied to you,* she says. Leona lumbers up behind him in her wedding dress, the fabric stretched over her pregnant belly. But she's not Leona, she's Livie. A very pregnant Livie, her eyes mournful. Astrid steps back, her stomach cramping. She never expected Trent to marry Livie!

She pops awake gasping for air, a crushing sadness in her chest. The muddled dream fades into its own twilight world, lost in the bright morning. The events of last night feel surreal—finding Thomas and Livie in the cottage, Beatrice showing up, a possible boat prowling along the shore. Boats pass this way all the time—families on outings, anglers, or diving boats. But three days in a row? If she can find a pair of binoculars in the house, she could walk the beach and see if she can spot a man gazing back at her from the deck of a boat. *Could he be Len Wilkers?* she thinks. *He lives on a boat down in Seabank.* But he has no reason to harass her. He has no reason to even know she's in town or that she's looking into Nina's death. Unless someone told him. But who? And why?

A faint whirring sound comes from somewhere in the distance. A crow caws in the woods. She yawns, gets out of bed, and pulls on her robe. The air is cold in the house—it never gets quite warm enough in the mornings and evenings, and sometimes it's too warm during the day. Old Victorians never keep a constant internal temperature, but she supposes this is what gives them character.

She goes down to the kitchen to make coffee, looks out the window toward the backyard. The cottage gazes at her benignly, as if it never hid two lovestruck teenagers inside its walls. As the coffee bubbles in the carafe, the whirring sound grows perceptibly louder—it's like water running through the pipes in the house. A tap is on somewhere. Did she leave the shower running?

She checks upstairs. None of the faucets are on. They aren't even dripping. She goes back downstairs. Yes, the rush of a faucet is louder on the first floor. But all the taps are turned off down here as well. Perhaps the sound is coming from outside.

She ties the robe around her waist, slips on garden shoes, and steps out onto the front porch. The morning air blows in clean and cool through her pajamas. One of the ceramic birdbaths has fallen from the railing and lies broken on the wooden slats of the porch. She picks up the pieces and sets them on the small bench next to the front door.

The green garden hose is attached to the faucet on the outside of the house, below the living room window.

She stares at the hose, trying to remember if she attached it to the faucet. The faucet is slightly leaking, a slow drip running down the hose to the ground. *It's turned on—it's running.* The hose extends down through the grass, into the driveway, and . . . in through the passenger window of her car.

Her heart flips over. *What the hell?* She dashes down the steps, turns off the faucet, then races through the damp morning grass to her rental car, her heart in her throat. Someone jimmied the window from the outside. It's halfway open, the hose wedged in and snaking down onto the floor mat. The car is already half-full of water, like a metallic swimming pool, and utterly, completely ruined.

◆ ◆ ◆

Half an hour later, Conor comes out of the woods, shaking his head. "No sign of anyone," he says. He searched the premises and took photographs of the car, the hose, and the surrounding area. No obvious footprints remain on the dry ground.

Astrid sits on the porch steps, hugging her middle. He comes to sit beside her. "We've got to stop meeting like this," he says. "And it's only Wednesday."

"What's next?" she says, a deep pressure on her chest. "My flight is in two days, but I can't leave. Not now. What about Aunt Maude?"

"You shouldn't stay here. Any idea who might have done this?"

"No, but I found Livie and Thomas Michaels making out in the cottage last night."

"What?" He laughs incredulously. "Wonders never cease."

"Beatrice came and retrieved him, and Livie rode her bicycle home. Thomas said he saw someone on a boat near the shore here three days in a row, possibly looking through binoculars. He couldn't identify the man or the boat."

"How do you know Livie and Thomas aren't your culprits?"

"Why would they return to vandalize my car? I didn't tell anyone about them. Beatrice came over but not because I called her. She figured things out herself."

"Well, I'll talk to those kids, see what I can find out. You'll want to get in touch with the rental car company—and your insurance company. And you might want to change the locks on the house." He heads back to his car.

"Wait!" Astrid says, running after him. "Didn't you say Len Wilkers is still around, living on a boat in Seabank?"

"Thirty miles from here. You're not going to approach him."

"Why not? Someone has been prowling around, trying to scare me away, destroying my car, and Thomas saw a boat three days in a row. Len Wilkers is in that picture, the one in the file. If my mother had an affair with him, maybe my sister was *his* biological child. Maybe he was somehow involved in Nina's death."

"And your mother knew?"

"I don't know . . . Maybe she imagined she drowned Nina, but he'd already done it. Maybe the letters implicate him, and I haven't yet figured out how. You said he was in the woods that night. My dad saw my mother on his boat. Now a boat's prowling around."

"There are things about Len Wilkers that you don't know. A neighbor once accused him of molesting her four-year-old daughter, before your sister died. No charges were filed."

Astrid gasps. "You didn't tell me this!"

"I didn't know you were planning to interrogate the guy!"

"Those details were not in the file on Nina!"

"The information came in later. Len Wilkers used to be Len Walker. He lived in Port Orchard with his wife and daughter. He later changed his name to escape the public eye. Someone tipped off my dad with an anonymous call."

"Len . . . *Walker* wasn't arrested for what happened with his neighbor? Why?"

"Your guess is as good as mine. Not enough evidence, probably."

"Nina could've been his . . . or he intended to molest her . . . but there was no sign that she had been assaulted."

"Maybe you or someone else interrupted him," Conor says.

"My mother, maybe?"

"Or you."

"I didn't see anyone . . . but he could've been there."

"If you're going to kill someone, drowning them is a good way to do it. An adult could hold a child underwater without creating a bruise. Maybe he lured Nina into the water under some pretense. He could've told her they were playing a game. But someone interrupted him, he left, and Nina drowned."

"Accidentally. Or . . . not."

"Exactly. The other child was only a little older than Nina."

"I have to talk to him."

"What good will it do? He'll deny everything."

"So what? He might let something slip."

Conor laughs and gestures to her car. "Looks like you're here for a while anyway. I have to head out on another call. I'll drop you a line later. If you still want to go, I'll go with you."

After he leaves, Astrid inspects her ruined car. "He's right. I'm stranded. Except . . . maybe I'm not." She retrieves her aunt's key chain. The Honda Accord key opens the car, and in the driver's seat, she adjusts the mirrors. Aside from a few library books on the passenger seat, the interior is clean and smells faintly of lavender. In a small compartment to the left of the steering wheel, she finds the current registration and insurance card.

After annoying calls to the rental car and insurance companies, she powers up her laptop and googles Len Wilkers. She finds no mention of the accusation against him when he was Len Walker, probably because no charges were filed, and nobody went public. He traveled a lot after Nina's death, diving in Europe, Canada, South America, perhaps seeking to escape scrutiny and accusatory stares.

But now, he's back, and his social media accounts show public photographs of underwater wrecks he has explored, other colorful images of Pacific Northwest ocean life, and a few of his commercial dives, in which he scouted fallen bridges or the safety of underwater docks and other structures. He certainly has a life. He looks very much the way he looked in the photograph from the party, only older, his hair gray. He still has ropy muscles. He is smiling in every picture. He does not seem damaged by the suspicion that once fell upon him.

She showers and manages to maneuver her aunt's Honda out of the driveway, around the rental car. She stops at the hospital to visit Aunt

Maude. Her cheeks have acquired a little color, much to Astrid's relief. A succession of Maude's friends from the local wilderness society, the library foundation, and her book groups has been stopping in to sit with her, and Livie has been a regular, too.

"I'm borrowing your car," Astrid whispers to her aunt, then squeezes her hand. "You would approve of my investigation, I hope. I'll report in later. You concentrate on waking up." Then Astrid drives south out of Heron Bay along a wooded, sometimes pastoral coastline.

The town of Seabank is small, lined with motels and country restaurants. The houses are set back from the main road. As she follows the signs to the harbor, she pictures Aunt Maude lying in her library next to her desk. If Len Wilkers has been harassing her, did he break in looking for the letter? Did he attack Aunt Maude? If so, how would he have even known about the letter in the first place?

The harbor is unexpectedly beautiful, the walkway along the water lined with shade trees and lush flora—hydrangeas, roses, rhododendrons, snapdragons, and various species of ornamental grasses. A soft breeze wafts in, the wind broken by the hills surrounding much of the protected bay. A few youngsters venture out in paddleboats, and gulls call overhead. A few small businesses—restaurants and marine-supply shops—have sprung up around the harbor. A sleek yacht is slowly venturing out as she parks in the lot near the shore.

She gets out of the car, cell phone tucked into her jacket pocket, and heads to the marina. The door to the main dock is locked. A young woman, deeply tanned, in shorts and a windbreaker, comes up behind her. "May I help you?"

"I'm looking for Len Wilkers," Astrid says. "I heard he lives here . . ."

"Len spends a lot of time on his boat, that's for sure," the woman says, grinning. A light dusting of freckles sprinkles itself across her nose.

I came to the right place, hallelujah, Astrid thinks. "Is there any way that I can talk to him?"

"Come on down, I'll show you." The woman unlocks the door and summons Astrid down the ramp. The dock floats above a deep bay, anemones and other sea creatures, in shades of white, yellow, and pink, growing out of the pilings beneath the water. The young woman leads Astrid along the main dock, and on docks branching out from the main one, large yachts are anchored. A couple of smaller boats are coming into the bay.

"Very end. The boat is the *Blue Descent*." The girl points toward the end of the dock, where a large boat, maybe thirty feet long, shows off its twin outboards and a cabin with an aluminum pilothouse door. The painted words *Blue Descent* gleam in slanted turquoise letters on the hull.

"He's in there?" Astrid asks, hopeful and also sweating a little with trepidation.

"Um, I think so," the young woman says, shielding her eyes. "He's there every day. Thought I saw him come down this way earlier. But you'll be lucky to catch him. I think he's heading out soon."

"Thank you." Astrid walks along the dock and reaches the boat just as someone stands up inside the pilot's cabin—a tall man who seems intent on his task at the helm. For a moment, in silhouette, he resembles the man she saw in the garden, looking toward the house. Then when the man in the boat turns, his shoulders seem too broad. But it could've been him.

Astrid waves at him, standing on tiptoe on the dock. "Hello, Mr. Wilkers?"

He comes out, holding a thick rope in his hand. He's athletic, his face craggy and creased. Tattoos peek out from beneath the short sleeves of his black T-shirt. She tries to imagine him taking her mother out boating all those years ago. Did he charm Rose Johansen into falling in love with him?

"You're looking at him," he says, walking out to the railing. "Who's asking?"

"May I speak with you? I think my parents used to know you a long time ago."

"I'm not that old." He puts the rope on a seat on the deck and motions to Astrid to step up onto the boat. "You want to come aboard for a bit?"

She hesitates. If he feels threatened—or even if he doesn't—he might take off and throw her overboard—

Don't go there.

"Sure, thank you."

He reaches out his hand and hoists her aboard, swinging her up onto the deck in one movement. The boat sways a little. He grins and gestures to one of the cushioned white seats on the deck. She sits in the sun, amazed at how clean the boat appears to be. *It must cost a fortune.* He has done well for himself.

"Who are these famous parents of yours?" he says, opening the door to the pilot's cabin and placing the rope inside.

"Rose and Bjorn Johansen. My sister, Nina, came with us to Heron Bay seventeen years ago—the summer she drowned in the reflecting pool up at the Michaels estate." There, she has said it. Her heartbeat pounds up through her head. The wind whooshes in her ears.

Len Wilkers freezes for a perceptible moment, his back turned to her, but then he seems to recover his composure and comes out onto the deck, arms crossed over his chest. "Is this a joke?" he asks, his voice heavy with suspicion. "I've said all I'm going to say about that whole fiasco." He looks uncomfortable with having her on the boat, his face suddenly hard. He pops mirrored sunglasses over his eyes. He gestures to the gleaming metal railing again, motioning to her to get off the boat.

"Did you have an affair with my mother?" She has been swiping through the pictures on her phone until she reaches the one taken up at the Michaels house on the eve of her sister's death. "You're in this picture, sitting right there . . ." She hands him the phone.

He sighs, takes the phone, and looks at the photograph. His lips tighten, the lines deepening on his face, but he does not remove the sunglasses. He hands the phone back to her, a tic in his jaw. "Yeah, I remember your mother. Long time ago, though. But I never slept with her."

"I know the investigation focused on you. I'd like to know what really happened."

"Here we fucking go again."

"My aunt thinks someone might have killed my sister. Not you—of course not you. But someone." The *not you* part is a complete lie.

He looks at her and bursts into laughter. She expects him to pick her up bodily and throw her off the boat. Instead, he starts pulling up ropes, untying the boat. She grips the railing. "I'll get down. I can talk to you from the dock."

He grins at her. "Think I'm going to throw you overboard, *drown you*?"

"No, not at all."

"Might not be a bad idea, huh?" He watches as she climbs down between the railings and lands on the dock.

"Have you been trying to scare me away? Did you leave me a nasty note and fill my car with water? Have you been hanging around in this boat near the dock at the Michaels house?"

"What the hell are you talking about?" He looks genuinely shocked, but then he starts laughing again, shaking his head as he prepares to take out the boat.

"I know about what happened when you were Len Walker. I know about your neighbor."

He looks at her again, the rope in his hand, his face going pale. "That was a load of crap. None of it was fucking true."

"Did my mother see you in the woods that night? She typed letters to my dad . . . I know you know about them. Were you out there that night?"

He looks at her blankly. "Letters. What letters?"

"My dad says you took her out on your boat. He saw her on your boat! Did you go into the woods to meet my mother? Or did she go out there looking for you?"

Len Wilkers pulls on a hat, goes into the cabin, comes back out. "Your dad needs a good pair of glasses. And your mother, she was a piece of work." He makes a swirling motion next to his ear.

"What does that mean? What did she do?"

He comes to the railing, leans over the side, looks up and down the dock. It's deserted. Out in the water, cormorants float on the waves. A gull sails overhead, calling out in a faint cackle. "Rose and I talked, okay? I promised to take her away from everything. She went on about traveling the world, about being free."

"When my sister was still alive." *But I thought my mother only wanted to escape after she lost her child.*

"She had ideas about us getting married . . . but she was just flirting, and I figured out pretty quick that she was full of all kinds of fantasies. I never had an affair with her, and I sure as hell never took her out on my boat."

Fantasies . . . The letters are full of them, too. "What reason do I have to believe you? Maybe you saw Nina in the woods, and you . . ."

He's finished untying the boat now. Starting up the motor. "I'm done talking to you." He disappears into the cabin.

"Damn it!" She lingers on the dock, then turns to leave. Conor was right—she had no chance of getting any information from Len Wilkers. She's halfway down the dock when footsteps race up behind her, and someone grabs her arm. It's Len.

She yanks her arm away. "What do you want?"

"I want to set the record straight."

"About what?"

He hands her a business card. "This is the attorney I hired when I was Len Walker in Port Orchard. Damien Leifsen. Leifsen and Benton."

"What about attorney-client privilege?"

"The website is on here. They list some of the cases they've won. No names, no dates. Read the story about the diver."

"What happened? Where is the family you had before? Your wife, Mrs. Walker?"

"I killed her."

"Seriously."

He makes a sour face, then shakes his head. "The strain of the accusations against me was too much for her. We split up. She got custody of our daughter. Not that it's any of your damn business. And one more thing, you're barking up the wrong tree." He points at her phone. "You should look at that other guy."

"Which one? That's my father—"

"No, the Michaels kid. The one with the floppy hair, became a writer or whatever. He had the eyes for your mother. Julian, that was his name. He followed Rose everywhere. She couldn't shake him."

CHAPTER TWENTY-SEVEN

Back at Aunt Maude's house, Astrid looks at the letters again. Could Len Wilkers be telling the truth? Her mother mentioned having to elude Julian. Could Rose have gone into the woods, followed by Julian? But why would he have killed Nina? *Did my mother have an affair with Julian? Is she covering for him in the letters?* But he was so young, practically a kid. Still, he said Rose was beautiful. Could she have seduced him? Perhaps he has something to hide, and he found out about the letters through his parents, if Aunt Maude mentioned to Beatrice what she'd found. He could've taken the ferry from San Juan Island.

He's in the photograph, after all.

And what about the accusations against Len Wilkers when he was Len Walker?

After trying to tidy the library, Astrid powers up her laptop on the desk, opens the web browser, and types in the URL for Leifsen and Benton. The firm specializes in defending clients against sexual-offense allegations. The menu options are About Us, Services, Areas of Expertise, Contact, and Case Results.

She clicks on the Case Results tab, which lists articles lauding Not Guilty verdicts in various cases, rape or pornography charges dismissed against clients, appeal wins, reversals of convictions. She clicks through six pages of articles before finding one titled **Police Drop Charges Against Diver.**

After reading through the article three times, she understands why Len Wilkers wanted her to visit this website. The neighbor girl used to come over and play with Len's daughter all the time. At one point, the girl said "the client" (Len) watched her in the bathroom and once touched her "private part." The police investigated, and as it turned out, both the client and his wife had helped the neighbor girl in the bathroom. She often had accidents and needed help to wipe or make sure her clothes were dry. Her mother questioned her, presented leading questions, and may have planted ideas in the girl's mind. Several witnesses observed the client to be a wonderful parent and to always act appropriately around children. The neighbor girl's mother had probably misinterpreted what her daughter was saying.

The client passed a polygraph exam, and a "psychosexual exam" suggested that he was unlikely to be a sex offender. Eventually, the police dismissed the case before the client, Len, could be arrested.

Astrid closes the website window and turns off her computer. Len's attorney presents a particular explanation of what happened. But perhaps the neighbor girl's mother remained suspicious of Len. Maybe others did, too. No wonder he changed his name. It's not clear what really happened. Astrid has no idea if a polygraph test is conclusive. But maybe Len Walker, now Len Wilkers, was himself a kind of victim. She does not know, and she likely never will.

He's clearly angry about having been accused—and then he became a suspect again, and Astrid returned to dredge up the past. She imagines him on a boat out in the bay, free and alone, away from civilization and suspicious gazes. Tying the boat to the Michaelses' dock and slipping through the woods to harass her and try to run her out of town. Is he trying to scare her away, fearing the police might harass him again? But how would he have known she was investigating? And if her mother accidentally—or deliberately—drowned Nina, how did he factor in? *Does he know what happened to Nina?*

Why would he implicate Julian?

Astrid rummages through her aunt's desk for the ferry schedule to San Juan Island. But she can't just show up there. She needs to find the number for Julian. Of course, it's not listed anywhere, but when she calls the Michaels house, Beatrice is more than happy to give her the number. "I'm sure Julian would love to hear from you," she says, using the word *love* again, and making Astrid believe it.

◆ ◆ ◆

Late Thursday morning, San Juan Island emerges from the mist like a mirage. Astrid leans over the railing of the ferry deck, inhaling the clean sea air, taking in the magnificent view of dense forests and rocky shorelines spilling down into the sea. A quaint town curves around a harbor on the east side of the island, protected from the wild Pacific winds off the western coast.

The captain has already announced the ferry's approach to the island, instructing drivers to return to their cars. As the boat maneuvers in toward the dock, she rushes through the passenger cabin and down the narrow staircase to the car deck. In her aunt's Honda, she sets her GPS to take her to Julian's home and drives a little too fast on the picturesque route along the south shore of the island.

Yesterday, when she called Julian, his voice sounded deeper and scratchier than she remembered. He said he was on deadline to turn in a manuscript but could spare a few minutes. *My wife is traveling, so I guess it's as good a time as any.* The towing company arrived to remove the rental car in the afternoon, and this morning, she caught the first boat to San Juan Island.

Now she drives past rolling meadows dotted with trees and finally comes to a boulder with the address glued on in ceramic letters. The dirt driveway winds down through a fir forest toward the sea. The house itself is a rustic, modern cedar two story blending into the woods and overlooking the rocky shore. Beneath a slanted metal roof, large windows reflect the sky and ocean.

She parks next to a black Audi and quickly checks her face in the visor mirror. *I don't care what I look like to Julian anymore,* she reminds herself, flipping up the visor.

She gets out and picks her way across the rocky driveway, past discarded flowerpots and an overturned wheelbarrow, and knocks on the front door. As if he's been waiting, Julian opens the door immediately. The past floods back to her—his piercing blue eyes, that roguish grin, the corner of his mouth turned up. His hair is still blond but threaded with gray. She can't stop staring into those eyes. They haven't changed. "Astrid," he says warmly, shaking her hand. "It has been . . . wow, how long? You grew up. In a good way."

"So did you," she says, barely able to catch her breath. She sees him as he was all those years ago, smoking his clove cigarettes.

"Come on in. You traveled a long way. I'm intrigued." He ushers her inside. She steps straight into a wide, open-air living room, the kitchen and dining room all part of the same space. A hall to the right leads to what she assumes are bedrooms. This is the second floor on a downward slope, the downstairs half built into the side of a hill. The house is furnished in simple, modern lines, a large window overlooking the water. An entire wall of the living room is a set of bookshelves. A gigantic telescope stands on a tripod right in front of the window, looking out upon the vast ocean and a distant island.

"Should I take off my shoes?" She looks down at the gleaming hardwood floor.

"No need—have a seat. Get you a drink?" He heads over to a wet bar.

"I'm all right," she says, the floor creaking beneath her shoes. She sits on the couch, feeling awkward.

"I'll get one for myself then. Helps me think." He pours a finger of Scotch into a thick tumbler and sits across from her. How easy it is for her to remember the crush she had on him, the fluttering in her stomach. It's as if no time has passed, except that he's older and a little thicker. She expected the spell would've worn off by now.

"Do you still smoke cloves?" she asks.

He smiles. "Gave them up long ago, not good for the health." He raises his glass. "You always wanted to try them."

"I never smoked," she says.

"Good for you." He sips the Scotch, places it on a coaster on the side table. A gold wedding band gleams on his left ring finger. "Strange, seeing you again after so long. You were so young and impressionable. But now you're a wise adult."

"Adult, but I don't know how wise." She looks around, notices his titles in a row on the bookshelves. "You always wanted to be an author. What's it like now that your dreams have come true?"

His eyes twinkle in the sunlight. "You're only as successful as your most recent book. Nothing that came before ever matters."

"I'm sure that's not true. People read all your books." *Although I can't bring myself to read even one,* she thinks.

He sits back, rests one arm over the back of his chair. "I always wondered what would've happened if you hadn't left town forever. After, you know." He waves his hand by way of explanation.

"You would've married your fiancée, and I would've gone to college," she says.

He leans forward, grabs his glass again. "Or maybe you and I, you know."

She laughs. "Seriously? Are you actually flirting with me right now?" She can see it now in a clearer way. He does make her flustered, but another part of her can see through him.

He sits back again. "Can't help myself. You and I." He moves his hand back and forth between them. "We had a connection from the beginning. Don't you think?"

"I was young and impressionable," she says. "And you're a husband and a father."

"Yeah, there's that, huh?" He looks into his glass, gulps the rest of his booze. He's starting early. He doesn't ask her about her own marriage, her own life. He just looks into his glass.

She reaches into her pocket, brings out the letters, and slides them across the coffee table toward him. "They're copies. The originals are safely hidden."

"That sounds intriguing." He snatches up the letters, reads them in silence. "The mystery deepens. Rose Petal was your mother. Shit." He runs his fingers through his hair, slides the letters back across the coffee table.

"Did you try to follow her when she left the party?"

"Oh yeah, like a puppy. Right. I might've gone off to have a smoke. My parents didn't like me smoking on the property. Your mother . . . what does she say about all this?"

"She denies writing these letters at all. She's in Europe. I haven't seen her in four years. The last time was when we met for dinner in New York. She was there for an art conference."

"Close relationship, huh?"

"What about your relationship with *your* mother? Did you see my father touching her earring that night? Pushing back her hair?" She points to the passage in the letter, where her mother accuses him.

"I never paid attention. And I sure as hell didn't stalk your mother." He turns his glass around. "I need another drink."

He was drinking back then, too, she thinks. "Unless there's more in these letters than I can see. Something that might incriminate someone else."

Julian gets up to pour himself another drink. "Wish I had more for you, Austen Girl." He lets the name slip so casually, as if she has not lived a whole life since she last saw him. But he never looked for her, never wrote to her, and the summer after her family left Heron Bay for the last time, he got married, and his wife had a child.

"Thomas is a nice guy," she says.

Julian looks at her, brows raised, and puts the bottle of Scotch back on the bar. "You met him. Oh yeah, my mother said you went over for breakfast or something. She's always *entertaining* people. Can't stop. It's in her blood." He sips his drink and returns to his seat.

She decides not to tell him about the flooded car, the note, the man in the woods. "Do you own a yacht?" she asks him.

He sputters, nearly spits out his Scotch, and laughs. "You mistake me for my dad," he says. "He's the one with money oozing from his pores. Couldn't you smell it when you were there?"

"You don't take a boat to Heron Bay."

"I ride the ferry like normal human beings."

She gets up. "Sorry I've taken up so much of your time."

He leaps to his feet. "Leaving so soon? I thought I could show you around town. The parks. Lend you a book or two." He winks at her, a barely perceptible flicker of his eyelid.

We are no longer friends, Astrid thinks. *Maybe we never were.* She sees in Julian now an illusion, a trick of the light. "The boat leaves in an hour," she says. "I don't have time."

"Ah, yes . . . we're slaves to the ferry schedule." He swirls the amber liquid in his glass. "You could stay. I mean, we have a guest room. Downstairs."

She pictures Julian sneaking up on her in the darkness, slipping into the guest bed while she sleeps. She used to fantasize about such a scenario, but now, the prospect scares her. "Kind of you, but I've got things to do."

"Maybe next time," he says, giving her a perfunctory nod.

"May I use your restroom before I go?" she asks, getting up.

"Down the hall, on your left." He gestures with his glass.

On her way to the hall, she stops to look at family photographs on a bookshelf—of Verne and Beatrice when they were younger. "Hey, that's Aunt Maude—and my mom and dad." She points at a photograph taken up at the Michaels mansion.

"Those are party pictures. And the older ones are cousins, grandparents, the whole shebang." In one faded picture, a little girl is running through a sprinkler, laughing, surrounded by family members at a garden party.

"That looks like Nina," Astrid says, squinting at the girl. Her features are not quite distinct—she is too far away in the picture.

"That's my cousin—she died before I was born. Flora. She was only four, I think. Meningitis or something."

"Oh, I'm so sorry. On your mother's side or on your father's side?"

"My mother's. Her older sister lived in France. Her husband was in the foreign service. She died a while back. I never got to meet her."

"And you and your wife!" In the wedding photos, Julian looks stunning in his tuxedo. His wife resembles a dark-haired, younger version of Beatrice with her aquiline, regal features.

Julian comes to stand next to her, too close. He smells mildly of sweat and alcohol. "Like I said, Lillian travels a lot."

"Is that why Thomas spends so much time with his grandparents?"

"My mother is good to him." He gazes at the photographs of him, Lillian, and young Thomas, as if looking for a life that no longer exists or maybe never did.

"Thomas doesn't spend a lot of time with his mother?"

"She keeps an apartment in Vermont. It's where she's from. Her family is there. She never wanted to return to the West Coast."

"You all don't get to spend much time together."

"We spend enough," he says. "You know what they say. We got married on my birthday so I would remember our anniversary."

Astrid forces a laugh. The house, she realizes, exudes loneliness, and Julian had everything going for him—looks, family, money, no tragedy in his past. He could've married for love, could've worked on his marriage. No wonder Thomas spends so much time in Heron Bay.

"Um, bathroom. I'll be right back." She slips down the hall, glances back over her shoulder. No sign of Julian, but clanging sounds come from the kitchen.

Heart pattering, she passes the open door to the bathroom and peers into what must be Julian's writing studio. Books and papers fill a set of bookshelves to the right, a computer with a printer and screen on a desk to the left. In front of her, a picture window overlooks the ocean. A sailboat drifts by in the distance.

She tiptoes to the desk. A ferry schedule lies open on a pile of papers, the morning sailings to Heron Bay circled. Is he planning on going, or did he already go? On a notepad next to the computer, Julian has jotted notes by hand. *Add scene on page 95. Revise investigation scene*, and other comments to himself.

Astrid glances back toward the door. Julian is still banging around in the kitchen. She pulls out her iPhone and snaps a few photographs of his handwriting. Then she rushes back out to the bathroom.

Inside, she catches her breath, tells herself to calm down. She scrolls through the photographs and pinches the screen to zoom in. Julian's handwriting looks similar to the writing in the hostile note, but she cannot tell for sure if the two samples match. The pushes and pulls look similar, the pressure of the pen, the slant. She needs more samples, but this will have to do for now. After washing her hands, she finger combs her hair and opens the door to find Julian standing right in front of her. She gasps, presses her hand to her chest. "You scared me."

"You okay?" he asks, giving her a peculiar look.

"Yeah, why?" She tucks her phone into her back pocket.

He glances down the hall, then over her head into the bathroom. "You took a while. I thought maybe you weren't feeling well."

"No, I'm fine," she says, hurrying past him to the front hall. *I have to get out of here.* Julian is right behind her. She steps out onto the porch. "Good to see you—"

"Sure you're okay?" he asks, following her outside.

"Never better." She turns and sprints to the car. Julian doesn't follow her, and the front door thuds shut.

As she drives back to the ferry landing, she takes deep breaths, gripping the steering wheel. *Did he see me slip into his writing studio?* But she heard dishes clinking in the kitchen. *Maybe I wasn't paying attention for a minute, and he came looking for me.* She didn't hear him approach the bathroom. *It doesn't mean anything. I'm paranoid.*

On the boat, she compares the photos of his writing more carefully to the threatening note. *Yes, the similarities are remarkable,* she thinks, *but they're inconclusive.* The *e* slants a little differently, but that could be due to the natural variation in one person's writing. How on earth will she obtain more samples? He's already suspicious. She could examine the signatures in his autographed books in the bookstore, but signatures are qualitatively different from other forms of handwriting. Even people who cannot write in cursive can learn to sign their names.

When she arrives at Aunt Maude's house, a brilliant orange sunset spreads across the sky. She can barely keep her eyes open. She's changing into her pajamas when the landline rings in the hall, an unfamiliar, shrill sound. She rushes to answer it. "Maude Dasgupta's residence."

"Ms. Johansen?" a tense woman's voice echoes at the other end.

"That's me," she says. *How do you know my name?* "Who is this?"

"I'm calling from Heron Bay Hospital. We've been trying to reach you all day. It's about your aunt. She's waking up. She asked for you."

CHAPTER TWENTY-EIGHT

As Astrid rides the elevator up to her aunt's room in the hospital, she focuses on keeping calm. Rose should be here, but then, she might not be much help, anyway. *I'll have to change my plane ticket,* Astrid thinks. She can't jet out of here tomorrow. She'll stay at least through the weekend, reschedule her flight for Sunday evening or Monday. Somehow, she will have to hold off her clients until then. At least she's not preparing for a court appearance.

"We're hopeful," Dr. Sawari whispers to Astrid outside the door to Aunt Maude's room. "But don't expect much. She's drifting in and out."

"Will she be all right? I mean, can you tell?"

"Not yet. She said your name and nothing else. We expect her to slowly improve, and then we'll be able to make a better assessment. Are you ready to go in there?"

Astrid nods and takes a deep breath. "What should I do? Should I talk to her?"

The doctor pats her arm, putting on that quiet, soothing smile. "Just let her know you're there. Let her do the rest."

Astrid exhales and goes inside. The curtains are open, sunset seeping in at an angle. Her aunt is slightly elevated on the pillows. Someone brushed her hair. Her eyes are closed. The monitor still beeps, but somehow the sound is softer.

Astrid sits quietly in the chair next to the bed again, rests her hand on Maude's forearm. Her skin feels a little warmer than before. "Aunt Maude. It's Astrid. I'm here."

No response at first. Maude keeps breathing evenly.

"Aunt Maude. Talk to me."

Astrid glances toward the door. It's still closed.

Aunt Maude's right eye opens slightly, and she turns to look at Astrid.

"Welcome back," Astrid says, bursting into tears. She wipes them away.

Maude blinks, then moves her mouth and squeezes Astrid's hand. Astrid leans in closer. "I'm here."

Maude nods slightly, still regarding Astrid through one half-open, watery eye. "Astrid," she whispers, then mumbles something incoherent.

"You asked for me."

Maude presses her eyes shut, her face tightening in frustration. Her mouth moves a little, no sound coming out.

"Take your time," Astrid says. "I'm not going anywhere."

Maude takes a shuddering breath, and her eyes open. The beeping of the monitor begins to grate in Astrid's ears. Maude's heart rate is increasing a little.

"You're going to be fine," Astrid says. "But don't strain yourself."

"Astrid—" And then Maude mumbles, "Careful . . . The letters . . ."

"I found them. The ones my mom typed. Those were the letters you wanted me to find, right? The ones in the book? You wanted me to analyze the signatures."

Maude shakes her head a little.

"What are you trying to say? I'm trying to decipher everything. The typewriting matches the machine in your study. The signatures match some of the postcards, okay? I interviewed Len Wilkers and Verne and Beatrice . . . Dr. Garwood says she never met Mom. I'm not sure—"

"Typewriter . . . library!"

The hair prickles on the back of Astrid's neck. "Yes, the typewriter is in the library."

Maude's eyes widen. She holds on to Astrid's hand. "Letter . . . typewriter. Rose . . . Petal."

Astrid lowers her voice. "She mentions Nina drowning and then seeing her . . . after she was gone. You didn't tell me. You worried I might not come here . . ."

Maude shifts beneath the sheets, the beeping speeding up a little again.

"Okay, I'm upsetting you," Astrid says, sitting back in the chair. "We don't need to talk about this now. Just rest. You need to get better."

"No," Maude says clearly. "Typewriter . . . was dropped . . ."

"You dropped the typewriter? But it's fine . . . It's not damaged."

The monitor beeps faster and faster. "No," Aunt Maude whispers. "No, no, no. You have it wrong! Out of order!" Her eyelashes flutter, and she closes her eyes.

CHAPTER TWENTY-NINE

Astrid presses her foot to the gas, forcing herself to slow down around curves. "I have it wrong?" she mutters. "But no, I have it right! Absolutely right! The typewriter is not out of order!" After Aunt Maude closed her eyes, she was asleep in a split second. The nurse ushered Astrid out of the room.

Back at the house, she brings the typewriter off the shelf in the library. It's in pristine condition, no sign that it was ever dropped. It still works. She paces the threadbare carpet, trying to figure out what to do. Could the word *dropped* mean something else? Someone dropped it off, someone borrowed it . . . or maybe the two words don't actually go together? Who might know the answer? How could she *have it wrong*? *Out of order?*

She calls Livie. "Aunt Maude woke up."

Livie starts to cry. "Hallelujah! I'll go and see her right away."

"My aunt said the typewriter was dropped. You work for her. Do you have any idea what she might mean? Was it out of order?"

"I move the typewriter sometimes when I'm cleaning up and dusting. She's not too strong anymore, so she asks me to carry the typewriter from the shelf to the desk and back. She always tells me to be careful not to drop it."

"And you never did. You never dropped it."

"No, I'm really careful."

"Did someone else drop it?"

"I don't think so . . . She said typewriters never really work right after you drop them."

"No, they don't." Astrid has learned in her profession that after a typewriter has been dropped, many parts become permanently damaged. And yet, Aunt Maude's typewriter works beautifully. "Well, she must've had it fixed by an expert, if this one was ever dropped."

"She has all her receipts in the file drawers. It would show the repairs."

"I found a receipt for a type slug replacement. But not a major repair like that."

"She had me drive it down to the repair guy for polishing and a new ribbon about a month ago."

"Heron Bay Office Machines?"

"Yeah. It's in the back of a big old house. You really have to look, but it's on Google Maps."

"Okay, good, thanks." Astrid hangs up and brings out the letters again. She reads through them, compares the typing to her retyped letters from the typewriter. They match except for a few quirks, the replaced type slug, the quality of the ribbon. She rechecks the file marked TYPEWRITER MAINTENANCE AND REPAIR. She lays out the receipts in order. Cleaning, alignment, adjustment, new rubber feet . . . type slug replacement. No mention of a dropped machine.

You have it wrong. Out of order.

"How, Aunt Maude? How do I have it wrong?" Astrid looks at the desk by the window, sees the faint image of her mother hunched over the typewriter, clacking away after Nina died.

Maybe Maude has another file of receipts. Astrid checks the file drawers again—nothing. She checks back through the log of maintenance. It stops at fifteen years ago. Before that, nothing. And yet, the typewriter was here.

She checks the typewriter's carrying case. There's nothing inside except the small brushes. Astrid puts the machine in its case. It's too late to go down to the typewriter repair shop this evening. She's exhausted, yet she doesn't sleep well.

◆ ◆ ◆

Friday morning, she's up early. She drives the typewriter down to the repair shop at 10:00 a.m., opening time. The GPS on her phone directs her right to a big white foursquare Victorian on a shaded side street. There is no sign for a shop—wait, there is, on the mailbox. In small letters are the words HERON BAY OFFICE MACHINES with an arrow pointing toward the rear of the house.

She walks around to the back door and steps inside. The typewriter feels heavy. She is greeted by the smells of old metal and rubber and cleaner and polish. Vintage typewriter ads adorn the walls of a back room, typewriters of various sizes and brands for sale on a high shelf unit to her right, next to tables and filing cabinets. To the left, typewriters are crowded onto more shelves and tables, repair slips attached.

She goes up to the counter, which looks back upon a cluttered workshop populated by typewriters in various states of disrepair—parts, innards, and shells laid out on workstations beneath blazing lamps.

A white-haired man, wearing a loose sweater and a beret, comes forward from the dark recesses of the back room, wiping his blackened fingers on a grimy cloth. "May I help you?" he asks kindly, his gaze dropping to the typewriter case.

"I hope you can," she says, lifting the case onto the countertop. "My aunt brings this typewriter here for maintenance. I think she has done so for years. Maude Dasgupta?"

"How is Maude? I hear she took a fall."

"Wow, word gets around in this town. She's still in the hospital."

He steps back and puts the cloth down on the counter. "I'm very sorry to hear that. She's one tough lady. She'll pull through. Tell her Peter McClain wishes her well."

"I certainly will. I'm Astrid. I'm wondering about this machine." She opens the case on the counter. "Was it ever dropped?"

"No, it's in fine shape. It's a wonderful machine."

"She said it was dropped. Out of order."

He thinks for a moment, hands pressed down on the countertop. "Well, she did drop a typewriter, but it was a long time ago now."

"You said 'a typewriter.' Not this one?"

"Oh no. The dropped one—it typed when she brought it in, but it wasn't going to work again. It was pretty much shot. She was broken up about it. She had that one forever."

"That one." The blood rushes in her ears. The humming of a machine in a back room seems to grow louder. "There was another one."

"Oh yeah—she pleaded with me to fix that thing." He shakes his head, wipes his hands on the cloth again. "I tried. Normally, I wouldn't. Not if a machine is dropped. But Maude has always been a good customer. So, I tried my darndest but . . . She wanted a replacement, but I didn't have another one exactly like it back then. She ended up getting this one here from somewhere else."

She points at Aunt Maude's typewriter. "Let me get this straight. This is not the dropped typewriter."

"No. It's the same model, but it's a different machine."

Astrid's heartbeat rat-a-tats in her ears. "So, the typewriter she had is gone—when exactly did she drop it? I don't have any record of that machine."

He gestures toward a back room. "I keep records in the office. Pretty much never throw anything away."

"Please, could you look? She had only one typewriter back then, correct?"

"Far as I know." He takes off his beret, smooths down his hair, replaces the beret. "I can look a bit if you want to wait."

"Yes, I can wait, please."

He bounces off into the back while she looks around at the ads and the typewriters on shelves. A drawer opens and shuts in the back room, papers shuffle. Finally, he returns with a few sheets of old paper stapled together. He places the papers on the countertop. "Looks to be around . . . fifteen years ago."

Astrid snatches up the papers and flips through them. *Bent typebars, broken ribbon cover, broken space bar* . . . And before that, maintenance receipts showing the typewriter was in good condition before it was dropped. A Corona Standard model like the replacement. But the serial number is different.

She looks up at Mr. McClain. "That other typewriter was the one she had in the house seventeen years ago. It would've been, correct?"

His eyebrows rise, then he lifts the beret and puts it back on again. "Yeah, for sure. It would've been. I took care of that machine for . . . let's see, something like ten years before she dropped it."

"And she's had this new one for almost fifteen years."

"Yup. Everything okay? You look a little pale."

"Yes, um," she says, flustered. "Where did she get this new typewriter if not here at your shop?"

"Oh hell, I can't remember now. Someone local. She never did say."

Astrid steps back, suddenly light-headed. Now what Aunt Maude said in the hospital makes sense. *You have it wrong.*

This typewriter on the countertop, which Rose used to type the letters, was not in Aunt Maude's library seventeen years ago. Aunt Maude didn't even own this typewriter back then. It was somewhere else entirely.

CHAPTER THIRTY

Astrid drives around town for a while, her mind whirling with questions. After picking up a sandwich at the Heron Bay Café, she sits at an outdoor picnic table and tries to clear her head. Did her mother type the letters in someone else's house? Was she somewhere else when she revealed all her thoughts, hallucinations, the worry that her husband was having an affair? If so, where was she?

Maybe Rose typed the letters in the town library. Or in a bookstore—anything is possible. It's clear that she typed the letters. The signatures, the content.

On the way home after lunch, Astrid dials Conor's number, and when he answers, she puts him on speakerphone and explains what she has just discovered.

"Where are you going with this?" he asks. "Are you talking to me in the car? You're breaking the law."

"Just come over," she says.

"I'm out on a few calls—I'll be there in a while."

She drives the rest of the way home, a little too fast. He's always out on other calls . . . but of course, he's working. He hasn't asked her out on another date. What does it matter? Soon, she will have this figured out, Aunt Maude will be home, and Astrid will leave Heron Bay.

Back in Aunt Maude's library, she reads the letters again. It's clear that they were typed on the machine that is here now. She tries to read between the lines. *What am I missing?*

The signature, *Your Rose Petal*, belongs to her mother. Everything she typed seems to check out—her grief, her belief that her daughter is still alive in some way, the break-in at the Michaels mansion. Her belief that her husband had an affair. But she doesn't mention her own affair—if she had one.

Astrid checks through Aunt Maude's filing cabinets again for the postcards bundled together from her mother. In an unsigned early one, there's an image of the Eiffel Tower in Paris with a hastily written note. *Wish you were here. Visited the Louvre and Rodin museums yesterday. You would love it here. See you soon.* The handwriting is very close to the writing in the signatures in the letters, although there is no actual signature on the postcard, which is dated in the early spring of 2004, when Astrid was twelve years old.

Your Rose Petal was likely written by the same person who wrote the postcards from Paris. Rose sometimes traveled on her own, even before the divorce. The important points are the same in the lettering, as Astrid discovered earlier. A few of the postcards are not signed; others are, the later ones when Astrid's mother had become an alcoholic. Her writing changes demonstrably.

Astrid looks up at the wall clock. It's late afternoon. How did so much time pass? Her muscles feel stiff. She pulls on her coat and heads out for a beach walk to stretch her legs. The clean ocean air refreshes her spirit. *What am I still missing?* Aunt Maude's voice echoes in her head. *You have it wrong. Out of order.*

By the time Astrid returns to the house, the sun hangs low in the sky. No word from Conor yet. She tamps down irritation, heats a frozen dinner in the microwave, and stands at the kitchen counter to eat. If Conor were here, she would cook him an elaborate pasta dish or maybe a stir-fry, light candles at the dining table . . . *Don't go there. You're flying back to California soon.*

After dinner, she returns to the library and reads through the letters again, trying to find another clue in the words. The sky dims, a ribbon of pink twilight unfurling across the horizon. The day has passed so quickly, and she's no closer to understanding Aunt Maude's cryptic words.

There's a tentative knock on the front door. She flings it open, expecting Conor. "Thomas, what are you doing here?"

He steps inside, his hair flopping over his eye. "The sheriff asked me about your car. It was towed?"

"Rental car. It was full of water. Somebody flooded it with the hose."

"That's terrible. I didn't do it."

"Okay, I believe you," she says, mostly to pacify him.

"I wanted to talk to you. You know the boat I saw? I think I know who it is. Could I come in?"

"Of course." She steps back to let him in.

He follows her into the kitchen, motions to the table. "Could I sit?"

"Be my guest. Would you like some tea? Juice? I don't have soda."

"Coffee would be good," he says, sitting at the breakfast table, hands in his coat pockets.

"After dinner? How about decaf?"

"Caffeinated is cool. I drink coffee all day. Like Lee Child. You know, the author of the Jack Reacher series? Lee Child drinks like, thirty cups of coffee a day when he's working. Thirty. No exaggeration." His brows furrow, his lips turned down. From this angle, she can see Julian in his features, but his nose and chin are softer, his complexion paler.

"Caffeinated it is. I'll join you in a cup, what the hell." She pours water into the carafe, grounds into the basket. Turns on the machine. "You're going to be a writer like your father now!"

"Livie says I could be. But I also want to be a physicist."

"Livie is a bit older than you, and I'm sure neither of you is set on your future."

"We are. Only Nana's trying to get Livie to leave town."

"What? She can't do that!"

"She's going to accuse Livie of stealing jewelry. She works for us, cleaning and stuff. Livie doesn't steal. I told Nana that would be cruel." His lips begin to quiver.

"Why would she do something like that? Just to break up you and Livie?"

He presses the back of his hand to his forehead. "She thinks Livie isn't good for me. She wants her to go to college in France. She thinks if she goes far away, I'll never follow her."

"You're not even out of high school."

"I love Nana. I don't want her to be so upset all the time. I also love Livie. I'm like, *caught*, you know." He sighs, his eyes a little wild, like he's a trapped animal.

"If you talk to your grandma, you should be able to work things out. Besides, your parents make decisions about things like this. With you, of course."

His face goes slack, his eyes dull. "Yeah, my parents. Right. They don't even love *each other*."

"Your grandparents are the ones you talk to."

He flattens the palm of his hand on the table. "Yeah, you know what? I don't want to talk about this anymore. It's like you're psychoanalyzing me or something."

"I'm not trying to do that. I'm just trying to talk—"

"About the boat. It came into the dock. The guy tied it up there. He walked up through the woods."

Astrid grips the edge of the counter, takes a deep breath. "When was this?"

"Yesterday. I was out hiking up at the lookout. I saw the boat tied up, so I went down to check it out. The man was already walking up through the woods. Then he disappeared. Same boat from before, I swear."

She pours two mugs of coffee, hands him one, and sits across from him, barely able to hold on to her own mug. "How can you be sure?"

Thomas shrugs. "It looked the same. White, same size. Normal-size guy, I guess."

She sips her coffee, trying not to show her alarm. "Must be coincidence. The forest has a lot of trails. I'm surprised more people don't hike through here."

Thomas gulps his coffee, slams the mug on the table. "No, it was him. Same guy, same boat. I got a lot closer this time. I went right up to that boat. I can tell you the name. It had big blue letters on the side. *Blue Descent.*"

CHAPTER THIRTY-ONE

Astrid nearly chokes on her coffee. "Are you certain about the name of the boat?"

"One hundred percent," Thomas says.

"I'll tell Conor. I mean, the sheriff." She looks out at the shadowy trees and shivers. Has Len Wilkers been watching her all this time, slipping through the woods to leave the note for her, to fill her car with water? Was he Nina's biological father? What reason would he have had to kill her? If he were guilty of assaulting his neighbor's daughter, he wouldn't want the past dredged up, new suspicion cast upon him. He lied to her about everything.

Thomas gets up and puts his empty mug in the sink. "The boat might be docked out there now. I could take you up to the lookout. You can see the dock from there."

"It's getting dark," Astrid says, gripping her coffee mug. "I should wait for the sheriff."

"Okay. Hey, thanks for the coffee."

"Thanks for the heads-up."

She walks him back down the hall. He stops and peers into the library. "Are those the letters?"

They're still laid out on the desk next to the postcards. "Yes, the ones my aunt found."

"Typed on that typewriter?" He walks into the room and touches the shiny black Corona Standard that she returned to the shelf.

"That's the one. I analyzed the typewritten text."

"You know for sure—that's pretty cool." He sits at the desk, making himself at home. He picks up a postcard. "Paris, whoa—awesome. My grandma promised to take me there. She loves Paris."

"My mother traveled a lot, too."

"This was 2004, a long time ago, like three years before I was born."

"I forget how young you are," she says. "You seem so grown up."

"I had to raise myself pretty much. Except for my grandma. She has always been around."

"It's good to have someone you can count on. Aunt Maude was—is that person for me."

"She owns a *lot* of books," Thomas says. He puts the postcard back on the desk, gets up, and runs his fingers along the spines of the books on the shelves. He pulls out a book and flips through the pages, his back to her. He shifts from foot to foot, occasionally running his fingers through his hair. Then he puts the book back on the shelf and pulls out another one. "*Robinson Crusoe. The Great Gatsby*, first edition. Jane Austen. My dad reads Jane Austen."

"Let me know if you would like to borrow a book."

"Hey, thanks. I might." He flips through the pages.

She looks at the letters. In the first letter . . . *I slipped inside and looked for evidence of you . . . If I hadn't found out about your betrayal . . .*

Rose broke into the Michaels house, and they never pressed charges. Her father insists there was no betrayal.

The second letter, a letter of confession: *The next thing I knew, she was floating in the water . . . I drowned her.*

Astrid takes a deep, shaky breath. Those words always throw her. And in the third letter: *But I tell you, our daughter never left us. I told Dr. Garwood . . . She stopped short of calling me delusional . . .*

She imagines her mother following the ghost of Nina through the forest. And long before the forest was formed, the land was covered in ice, until the ice retreated and left behind glacially carved valleys, and then hurtling forward in time, the Europeans arrived, bringing smallpox that killed nearly a third of the population of Native people. The ghosts of the past, of earth's history, haunt these woods, mingling with the present, the unknown future. The letters from the past. *Past, present, future . . .*

Out of order.

She thought Aunt Maude meant that the typewriter was broken, out of order. But what if she meant the letters are out of order?

After all, they're not dated.

Fingers trembling, Astrid shuffles the letters around, back and forth—second one first, first one second, third one first. What is the most improbable order?

That Nina died last, that my mother was seeing her dead daughter before she ever drowned. But that is impossible. *Nothing is impossible.* She has seen improbable outcomes. She glances over at Thomas, who still has his nose in a book. He glances sidelong at her, then looks back at the book.

She places the letters in a different chronological order. Backward. No, forward again. In the first letter, her mother is going to do something . . . *Wait. What if the last letter goes first?*

> But I tell you, our daughter never left us. I told Dr. Garwood . . . She stopped short of calling me delusional . . .

And then . . .

> I slipped inside and looked for evidence of you . . . If I hadn't found out about your betrayal . . .

And then, a confession:

> The next thing I knew, she was floating in the water . . . I drowned her.

Our daughter was there. The truth, the answer, nags at the back of her mind, but she can't grasp it . . .

Maybe the order of the letters was right to begin with.

Astrid rearranges them, puts them back in their original order. No, something is wrong, she can feel it.

She mixes them up again, ending with the drowning of Nina. How could Rose have seen her dead daughter *before she actually died*? The signatures match the letters. And only her mother used the nickname *Rose Petal*.

Wait.

Out of order.

Astrid picks up the postcard from France, dated 2004, bundled with the other postcards from her mother. She riffles through all of them. Something is off.

She goes back to the postcard from Paris. Nina was a baby. Rose could not have been in Paris in the summer of 2004. She was home in Seattle, taking care of an infant. Or maybe Rose went to Paris anyway, even with a baby.

I don't remember my mother leaving, Astrid thinks. She had a new baby! She didn't leave.

Astrid shuffles through the postcards. The handwriting is a little different in some of them, in those early, unsigned ones. She needs her equipment at the lab to properly analyze the details, but she can eyeball basic patterns in loops, pushes, and pulls. She assumed that because Aunt Maude was so methodical, she organized everything perfectly. But these postcards are from at least two different people.

Was I comparing the wrong postcards, the wrong handwriting, to the typewritten letters?

She assumed Aunt Maude had bundled together postcards from only her mother in different states of mind. *I should've known better. I should have seen . . .*

Astrid reads the letters again, trying to be completely objective. *Put aside the signature, Rose Petal. Look at the contents of the letter.*

The typist is haunted by the death of her daughter . . .

Nina.

Wait. No.

In the letters, there is no mention of the name Nina.

No mention of Nina.

And yet. *Your Rose Petal.*

Put that aside.

The mention of her husband's affair, breaking into the neighbors' house. Twice pregnant. The other child. Astrid.

But never any names. None.

A cold wind blows through her. "I had it wrong all along," she says aloud, sitting back, goose bumps rippling across her skin. "My mother did not type these letters. But I might know who did."

CHAPTER THIRTY-TWO

Thomas shoves the book back onto the shelf and turns to face her. "Who wrote those letters? If it wasn't your mom?"

She looks up at him, distracted. She was so deep into her analysis, she almost forgot Thomas was here. "Sorry, I was thinking out loud." *I can't tell him what I know—he has no idea.* Verne Michaels gave Aunt Maude her old typewriter, the one she dropped. He must've given her this one, too . . .

"May I see the letters? I'm good at puzzles." He comes close and leans over her.

"I'm not sure you could figure out this one." She hastily folds the letters, and she's about to shove them into a drawer when Thomas snatches them off the desk and stuffs them into his jacket pocket.

Astrid stares at him in shock. "Hey, what are you doing? Give those back!"

He holds up his hands. "Abracadabra. They're gone."

"Is this some kind of game?" *Does he already know?*

"Someone typed the letters on that old machine." He gestures to the typewriter.

A shiver runs through her. "Who owned that machine before, Thomas?" *Beatrice Michaels.* But how? Why? How would she know Rose's nickname? *So many unanswered questions.*

"I'm taking the typewriter—sorry about that." He looks around, making fists and then opening his hands. Sweat breaks out on his forehead.

The hair rises on the back of her neck. Instinct tells her to call Conor, but the phone is on a table behind Thomas. She would have to get past him. "Why are you protecting your grandmother, Thomas? Did she confess something to you?"

"My nana wouldn't hurt a flea." He paces back and forth in the library, hands in and out of his bulky pockets. "You wouldn't leave. You won't let anything go."

"You left me that note," Astrid says.

"It wasn't my writing," he says.

"It was also your grandmother's." The writing was similar to Julian's but not exactly the same. "You filled the rental car with water."

He says nothing, keeps pacing. "She said you would leave, and I would be able to find the letters, but I couldn't. Livie looked for them, too. She had the house key."

"I thought she was acting strangely. So it wasn't all about the lost camisole."

"I asked for her help . . . but then you found the letters. Too bad."

"Your grandmother is manipulating you!" Astrid says.

"Nana loves me—"

"Enough to bypass your dad and leave you the estate?"

"My grandparents are moving back to New York, where they lived before, closer to hospitals. I'm staying here. I love Livie. Nana will make Livie leave if I don't—"

"If you don't what?" Astrid is standing now, the arched doorway at the corner of her vision, how many steps away? Ten, maybe. Too far. Thomas would lunge between her and the door before she could get there. He is already between her and the telephone. Outside, the wind rushes through the trees.

"If I don't help her." He gives her a pleading look. "You're making me do this."

"Nobody can make you do anything. Your grandmother cannot *make* Livie do anything. She lives with her own parents. She's older than eighteen—"

"Nana has it on video—I loaned Livie a necklace of my grandma's when she wasn't home. I didn't know Nana put a camera in her room—"

In her room. Not *their* room, not the room Beatrice shares with Verne.

"Talk to your dad. You have the letters now. You can talk to your dad about your grandmother."

"No, I can't. It will mess everything up. He'll send me to a boarding school. It's what he wanted to do anyway—my mom, too. Nana convinced them not to."

Thomas is completely brainwashed, Astrid thinks. "You need to leave," she says in her most authoritative voice, hoping he will crack. She points at the door. "Right now. Or I'll call the sheriff." *Which I already did.*

Thomas grabs a pair of scissors from the penholder on the desk. For a split second, she thinks he's going to stab her, but instead, he cuts the telephone cord, then tosses the scissors onto the desk. "Cell phones don't work here."

Damn it. "You don't want to do this. Put the letters on the desk and go home, and I'll forget any of this happened."

"But you won't," he says in a slight whine. "I can't give back the letters." He fishes in his pocket and brings out something metallic, dulled by years. An old gun—probably from his grandfather's collection. He points it at her with a shaky hand.

Her lips go numb, her heart nearly stopping. *Don't show panic. It's probably not loaded. He's just a kid.* "You're not serious about this," she says. "Think what will happen if you get caught! You won't see Livie—"

"Shut up, shut up!" He steps back, holding the gun out, pointed at her head.

"Be careful—if it's loaded, it could go off." Her heart is beating in her throat.

"It's loaded. My grandpa taught me how to shoot cans—a long time ago, but I remember. I won't miss—"

"You don't want to shoot anyone. You're not like that. You could hurt *yourself* if you try to shoot it. It could backfire."

"I know how to use it," he says.

"Does he know you have it?" Her heartbeat races in her ears.

"Hell no. He'd beat the shit out of me."

Buy time, talk him down. Take a gun seriously, she tells herself, although a part of her doesn't believe he is actually doing this.

"You tried to scare me away. You knew your grandmother typed these letters. Do you even know why? Do you know what she might have done?"

"You have to . . . write a note, okay?" He waves the gun toward the desk. "Sit back down and write what I tell you."

"What if I let you leave and forget this ever happened?"

"Now! Just sit." He starts to cry a little, then stops and steels his expression. "Do what I say. Take out paper and a pen. Now."

She opens the drawer, takes out paper and pen. "Let's talk about this. This isn't who you are."

"What are you, some big-time counselor now?" He's growing bolder now that he's holding a gun.

"You're a promising young man. I want to help you. We're friends."

He laughs—an unfamiliar, grating sound. "How can we be friends? Write." He stands in front of the desk, pointing the gun at her head.

She should be more afraid. *Maybe I am, maybe I'm in shock.*

But part of her still doesn't even believe this is happening. She will wake in her apartment surrounded by boxes. She is hyperaware of the rush of air through the vents, the distant, relentless tide, back and forth. The pull of the moon, which is just now rising, indifferent to the crisis below.

"What do you want me to write?" she asks.

"You're depressed. You drowned your sister."

"Her death was already ruled an accident—years ago."

"You've always been guilty. You can't forgive yourself."

"Why not take the letters and go? I'll leave town. I was going to leave anyway."

"Write that you can't go on." His voice cracks, and she feels he is reciting words someone else gave him.

"Nobody is going to believe that." She tries to hold his gaze, willing herself to ignore the gun. He won't look at her. The gun wavers in his hand.

"Hurry up." He is sweating profusely now.

"Len Wilkers never had anything to do with this. Did he? How did you know the name of his boat?"

"We have something called *the internet*." His voice is as shaky as the gun. He shifts his weight and hardens his jaw. "You killed your little sister. You were jealous. You held her head underwater and now you can't live with yourself."

"Why do I have to confess?" she says, trying to keep her voice calm. "I didn't do anything. It has been a long time."

"People feel guilty forever. Hurry up."

Her hand shaking, she writes what Thomas wants her to write.

I held her underwater . . .

I can't live with what I've done . . . I am a killer.

She slants the handwritten words to the left, the opposite of her normal style, so that Conor will know she was under duress. He may not see the note in time. But surely, he will know the truth.

"Are you finished?" Thomas snaps, the gun still pointed at her.

She nods, sitting back in the chair, looking down at her strange handwriting.

"Sign it, now!"

She signs the letter. "Now what?"

"We go." He nudges her to her feet, and she walks to the back door, aware of him behind her. She puts on her sneakers, laces them up.

"What if nobody finds the note?" she asks.

"The sheriff will come looking for you. Somebody will find it."

"You don't have to do this. The sheriff will know you've been here."

"Nobody will know. I'm not even here. I'm on a boat home."

"Someone's giving you an alibi? The sheriff will see through it. He'll know you're a murderer."

Thomas pushes her outside into the blustery night. "This isn't a murder—it's a suicide."

She can hear her own labored breathing, and he shoves her toward the trail. She considers taking off, running, but he'll shoot her. They follow the trails winding through the woods. "We can go back," she says.

"Shut up."

She takes a turnoff heading to the beach, but Thomas yanks her arm and spins her toward the uphill trail. They're taking the switchbacks now, up and up, the gun pressing into her back. Her breath comes in shallow, ragged gasps. The gun could go off accidentally, at any moment. The foliage rustles, birds flitting in the shadows, unseen. *This can't be it,* Astrid thinks. *I have to get word back to Conor, to Aunt Maude. Beatrice typed the letters, but why? And how did she know Rose's nickname? Why use it?* "Thomas, your grandma isn't the person you think she is."

"You're framing her. She said she saw you."

"No, she didn't. She's lying," Astrid says, stopping on a steep incline.

Thomas prods her forward. "You held her underwater. My nana saw you, but she didn't want you to get in trouble. You were a kid."

Astrid can't catch her breath. "Why would I do that?"

"You hated your sister. You were jealous of her. Nana said your mom loved her more. You feel so guilty, but those letters make it look like Nana did it. But she would never do that. Ever."

Astrid starts laughing, gasping for breath, stumbling along the trail. "You really believe this?"

"I wasn't even alive. I believe her."

"What she's telling you is wrong." They're at the top, the sign ahead of them illuminated beneath the moon: FALLING CAN BE DEADLY . . .

Please Stay on the Trail. The wind is blowing, whipping back her hair, and she realizes that everything Thomas has told her, about her culpability, was already inside her. She believed it herself.

"Go," Thomas says, pushing her. "You're going to jump."

She slides dangerously close to the edge. Time slows. The dashing of the surf against the rocks below seems suddenly muted. She stands at the edge of a precipice, the ocean rippling away to the horizon. Moonlight plays upon the water, and she imagines all the ships that have passed these shores, the wooden boats that furled their sails while navigating into the harbor. The forests that once grew densely all the way down to the water. The sea will rise and erode the shore, and one day, this cliff will be gone. She is not the first one to die here, and she will not be the last.

She turns to face Thomas, the young and uncertain teenager. "You don't want to do this," she says. "You know it's wrong."

But his eyes are metal. Nothing penetrates. He points the gun at her. "Jump."

"What if I don't die? What if I hit my head on a rock and—"

"You will. We're high up."

"Is this what you want for the rest of your life?"

"You did this," he says, stepping closer to her. The gun shakes in his hand. Beatrice has him wrapped around her finger, with her lies, her frailty, a promise of inheritance—or the threat of losing it.

"You're not going to shoot me," she says. She teeters at the edge, trying not to look down. Her foot slips. She scrambles up onto the embankment.

"Why wouldn't I?" he says.

"Because you don't want to kill anyone. You want to protect your grandmother."

"You have no idea what I want," he says, taking another step closer. The wind ruffles his hair.

Just past him, she can see the opening in the woods to the trail. A huge boulder with smaller rocks scattered on the ground.

"You know an old gun like that is traceable, and the evidence will still be in my body." She does not know if this is true, but she has nothing to lose.

"There won't be any gun. It'll be long gone."

"Stop now—turn and walk away. We can say this never happened."

His face crumples. He gestures with his free hand. "But it happened, didn't it? You wrote that note, and we're here now." He starts to cry a little again, a hiccuping sound. He wipes away the tears, keeps his grip on the gun.

There's a crackle in the woods—a deer or a raccoon—and in that moment, Thomas falters, turning slightly toward the sound. Astrid lunges for him, knocks the gun, and it arcs through the air in slow motion, landing in the dirt. He staggers backward, and she scrambles across the ground, but he yanks her arm, nearly pulling it from the socket. She manages to stumble away. He shoves her, and she falls into the dirt, the wind knocked out of her. This can't be happening. She and Thomas were supposed to play duets together. He needs to start school. He's throwing his life away.

The gun—where is it? There, glinting dully in the moonlight. She manages to kick it toward the brush. Thomas leaps for it, swipes at her face—socks her in the cheek. Pain blasts through her, a shattering detonation. *My bone is broken,* she thinks.

She can feel herself falling, spots bursting out in her vision. As the world spins, she crawls toward the rocks. She must've kicked the gun in this direction. Thomas grabs for her pant leg, almost catches her. "Thomas, stop!" she shouts. "You . . . can . . . stop."

But he keeps coming, a wild look in his eyes. *There's no reasoning with him,* she thinks in a panic. He's pulling her toward him, his grip tight on her pants, nearly ripping them off her.

She kicks hard, keeps kicking until he lets go for a split second. Then she twists away and rolls on the ground, feeling around for a weapon. Something, anything. She grabs the nearest rock, swings around, and punches him hard in the nose. The cracking sound makes her wince. He lets out a strangled cry and presses his hands to his face. Blood seeps from his nose.

She drops the rock, her hands shaking, gets up, and lurches toward the trail. "Get back here!" Thomas slurs behind her. He still has the letters. The evidence. But if she turns back toward him . . . *Go, leave, now,* she tells herself. She blunders forward, and then, not looking back, she breaks into a run.

CHAPTER THIRTY-THREE

When she reaches Aunt Maude's garden, her lungs screaming, Astrid dares to glance back over her shoulder. No sign of Thomas. What if he fell unconscious? What if she killed him? *No, I only broke his nose. I acted in self-defense. Don't think about it now.* She bursts into the house through the back door, locks it after her, flips on the kitchen light. She stops to catch her breath, then rushes into the hall and picks up the phone. No dial tone. Did Thomas cut both lines? But she didn't see him cut this one. Sweating, her heart hammering, she runs into the guest room and grabs her cell phone, purse, and the keys to Aunt Maude's Honda. Surely Conor is on his way by now.

A clacking sound stops her cold. She holds her breath. Again, more clacking. *Coming from the library.* For a split second, she imagines her mother in there, tapping out a letter to her father.

Barely breathing, Astrid grips the keys in her hand and walks down the hall, a board squeaking under her shoe. No use in trying to be quiet. Whoever broke into the house must've heard her come back in. She stands in the doorway to the library. Beatrice sits at her aunt's desk, the typewriter in front of her, a sheet of paper in the machine. The note Astrid wrote sits next to the typewriter.

"What are you doing here?" Astrid blurts. "I didn't see your car."

"I parked on the road." Beatrice looks up at Astrid, not seeming to see her. "Verne should've kept this typewriter. He never should've given it away."

"Do you know what your grandson has been up to?"

Beatrice scrapes back the chair and leaps to her feet. "Where is Thomas? Is he all right?"

Astrid leans over the desk and grabs the letter she wrote. "He tried to kill me. But you knew that, didn't you?"

"He—what?" Beatrice blinks, her eyes wide. "He would never do such a thing. Where is he?"

"He's alive, which is more than you wanted for me, isn't it? He's got the letters, the ones *you* typed."

"I have no idea what you're talking about." Beatrice's voice becomes feathery, ragged.

"Now you *are* starting to sound like my mother."

There's a flash of movement in the woods. Beatrice turns toward the window. "Well, I knew she was out there."

"Who?" Astrid says, the hair prickling on her arms. *Beatrice said* she.

Beatrice stares out the window, entranced, then turns and sits in the chair again, sliding it back to the desk. She rests her fingers on the typewriter keys.

Astrid walks up to the desk. "I know you typed the letters on this typewriter when it belonged to you. But why did you pretend to be my mother?"

Beatrice laughs softly, pretends to type, her fingers barely touching the keys. "I never had to pretend to be anyone."

"You typed the letters to Verne? You signed my mother's name."

"It did surprise him," she says, the right corner of her lip rising. "Your mother was a home-wrecker."

"You broke in here looking for evidence of Verne. It wasn't the other way around. My mother never broke into your house. That was a lie."

Beatrice rests her hands in her lap and sits up straight. "I came to know this house better than I ever knew my own. Do you know how much I loved Verne? Still love him?" She swivels in the chair again to look out into the darkness.

"Who are you seeing out there?" Astrid asks. She thinks of the letters. *Our daughter . . . in her white, fairy-tale nightgown.* "Oh my God. You had a daughter, didn't you?"

Beatrice doesn't reply. She just stares off into the night.

"At Julian's place, I saw photographs of your niece. Flora, isn't it? She looked like Nina. But Flora was your daughter, wasn't she?"

"You saw Julian? How is he?" Beatrice turns back toward the typewriter, her face placid.

"You were seeing your daughter everywhere. You said your niece died, your sister's daughter, but then you said you were an only child. How could you be both? Julian said your older sister died. Did you ever even have an older sister?"

"Julian should visit more often," Beatrice says plaintively.

"He never knew. He still doesn't, does he? He thinks Flora was his cousin who died before he was born, and you never told him the truth. Verne went along with your charade." Astrid is only guessing, going out on a limb. She watches carefully as Beatrice's expression goes blank, then her face slowly implodes. Her lips tremble, tears spilling from her eyes.

I never again wanted to see grief on a mother's face, Astrid thinks. "How many years has it been now? How long has Flora been gone?"

Beatrice gets up and totters to the doorway. She grips the doorjamb for support.

"You never named your daughter in the letters," Astrid says. "Flora is such a lovely name."

"Oh, Flora, Flora," Beatrice whispers, turning toward Astrid. "Verne wanted that name. It was his mother's . . . I went along, but I was never fond of his mother. So, I couldn't bring myself to write the name." Her voice breaks a little.

"But why did you lie? Why did you say Flora was your niece?"

Beatrice sniffs a little but does not reply.

"I'm sorry you lost your daughter," Astrid says. "I can imagine what it was like—"

"How could you possibly? Imagine?" Beatrice snaps, her face turning to stone.

"I lost a sister! And you might have killed her. Why? Did you hold her underwater?"

Beatrice looks off down the hall, her chest heaving, her hand still gripping the doorjamb. "Thomas has the letters. Where is Thomas? I tried to find them. I did."

"Was Nina Verne's biological daughter? Was it revenge? Why, Beatrice?" Her voice shakes with rage. *Calm down,* she tells herself. *Beatrice didn't know what she was doing. But she is responsible. I had nothing to do with my sister's death. I was only a kid.*

Astrid yanks the paper out of the typewriter. Beatrice has typed gibberish, random letters and numbers.

The older woman crumples to the floor, her shoulders shaking. She sobs silently, with abandon, all her composure dissolving.

There's a commotion in the woods. Astrid rushes to the window. By the light of the moon, she can see Thomas stumbling into the garden. Blood runs from his swollen nose. He appears dazed. He staggers up the front steps and bangs on the door. He's yelling incoherently.

Please let the door hold, Astrid thinks. "Beatrice, tell Thomas to stay back."

Beatrice doesn't reply. Her breathing is labored—she collapses on her side on the floor, curled into a fetal position.

"Are you all right? Talk to me!" Astrid kneels next to Beatrice, who is sweating, her skin pale.

More banging on the door. The wood begins to splinter. Thomas is yelling, cursing Astrid as a siren approaches, growing louder. A car rumbles up the driveway, and the room fills with blue light.

CHAPTER THIRTY-FOUR

Ten days later

At the top of the hill, the pastor is already reading from scripture. The memorial service is small, a tight-knit group of family members and a few friends. Beatrice wanted to be buried with stone sculptures on her grave. The smallest statues have been transported here—a squirrel, a rabbit, a fox—each one a couple of feet tall. The gigantic statues are still in the woods, where they will crumble and disappear, eventually lost to time.

Thomas stands near the grave with a police officer by his side. He was allowed out of juvenile detention to attend the service. He looks like a pale sheet of paper. He stands between Julian and Verne, everyone dressed in black. And the statuesque, stunning woman with flowing, dark hair, straight off the cover of *Vogue*, is Julian's wife. She stands apart from the rest of the family, pushes her hair back, and looks down at the grass while the pastor speaks of walking through the valley of the shadow of death.

Astrid sympathizes with the boy, who has lost the woman who showed him the most affection, albeit in a manipulative way. Other family members gather around, dressed impeccably.

All in black, Livie stands off to the side, away from the Michaels family, with her parents and a boy and girl who might be her siblings. Among a small group of Beatrice's friends, Astrid spots Dr. Garwood.

"Are you sure you want to be here?" Astrid asks Maude, who is a little wobbly on her feet.

Maude nods. She insisted on honoring the Beatrice she had once known, the kind and generous neighbor.

Thomas won't catch Astrid's eye. A bandage covers his swollen, bruised nose. He stares longingly at Livie, but she won't return his gaze. Her mother, who looks remarkably like her, with reddish curls, holds on to her daughter's arm. Livie's father is a thin, receding sort of man—in his affect and his hairline.

It's Verne who catches Astrid's eye. He keeps looking at her. He is not crying, but his shoulders are slumped, his face sagging with weariness. He seems lost in an oversize black suit. *Some broken things can never be fixed,* Astrid thinks. She still has a bruise on her cheek where Thomas struck her, but she was not badly injured, at least not physically.

After the service, as everyone offers condolences, Aunt Maude and Conor move off toward the car. Astrid approaches Dr. Garwood. "You knew Beatrice typed those letters. She was seeing you. But you didn't tell me."

Dr. Garwood gives her a sad, sympathetic smile. "You know I couldn't."

"I understand, I think," Astrid says. "But she could've been dangerous . . ."

"The letters were typed years ago. I'm sorry about what happened. I didn't realize Thomas was involved."

"Well, it's all over now, isn't it? Beatrice is gone. Maybe I pushed her too hard." Astrid turns away.

Dr. Garwood grabs her arm. "She had heart trouble. She chose to go to your aunt's house. If she hadn't collapsed there, it would've happened somewhere else."

Astrid pulls her arm away and gives Dr. Garwood a polite smile. "Thanks for the reassurance," she says and heads for the car. She spots Verne rushing across the grass toward her. He walks with that familiar left-leaning lope, and she flashes on a distant memory of that night long ago, when she followed Julian into the woods.

"It was you," she says when Verne catches up to her.

"Excuse me?" he says, a little breathless from exertion.

"The night my sister drowned, I saw you in the woods. I thought you were Julian. Why didn't I realize?"

"We see what we want to see." He looks down at his shoes, then at her, his eyes red-rimmed and puffy. "We should talk. But not here. Not now. I have something to give you."

"I hope it's not a gun or a typewriter."

"Tomorrow morning, at the house."

"All right. But I can't stay long." She glances back at Conor, who is walking Aunt Maude to the car. He looks over his shoulder at her and raises his eyebrows. Astrid waves at him and looks at Verne again. "What about Len Wilkers? My dad saw my mother on his boat."

Verne chuckles, shakes his head, and shoves his hands into the pockets of his pressed black trousers. "Did he now? What did he think he saw?"

"Her hat . . ."

"But not Mr. Wilkers. You forget," Verne says, winking at her. "I had a boat, too."

CHAPTER THIRTY-FIVE

"Are you sure you want to do this?" Conor asks the next morning, getting out of the car. He parked at the bottom of the Michaelses' long, winding driveway, which opens onto Uptown Road.

"I need answers," Astrid says, "and Verne Michaels might be the only one who can give them to me."

Halfway up the driveway, a For Sale sign, posted by Heron Bay Realty, is prominently displayed beneath a cedar tree. The forest here smells sweet, like autumn. Dry fallen leaves blanket the soil. Birds twitter through the undergrowth. Conor reaches for her hand again as they walk, and it feels natural to hold on to him. She feels a strange flutter of anticipation, a sensation she hasn't had in years.

As they approach the Michaels mansion, the family's unspoken secrets seep from the stucco siding. Why didn't she notice the mossy steps before? The cracks in the patio stones? The house gives off an air of neglect.

So much heartache hides in these walls. No wonder Julian rarely comes back here with his son, and yet, he didn't move too far away. He must have felt his mother's character, the grief she carried with her, the way her emotions twisted into knots. Her delusions.

Before they even knock on the front door, it creaks open, a thin young woman answering, bucket in hand. Not Livie. She quit. "You're here to see Mr. Michaels," the young woman says. She's wearing vinyl cleaning gloves. "He's in the study." She nods to the left, down the hall.

They step inside the foyer, which opens into the spacious living room with sliding glass doors leading out to that expansive patio. Astrid can see the ghosts of partygoers clinking glasses, laughing and dancing to the music from a live band.

On the walls, photographs of the family depict happier days. They're laughing and running on the beach, Julian graduates from university, he poses with his wife and son, Verne and Beatrice gather with other relatives. And the little girl, Flora, runs on the beach, holding a plastic pail and shovel.

Astrid aches for the family's loss, for Beatrice's loss—for what it led her to do. And for Verne, a man of whom she knows so little. How did he react to the loss of little Flora? By leaving his family, leaving reminders of her, and seeking solace with another woman? Were there more women than her mother?

Conor seems to sense her nervousness. He holds her hand again as the housekeeper leads them down the hall, a bucket of soapy water weighing down her right arm. She nods through an open doorway. "Go on in," she says and lumbers off down the hall.

Astrid goes in alone. Verne Michaels is sitting behind a gigantic, antique desk, his tall frame silhouetted by the window behind him. All along one wall, legal textbooks fill the bookshelves, the spines nearly identical. Astrid takes the single chair on this side of the desk.

He looks up at her. He's writing by hand in a ledger. The room lacks a computer or even a typewriter. Stepping into his office is like stepping back in time to the smells of ink, rubber, and leather.

He closes the ledger and sits back in his chair, looking at her. She tries to imagine what her mother saw in him. Power? Sympathy? A man who paid attention to her when her husband was always distracted? Oh, he is still handsome, still authoritative.

She pulls the three typewritten letters, which Conor retrieved from Thomas, out of her pocket and slides them across the desk. "These were in a book, in the box of books you donated to the library. Aunt Maude told me. You knew the letters were inside. You addressed the box to my aunt."

He does not pick up the letters. "Did I? Or perhaps it was an accident. I was cleaning out the house, you see. Preparing to put it on the market. I didn't mean to donate that book—it must've been stuck in with the others. The letters were in there for so long . . . I think Beatrice had forgotten they were there as well."

"No, you knew. Tell me why you decided to give them to Aunt Maude."

"I didn't decide, but somehow—I'm not sure how—Beatrice found out and went over to see your aunt."

"You should've told the sheriff!"

"There was nothing to tell. Beatrice had nothing to do with what happened to your aunt. Maude must've fallen. I regret that she was injured."

"Do you regret your affair with my mother?"

He swivels in his chair to look out the window toward the stone patio. "Oh no, never. I used to sit in here sometimes and watch our guests. The patio goes all the way around. I saw your mother walking back here on her own, and I thought she was the most beautiful creature I'd ever seen."

"More beautiful than your wife."

"Oh, without a doubt. Rose couldn't see me watching her. I sat here in the dark and admired her for quite some time. I watched her smoke a whole cigarette."

"My mother didn't smoke."

"Oh yes, she did. But only now and then. And not when she was pregnant."

"How do you know that?"

"She told me. She wrote to me. And, of course, I asked about the baby."

"You thought it might be yours."

"Why wouldn't I? She told me she was taking birth control pills, but evidently, she wasn't. Or they failed."

Astrid feels the sting of her own lies to Trent—lies that she cannot take back. "Beatrice was beautiful," she says. "And elegant and generous in her own way."

"We did love each other, at first. But then."

"Then Flora died."

"Every time I looked at Beatrice, I saw Flora. It was unbearable. Something changes in a marriage."

"Why did Beatrice pretend Flora was her niece?"

He swivels back to face Astrid. His eyes are still a little red—perhaps from tears, or perhaps he's merely tired. "At first, when Flora got sick, Beatrice thought she had a cold. Flora was always catching whatever virus was going around. But when I got home from work that night, I realized that our daughter was extremely ill. I couldn't wake her. We rushed her to the hospital, and the doctors diagnosed her with a rare form of meningitis. She died a day later. Beatrice was devastated. She felt responsible. She thought that if only she had tried to wake Flora . . ."

"But how could Beatrice have known? It wasn't her fault."

"I tried to tell her, but I could not console her. We were living in New York at the time. I brought her to Heron Bay for a change of scenery. Nobody here had ever known Flora. But when a guest saw a photograph on the wall, Beatrice made up a story about a niece. Just like that. She could keep her own daughter alive in her imagination, while telling everyone that someone else had died."

"You went along because—"

"The story comforted Beatrice. How could I contradict her? But her delusions were more difficult for me. She often believed she actually saw Flora. The psychiatrist didn't help."

"Did Beatrice know about you and my mother back then?"

"Oh, I think she suspected our attraction to one another. Your mother and I did not act upon our feelings for a few years—until one day, we did."

"Beatrice typed the letters after she found out about the affair."

"I meant to destroy them." He riffles through the letters with gnarled fingers. He looks up at her, and she catches a glimpse of the man he used to be. Striking, forceful. But her fourteen-year-old eyes were set on Julian all those years ago.

"Beatrice tried to kill my aunt to get those letters back," Astrid says.

"It was an unfortunate accident. Beatrice didn't hurt anyone. I'm sure she simply went there to retrieve the letters and avoid a scandal. Our grandson's name dragged through the mud. The wrongful-death lawsuit, which was sure to happen, would've been the end of us. And Beatrice hated reminders of your sister. Nina looked far too much like Flora."

"You had the letters seventeen years ago. The confession! You should've gone to the police."

"The letters were full of imaginings. Made-up stories."

"When Beatrice typed you those letters—where were you?"

"I'd returned to the city for work. You probably don't remember, but I was not in many of the photographs."

"Before that, you were in Aunt Maude's house with my mother? That was pretty brazen."

"Now and then, yes." He smiles slightly.

"Did you love my mother?" she says, leaning forward. "Or was she just a dalliance?"

He looks right at her. "Yes, yes, I did. I would've left my wife for her."

"But you didn't."

"Well, that was not my choice. You should know that by now. I wanted to be with your mother. Your father was in love with the forest. And my wife was . . . unbalanced. She thought she saw Flora quite often, actually."

"And then she just . . . at that pool . . ."

He leans forward and points a finger at Astrid. "Nobody knows what happened at that pool. Nobody. Beatrice was in a fugue state. A dream state."

"But she was an adult, and she was there. She confessed."

"Nobody will ever know for sure."

Astrid grits her teeth, looking around at the ostentatious house, the gilded law books. The evidence of indulgence. "That night, you were with my mother at the house, after my dad left the party. Beatrice went looking for you. That was when she found Nina at the reflecting pool."

"If you say so," he says, a faint smile on his lips.

"My mother did come home. She was talking to you. Then you left. I wish I'd caught up with you in the woods."

"I did not see your sister. I did not know she was out there." He looks at her directly, and she doesn't know if he is telling the truth. But what she heard and saw that night did not come from her imagination. It was all real.

On her phone, she swipes through to the photograph taken that night. Her mother is staring off toward the front of the picture. "My mother was looking at you. That was your Bulova watch."

He brings the old watch out of a drawer. "I always keep this. You see, your mother gave it to me."

"You let her go on believing that she was responsible for Nina's death. You let her blame *me*."

"Why should anyone blame you?"

Why? She gapes, unable to reply.

"Beatrice was angry with me, after she found the letter from your mother—she started signing her letters the same way, *Rose Petal*."

"What letter from my mother?" Astrid grips the arms of the chair.

"Indeed. I didn't know she had typed me a letter about our child, Nina. She said she was almost certain Nina was mine. My wife intercepted the letter, and . . . the cat was out of the proverbial bag. Your mother thought I had rejected her because I never replied. But I had no idea about the note, about Nina . . ."

"That was how Beatrice found out about my mother's nickname."

"Yes, Beatrice held on to the letter. I returned to the city for a while. Then she began sending me letters signed by your mother. Fantasies, delusions. That night, I returned . . . I was at Maude's house, hashing things out with your mother . . ."

"You and my mother came upstairs to check on Nina. My mother said, 'Such a likeness . . . I swear.'"

"That was when I knew—what my wife never told me, the message that she had intercepted. Your mother told me that night when I came back. I was leaving to confront my wife—"

Astrid draws a sharp breath, the air filled with poisonous lies. She could scream, run, throw something. "My mother said she was coming from the party—"

"She had to say that, didn't she? She was on her way back there looking for your father, to see if he'd returned. But where was he? Your father had absconded and abdicated his responsibilities. Why didn't you blame him?"

She gets up and steps back. "I'm growing weary of the blame game. I lost my sister. And so much more."

"So did I," he says, his eyes tired. "I said I needed to give you something." He reaches into his desk drawer and pulls out a folded, faded piece of paper. He gets up and hands it to Astrid. As she unfolds the paper, she can see that the letter was typed on a different typewriter, not the one now in Aunt Maude's library.

> Dear Verne,
> These last days with you have been a wonderful escape, but we can't go on like this. I love Bjorn. I can't leave him. But you deserve to know. I believe that Nina is yours. The timing is right, as you said. Strange to think you lost a child so much like Nina, and now here she is. She will need your support.
> At times, I think Bjorn knows the truth, and I feel him drifting away. He tries to love Nina, but I catch him looking at her askance. I'm full of regret and fear.

It took this possibility of losing him to make me realize that I can't live without him.

The nickname he gave me, I must keep for him now—I am his Rose Petal, no longer yours. I could have loved you, Verne, if we'd met in another time or in another universe. Maybe I would've been Your Rose Petal instead.

With gratitude,
Rose

CHAPTER THIRTY-SIX

Six months later

Life is slower here in Heron Bay, the sounds different, following the natural rhythm of the ocean. On her morning walk, Astrid stops to watch a great blue heron standing motionless in the shallows, its reflection rippling in the calm water. In the distance, a harbor seal surfaces, spouts, and draws a breath, then dives under again. Cormorants with long black necks and narrow beaks ride the waves, occasionally ducking under to catch fish. Stray northern seabirds, lingering here although springtime has come and they can fly back north, bob on the waves in spectacular black and white.

She has also come to know the wildlife dwelling in the protected forest behind the house, extending north along the coast, past the old Michaels house on the bluff. She has not yet met the new owners. She has been back here only two months.

Her past life is fading in the rearview mirror. Back at her Vallejo apartment, when she was packing up, she invited Trent to come over and talk to her. He didn't want to come at first. He made excuses. But when she told him she was moving to Heron Bay, Washington, he exhaled as if relieved, and he agreed to stop by to say goodbye to her, and to listen to what she had to say. He sat in her diminutive living room, his shoulders hunched, looking around at the boxes as yet unpacked. She planned to simply forward them to Heron Bay. She felt a stab of nostalgia when he refused a cup of coffee but took a cup of herbal tea, then tapped on the side of the cup in his thoughtful way.

For the first time, she explained to Trent that she'd been charged with babysitting her sister that night, that Nina had drowned in shallow water, that Astrid had followed someone she believed to be Julian, her teenage hormones getting the best of her. She told him about all the nightmares, about how she didn't trust herself to take care of a child. "I should've told you all this before, when we were together. I shouldn't have hidden the birth control pills."

Trent nodded, frowning, a fleeting look of sadness passing through his eyes. But she knew in that moment that he had really loved her. *Some broken things can never be fixed,* she thought.

He did not accuse her or admonish her. He simply got up, took a deep breath, and gave her a hug. "I wish the best for you, Astrid," he said.

"And I for you," she replied.

As he opened the door, he turned to face her. "We were both responsible for what happened to us," he said. "It wasn't because of the birth control pills, or what you kept from me . . . We could've dealt with that."

Flustered, she said, "But you said my lies broke us."

"My expectations, your lies, we didn't meet in the middle. I could've been more understanding. I could've asked you what you wanted. I've learned a lot since then."

"Well, you got what you wanted. You and Leona will have a family."

"The pregnancy," he says. "It wasn't planned. She was using birth control . . . but it failed. She got pregnant by accident."

Then he left. Astrid felt, afterward, as if a weight had been lifted, her assumptions turned upside down.

She did not speak to Leona again, and she has removed her former best friend's contact information from her phone. The gap in Astrid's heart is beginning to fill with new friends, and there is much work involved in transferring her business to Heron Bay. She is looking to the future.

She helps her aunt walk out through the garden toward the cottage, one step at a time as Maude leans on her cane. "I should've told you about this years ago," Maude says, taking the path slowly. "Your mother felt Nina here. I couldn't begrudge her that. I feel her here, too, but not in the same way. I cherish my memories of her. But I wasn't going to let grief drive me away from my home."

"I'm glad you stayed." Astrid holds her aunt's elbow.

Maude chuckles and waves her hand dismissively. "Oh, honey, you fuss over me. If I fall, I'm just going to land in the dirt."

"I worry—you hit your head."

"Not because I'm unstable. Beatrice pushed me, remember?"

"The thud I heard in your voice mail—"

"Honestly, I don't remember even calling you. Beatrice must've come in and shut the door. I don't remember anything after I got home from my beach walk. Perhaps that's a blessing."

"You said in your message that you meant to tell me about the key."

"Only that I'd left an extra house key under a flowerpot on the porch. I was planning to go for a walk—and I thought you might arrive while I was gone."

"That's it? It was that simple?"

"Sometimes a key is just a key," Aunt Maude says and winks. "Come with me. I want to show you something."

"Are you sure you should be taking long walks yet?"

"If not now, then when?" Aunt Maude grins. She looks vibrant, ageless. "I've been given a second chance, which is more than I can say for poor Beatrice."

"You still have compassion for her." Astrid walks beside her aunt on the stone path that winds past the lavender beds, the rosemary and tiger lilies, the gardens surrounded by stone borders.

"She suffered a great loss—she was not so different from your mother. But Beatrice was even more lost, you see. I truly believe she died of a broken heart."

"But Flora died so long ago. When Beatrice saw Nina in the reflecting pool, her little girl had been gone for many years."

Aunt Maude stops and holds Astrid's wrist, forcing Astrid to stop walking, too, and look into her aunt's eyes. Reflecting the sun, they look light brown, almost golden. "You of all people should know that grief pays no heed to the passing of time," Aunt Maude says. "When you've lost a loved one, twenty years could be one year. One year could be one month or no time at all. Sometimes when I wake, I feel your uncle Raj next to me. I can hear his voice suggesting we hike up into the mountains. *Day trip,* he used to say. *Let's pack a lunch.*" She touches her temple. "He's in my head all the time. Beatrice—I understand her."

"Aunt Maude, she nearly killed you."

"She wasn't herself."

"Maybe she was. And my mother?"

"She thought Nina was sending her signs. It was her spirit, you see. But then Rose closed down completely. She thinks she has moved on with all that traveling, but she has barely taken one step away from the reflecting pool."

One step away. Astrid's mother fled as far as she could from pain, but pain stuck to her like burs wherever she went. "She's like one of those crumbling stone statues."

"I would not be so unkind. People grieve in different ways."

"And Beatrice? She saw her daughter alive and running away from her. And then she manipulated Thomas. He was conflicted . . . I don't think he's bad at heart." But Astrid still dreams of that antique gun pointed at her.

"Nobody is born bad at heart. Life wears us all down." Aunt Maude stops at a mossy stone bench in the garden. Astrid has never seen this bench. She hasn't taken a slow stroll through her aunt's complex garden in years. She was too focused on finding the letter, on solving her sister's death. In front of the bench, a brick border surrounds a lush garden. The daffodils and cherry trees are bursting into bloom. In the center of the garden, a beautiful Japanese maple grows like a large umbrella. Beneath the maple, a flat white stone is dusted over with dirt.

"This is a special place," Aunt Maude says, pointing to the flat stone. "Would you clean that off, please?"

Astrid crouches and wipes off the stone, revealing the engraving: NINA's GARDEN. "Aunt Maude, this is lovely!" Tears come to her eyes.

"I knew you would like it."

Astrid sits beside Aunt Maude on the bench, and they're both quiet for a time, breathing in the sea air, listening to the chatter of birds, the distant surf. "I didn't know this bench was here or this little garden," Astrid says. "I can feel Nina here. It's beautiful."

"Come on, let's see your new office." Maude gets up and they both head down the path. Morning sunlight reflects off the windows of the cottage. The business sign sits outside the door, waiting to be mounted on the wall. PACIFIC DOCUMENT EXAMINER INC. When Astrid looks through the windows, excitement stirs inside her. "It's a work in progress," she says, opening the door.

Inside the cottage, Maude exclaims, "Oh my, this is state-of-the-art."

"Well, it's only a lab with some bookshelves and filing cabinets."

"It's so you. All this equipment . . ."

Aunt Maude goes to the storage cabinets in the kitchen, opens one, and pulls out a couple of boxes. Then she motions to the back wall. "Check the cubbyhole behind there."

Astrid reaches in and finds a false back in the cabinet, hiding a cubbyhole. She pulls out something soft, partly deflated. In the light, the silver ball is dusty, its sheen dulled by the passing of time. But it's definitely Nina's.

"How did this get here?" Astrid asks, her throat closing.

"I found it floating in the water," Aunt Maude says. "I hid it under my coat and threw it in my car. Later I brought it here. Nobody noticed. Nobody looked in my car."

"But why didn't you leave it in the pool?"

"I was worried that you or your mother had left it there. I wanted to protect the people I loved. I never thought either of you would've deliberately drowned Nina. But someone left the ball there . . . Then later, I found the letters. At first, I thought your mother had typed them. But she mentions making a casserole. Rose was not a fan of cooking! The casserole was Verne's favorite dish, not Bjorn's. Beatrice often came over to pick the vegetables from my garden . . . I realized she must've been the culprit, and I came to understand the correct sequence of the letters. I knew she had probably lured Nina into the water."

"How did Beatrice even know you had the letters?"

"Well, I tipped her off. Silly me. I asked her if she'd used a typewriter years ago, the one in my library. And Verne told her he had donated the books! She came to the house . . ." Maude places the silver ball on a bookshelf.

"I'm glad you're okay." Astrid squeezes her aunt's hand. "I do have one question, though. In that old photograph, Beatrice was barely a blur in the background, but you wrote 'killed Nina??' on the back."

"That first word was *Rose*. The photograph came with the letters. It was wedged between two of them. I thought she had typed those letters at first, like I said. Come on, let's go."

They head back up to the house. Aunt Maude sinks into her wheelchair on the front porch. Her cheeks are pink—her hair shines in the sunlight. If it's even possible, she looks healthier than she did the last time Astrid saw her, although her legs are still shaky.

Astrid takes the rattan chair next to her aunt, leans back, and rests her feet on the ottoman. "Did you have another reason for calling me back here?" she asks. "Or was it just the letters?"

Maude tilts back her head and closes her eyes. "I've wanted more than anything these last years for you to come back. I finally found a good excuse. I'm sorry I put you in danger. That was never my intention."

"You were in danger, too." Astrid looks up toward the Michaels mansion. "I'm glad they're not there anymore. Such a relief that the house finally sold."

A car climbs the driveway—the Subaru belonging to Astrid's father. He's not carrying a suitcase. He's on the way somewhere else. She gets up to greet him, and he hugs her tightly, so much unspoken passing between them, so much unsaid.

Aunt Maude gets up, holding the railing with one hand, her cane with the other. "Bjorn," she says.

"Maude," he says, giving her a nod. "Good to see you up and about. How are you feeling?"

"Right as rain," she says.

"I, um, need to talk to Astrid, if that's okay," he says. "I can't stay long. I'm on a field trip—"

"Counting what this time?"

"Monarch butterflies. I'm part of the project to give them a highway of respite along their migration routes."

"So you are," she says, sitting in her wheelchair again. She rests her walking stick against the railing. "Go on then."

Astrid goes inside with her father, into the library. He looks around uncomfortably, glances at the typewriter on the desk. He backs out of the room. "Could we walk, maybe, in the backyard?"

"Sure." She pulls on her sneakers, and they go outside.

"Are you still traumatized from what happened with that boy? And Beatrice?" he asks, walking with his hands behind his back.

"That's a pretty clinical way of asking if I'm okay—"

"Are you?" He glances at her sharply.

"I'm fine. I don't dream about Nina anymore, either. At least, not the drowning dreams, now that I know what really happened."

"I should've been here—I shouldn't have left."

"It's all in the past."

"Not entirely," he says, stopping at the cottage to look at the business sign.

"What do you mean?"

"The night I went back to the city. When your mother and I fought, and I told her I would leave her . . ."

She sits on the stone steps outside the shop. Says nothing. Braces herself for what might be coming.

"I went back to our house to get the results of the paternity test."

"What?" Well, she thinks, she should have expected this, too.

"I had a neighbor pick up mail for us. I knew the results would be coming. I asked him to let me know if any mail came from the lab."

"And?" She holds her breath.

"I never told your mother. She never knew the results. Never knew that I even did the test. Because Nina was gone, and it didn't matter anymore." He sits next to her, bends his head forward.

She drapes an arm around his shoulders. "You don't need to tell me."

"She hated me for questioning her. And I hated myself." He pulls an old piece of paper out of his pocket, a tattered envelope.

"You kept it all these years," she says.

"How could I not?" He hands it to her, wiping his eyes with the back of his sleeve.

She pulls out the test results and reads them in silence. Then she looks at her father, tears in her eyes.

CHAPTER THIRTY-SEVEN

"Mom," Astrid says into the phone.

"Astrid, how are you? So much has happened! Luigi told me Maude tried to call this morning—I was at the gallery. I hear she's walking quite well on her own. Physical therapy has done wonders."

"Yes, we're all happy," Astrid says.

"You'll all have to meet Luigi. Are you coming to Italy anytime soon? It's lovely here, nothing like anywhere in the US. The sun shines so brightly."

Nothing like anywhere. Her voice sounds too bouncy. Maybe she's been drinking. Maybe she is overcompensating for the grief that must follow her everywhere. The bright sunlight keeps the shadows at bay.

"But where are you exactly?" Astrid asks. She often has to ask this question when she speaks with her mother.

"Praiano."

A man yells in the background in rapid-fire Italian, another man replying as if angry, but they laugh, and more voices join in.

"The name sounds—"

"It's a cliffside town on the coast," Rose says. "You really should visit. It's a great jumping-off point for visiting all the lovely beaches and towns and churches here. And the food is to die for. I never get tired of this place, no matter how long I'm here. And the birds. I've been drawing birds, only because Luigi is an artist. He's well known here.

He's wonderful. He's so open to other cultures, to other ways of seeing. He's also a fabulous cook."

"Sounds like you're having a marvelous time," Astrid says.

"Oh, I am! I'm sorry I haven't been in touch. Time gets away from me. But if you come, we could go to Capri island—although it's quite a retreat for celebrities."

"It does sound like a great trip." Somehow, Astrid feels closer to her mother when they don't speak. She can hold on to some idea of her, some hope that she might one day become the mother Astrid needed her to be, the sister Maude needed her to be. The mother who would've dropped everything to fly here to sit by her sister's bedside, to hold her hand and help Astrid figure out what happened to Nina. To grieve with her. To just chat and be present. But Rose does not want to be a sister or a mother, not anymore. She wants her own life.

"I'll send you some of my drawings," Rose says.

"Yes, sure." Astrid looks toward the doorway. Her father is standing there, and suddenly she wants to go and hug him. "Mom. I need to talk to you about something."

"Oh no, should I sit down? This sounds serious. Haven't we all been through enough?"

"It is—there's a lot of noise in the background."

"We're having a dinner party to celebrate Luigi's new show at the gallery." Astrid imagines the bright blues and azure seas down the cliff from her mother's villa in Praiano and wonders if Rose ever even thinks of Heron Bay. The background noise quiets. "Okay, I'm in a different room. What is it?"

"I'm sorry . . . I thought you wrote those letters, the confession. But it was Beatrice."

"I told you it wasn't me."

"I know. She confessed to drowning Nina . . . Maybe because she thought Nina was Verne's biological child."

Rose goes silent, and Astrid half expects her to hang up. Her father has crept silently into the room, waiting. "That's a terrible accusation."

Astrid says Beatrice was there, that she let Nina drown, according to her letter. "I thought you would want to know."

"You go to that god-awful place and turn over stones, and you find out this horrific thing, this letter—and you tell me about it. What can I do about it now? What can I do?"

"Beatrice died . . . but you might . . . I don't know how you feel about it, about her."

"I vowed to Luigi that I would be a calm person. I am a calm person."

Astrid holds the phone away from her ear. "I only wanted you to know. And I wanted you to know that I know about your affair with Verne Michaels. I know—"

"Well, you were going to find out someday. Luigi and I have a motto, that we only look forward. That's why I'm here. That's the only way I could make a life."

"I know you came home that night. I heard you come home with Verne Michaels. And then you left again. I'll never know where you went—"

"You're too preoccupied with the past," her mother says, her voice high pitched. "The therapist we sent you to should've helped rid you of that."

"Rid me? Like what, doing laundry and washing out dirt?" *My mother is not answering my question.* Rose deflects difficult subjects with a slice to the jugular.

"Well, a good therapist will help you come to terms. I've said it before."

"Did a therapist help *you* come to terms?" Astrid asks, incredulous.

"I had a very good one. But I worry about you. It seems you've still got a problem."

You've *still got a problem.* Astrid wraps the phone cord around her wrist, looks out the front window at the shape of Aunt Maude on the porch, sitting back in a shaft of sunlight, relaxed. Rose rarely answers a difficult question by revealing her own emotions. Fear, vulnerability, sadness, grief. Her favorite words are *you have a problem*. "This isn't about me having a problem," Astrid says quietly. "Grief doesn't get scrubbed away down a drain. A therapist doesn't work through it, and you're done. It's something that stays with you forever. It becomes a part of you."

"I'm concerned about you."

"Since when?" *If you'd been truly concerned, you would have asked me how I was all those months after Nina died. You would not have lost yourself in pills and booze; you would have come back here when Maude hit her head and lay in a coma in the hospital.*

"You seem unstable," her mother says, an edge beneath her words. Blame, reproach.

"I was only fourteen. You and Dad made me babysit Nina every time you went out. You asked me how hard it could be to watch her for two hours, but the truth is, it was really hard. I was a kid."

"You're so confrontational!"

"And you and Dad knew she tended to wander off—and when she did it again, you had already been at home with Verne. And yet. You never came to me and said it was an accident, that you forgave me for anything, that it was nobody's fault."

In the silence, Astrid almost thinks her mother has hung up. But then Rose says, "You haven't moved on with your life. I wish you would."

"All right, Mom, thank you," Astrid says.

"Is there anything else? I've got to go."

"Um, Dad wants to talk to you. He has to tell you something." Before her mother can protest, Astrid covers the phone. "Dad."

He takes the receiver from her, his brows rising. She leaves the room and shuts the door. Rose, all sweetness and light, will never apologize for being a half-absent mother. For being a fallible human being. She has no idea that she was anything other than perfect.

Astrid joins Aunt Maude on the porch.

"How did it go?" Maude asks, opening her eyes and smiling.

Astrid leans back in the Adirondack chair. "She never changes."

"Some people don't. They develop a way of coping when they are very young. And they keep doing it. Your mother is like that."

"The thing is, if she would ever stop saying 'you' and deflecting everything onto me, I might be able to have a real conversation with her. I love my mother. I'm sorry she lost her daughter. It's very sad—it's a grief nobody should have to bear. I lost a sister. We could have shared in that grief."

"She doesn't want to," Maude says.

"I know now that she never will. And she will never say she's sorry for blaming me. Maybe she still does blame me."

"It's easier than feeling the grief and owning it," Maude says. She reaches out her fragile hand and holds on to Astrid's. "I can share the grief with you. I miss little Nina. I spent many nights crying about her. I still do. Bad things happen to good people, and I've struggled with that over the years. I've struggled with why she died, how she died—and now we know."

"I feel it, too. Mom can't forgive me. But I forgive myself. It does help to know Beatrice did this. I couldn't have saved Nina, not really."

Her father's deep, soothing voice rumbles in the other room. The sound takes her back to her childhood, when her parents spoke secretly behind closed doors. Sometimes they laughed, sometimes they argued, but often, there was great happiness. When the family took a walk together, Nina often rode on her father's shoulders. He started to run, and she screamed with laughter. Rose smiled and watched them go. Astrid can see the past, both a blessing and a curse.

She knows what her father is saying now. She saw the DNA results for herself. Perhaps not revealing the truth was Bjorn's way of punishing Rose for the affair. But he is telling her now that he knew for certain seventeen years ago that Nina was his own biological child.

CHAPTER THIRTY-EIGHT

After her father leaves, Astrid goes upstairs to the room in which she slept seventeen years ago. She has moved back in here, painted the walls bright blue, and added her own furniture. No trace remains of the teenager she once was. She even painted over the graffiti in the closet. She keeps the new version of *Gone with the Wind* on the shelf along with other books she brought from California. Her clothes hang in the closet.

She opens a desk drawer and brings out the Kashmiri box, opens the lid, and takes out the tickets and the printed wedding photograph. After lingering a moment on the smiling picture of her and Trent, she rips it up and throws the shreds, and the tickets, into the paper recycling bin under the desk. She places the container of birth control pills into a postage-paid mailing envelope for properly disposing of pharmaceuticals. Why did she keep the half-used prescription? She should have tossed it long ago. But she kept it like an albatross around her neck.

All that is left now is the wedding ring in its velvet box. She takes it out. The gold glints, forever untarnished. She puts the ring back in the box, places the box in a little gift bag. Livie is leaving town soon, moving to Los Angeles, where she will attend university. The ring will go with her, a gift from a friend.

The doorbell rings, followed by footsteps and voices downstairs. "Astrid!" Aunt Maude calls up the stairs. "You've got a visitor!"

That fluttery feeling returns to Astrid's chest, the delicious sense of anticipation, of impending adventure. "Be right there!" She rushes to the mirror in the bathroom, quickly brushes her hair and adjusts her blouse, then races down the stairs. Aunt Maude has gone back out to sit on the deck, but Conor is standing in the foyer, dressed for a day off in a T-shirt and jeans, his hair slicked back as if he has just showered. He looks impossibly handsome. Astrid wants to tumble right into his arms.

He grins at her and holds up a paper bag. "Thought I'd check in on you," he says. "I brought bagels."

"My favorite!" She hugs him, delighted to feel his solid warmth against her.

In the kitchen, they sit side by side in the breakfast nook, eating.

"I like what you've done with the cottage," Conor says. "You'll have to tell me what all those gadgets do."

"Of course . . . I'm just getting settled in."

"I'm glad you're back. Did I tell you that?"

"Me too. I never thanked you for all your help."

"You helped me, too. The case haunted my dad, and it haunted me. Now I can put it to rest."

"If Beatrice had lived, what would've happened to her?"

"I would've had a difficult time charging her with anything. Maude doesn't remember what happened in the library the day you arrived. And regarding your sister's death, the letters were flimsy evidence at best."

"Verne had those letters all these years. Could you charge him with obstructing justice?"

"He thought Beatrice was delusional. We would have to prove that he actively hindered an investigation. That would be a tough mountain to climb. And since we're not charging Beatrice . . . Well . . ."

"Okay, I get it," she says, nodding. "What's going to happen to Thomas?"

"He's a juvenile. We'll see."

"He did all that because he wanted to protect his grandmother. And his inheritance!"

"Yeah, go figure." He gives her a quizzical look. "Come to dinner at my house Saturday? You haven't been back there in, what, seventeen years? I'll make you my famous veggie lasagna."

"I'd love to," she says.

When they finish the bagels, Conor washes the plates and loads the dishwasher. He's getting comfortable here. "Come on," he says and leads her into the living room. He opens the record cabinet. "Remember this album?" he says, taking the record out of its sleeve. *Saturday Night Fever.*

"I do. We danced—"

"To the fast songs. But you didn't want to slow dance with me."

"I know, I'm sorry." She takes the record from him, places it on the turntable, and switches on the power. The needle moves automatically to the first song. She skips forward to "How Deep Is Your Love," turns up the volume. "But I do now. Would you like to dance?"

"Don't mind if I do," he says, smiling and pulling her close.

ACKNOWLEDGMENTS

Thank you to my brilliant editor, Danielle Marshall, and the entire amazing Amazon Publishing team. As always, my savvy agent, Paige Wheeler, keeps me on track. I'm indebted to Amy Camp, former police detective, for details about police investigative procedure, for her wonderful brainstorming ideas, and for reviewing an early draft of the manuscript.

I'm grateful to Kathy Carlson, CFDE, CQDE, for allowing me to interview her and for generously offering her expertise, insight, and considerable experience as a certified court-qualified forensic document examiner. Any errors are purely my own!

Thanks also to Fran Matera, RN, MSN, TCRN, for medical details and information about how to respond to a drowning. Author Barbara Sissel is a wonderful friend, and I deeply appreciated her editorial feedback on an early draft of the manuscript.

As always, I rely on my writing-group colleagues, my friends, my brain trust: Susan Wiggs, Sheila Roberts, Kate Breslin, Lois Dyer, Anne Clermont, Sandy Dengler, Leigh Hearon, Maureen McQuerry, Warren Read, Patricia M. Stricklin, Jana Bourne, Terry Matera, and Randall Platt.

I produced the first draft of this manuscript on manual typewriters from my collection, and the novel contains details about the maintenance and repair of these remarkable machines. I would be lost without knowledge and guidance from Matt McCormack, owner of Ace

Typewriter & Equipment Co.; Paul Lundy, owner of Bremerton Office Machine Company; and all my typewriter friends.

Thank you to my family, friends, reviewers, and loyal readers! I cannot express the depth of my gratitude to the late Marilyn Lundberg McConnell, who was a great light in my life. Without her profound influence, I never would've become the writer—and person—I am today.

ABOUT THE AUTHOR

Photo © 2015 Carol Ann Morris

A. J. Banner is the bestselling author of *In Another Light*, *The Poison Garden*, *After Nightfall*, *The Twilight Wife*, and *The Good Neighbor*. Banner grew up sneaking books from her parents' library, reading Agatha Christie, Daphne du Maurier, and other masters of mystery. She received degrees from the University of California, Berkeley. Born in India and raised in North America, Banner lives in the Pacific Northwest with her husband and five rescued cats. For more information, visit www.ajbanner.com.